Ada
King

by E.M. Faulds

DEDICATION

For Douglas, Alex, Leonne and Una and all my Scottish family. For Mum, Dad, Megan and John and all my Australian family. Special thanks to Mr & Mrs Wootton for providing a writing bolthole. You'll find I borrowed your names for a pair of comic relief characters.
To my friends across the world: a lot of me is in here, therefore some of you is, too.

CONTENTS

PROLOGUE

As she lies back in the deep tub of blue plastic, there is a fizz of bubbles that escape from her hair and skin. Butterfly flits across her view. She contemplates buoyancy. *Is this why Ikatere does what he does?* Ears underwater, she brushes her fingertips over the thin, outer cartilage which sounds like a drawn-out snare drum roll. She brushes the back of them, close to her skull, and it thunders. It had been a long time since she'd even thought of a bath – the rains were holding off. Each of her friends had donated some of their fresh water rations, a gift of staggering generosity, consideration. The awning flaps in the wind, showing glimpses of masts swinging metronomically as the raft bobs on the choppy, sunny waves. It is a perfect day to be in a raft city, the tangle of floating communities which forges this vast ocean towards the sun.

Which ocean? After long enough, all oceans become one ocean, all people one people. All wars are civil wars.

The city's clean masts and towers are at odds with the lower structures – flotsam and jetsam rescued from the sea and welded together, a riot of colour glinting in the sun – cathedrals of bamboo, man-o-wars of fibreglass and plastic, tentacles of delicate kelp, tenements of sailcloth and, everywhere, rope, joining the city, grasping it with fingers of many colours that sometimes bind the uprights

1

like weeds and sometimes trail diagonally with laundry-prayer-flags fluttering in the wind.

She knows she doesn't have long. Agung will come to interrupt. Today is the day they turn on the mindfields and she has paused from her work only at Ikatere's insistence that she is too fraught, too tense. He does not understand as she does the consequences of what they are bringing into the world today. But he was right to make her pause for a moment and let the warm water caress her skin. Agung will come soon.

Agung. Leader of the Rafters and a man whom she has never seen equalled in determination and wit. If she had met him out of context, she would never know it from his face and expression – a sleepy, round-faced man. She would never have guessed that he had the gumption to uproot an entire community and bring them out here to freedom. She would never have guessed the deviousness with which he planned to give his people the edge during the tumult that is the time called now. Agung the sharp. Agung the brilliant.

Agung brought her here. Her name is Ada King and today she will become the mother of a new way to be human.

PART I - MOTHER

Ada's first memory of her mother:

The closet was black. The tails of coats brushed her face and the plastic smell of shoes huddled around. Ada was frightened and alone. She began to sob a little. She knew it was naughty to cry, but she was so lonely. It must have been hours since her mother squatted down and deposited her in the closet, closing the door into terrifying darkness. Hours so long, her mother must be gone forever. She began to wail and splutter a little. It was then that her first companion came to her.

She sat, open-mouthed, as the butterfly of blue and yellow faceted, inky eye-spot wings fluttered and floated, illuminated by some power of its own in the darkness. She watched until her mother opened the door and gathered her up into her arms, sobbing. Ada tried to reach chubby little fingers to Butterfly as it floated over her mother's shoulder, so close, never quite reaching. A peal of laughter gurgled up through her.

Ada's last memory of her mother:

Ada was walking down the corridor to class, books in hand, head down beneath a curtain of defensive hair. She peered up at the approach of sharp-edged footsteps, ringing out in a world of rubber plimsolls' squeak, expecting a teacher. The woman was tall, thin and dark and her face tensed for a moment as their eyes met. Ada's lips tingled with a shock of recognition but stayed closed. Blotches of yellow appeared rapidly on the woman's cheeks and jaw. Until that moment, Ada had thought that it was only an expression that people went pale with fright.

For many years afterwards, Ada would second-guess the flinching muscles that sat at the top of the woman's cheekbones and at the blunt end of her eyebrows. She would question the mottled whorls of parchment-coloured skin. Was it recognition? Surprise? Fright? Disgust? Did she care but say nothing, acknowledging that all children belonged to the state? Did she care at all? Was she even who Ada thought she was?

The woman turned away and walked; tick-tack of hard soles back down the corridor. The angle of tension in a pair of shoulder blades beneath a powder blue sweater became Ada's engram of the human who was her mother, and her final memory of her. A strange and unpleasant taste grew in her mouth whenever she thought of it.

1. SCHOOLING

Ada watched the glitter of dust motes in the yellow light that fell onto the honey-coloured wood of her desk. Everything was a version of yellow or grey in this place, she thought; yellowing lining paper peeling from the classroom walls, grey linoleum underfoot; buttery yellow paint that peeled from the door, greenish-grey grime around the handle. But she liked the fall of sunlight on her face. Butterfly floated with her gaze, serenely, not even stirring the dust particles. "Ada King," the Home Sister barked. "Stop daydreaming." Ada turned back to her exercise book and stopped chewing her pencil. A scattering of eraser droppings covered her page already. Butterfly had taken up her position over the numbers again, hiding them with her wings.

Ada's belly chose that moment to gurgle, audibly, sending a wave of giggles through the class. "Enough," Home Sister Dolores warned the girls. "Bellies will rumble 'til Middle Bloc tumbles," she intoned, and that was the end of the matter as far as Dolores was concerned. Ada tried to ignore the dread that this simple rhyme would be taken up in the break-time and used by her classmates to torment her somehow. She tried, but her mind would not cease churning out possible combination chants. "Bellies will rumble 'til Ada tumbles," accompanied by a shove, or,

"Ada's a dumble, see how she tumbles," and so on.

Butterfly would not go away and Ada swiped at her with a ruler, smack on the desk, gunshot-loud. "Out, Ada King," Dolores shouted, and Ada followed her stony point to the door with dragging feet. Laughter that could no longer be contained followed her exit. "I have just about had enough of you, child," Dolores hissed as she joined Ada in the hall. "Why are you being so disruptive?"

Ada tried to explain to her shoes. "I can't see the numbers because Butterfly keeps covering them with her wings and I.."

"Butterflies? What...? You do know that lying is a transgression against the state, don't you?"

Ada looked up and out of the corner of her eye. The painfully tight ponytail, the flared nostrils with little brown hairs and the lips pressed tight and white loomed down at her. "I'm not lying. I wouldn't..." The Sister grabbed Ada with a fierce grip just below the elbow and produced a ruler from somewhere like a magic trick. Ada had time to realise that the classroom had gone preternaturally quiet just before her backside stung five times. Butterfly treacherously brushed at Ada's cheeks.

As she was sent back in, she kept her body rigid and straight and sat down slowly, closing her eyes only briefly as she did. She picked up her pencil and began to write numbers, any numbers, through the rippled glass of tears.

"I just can't understand how your marks could be this bad," the Home Mother said in a strident voice. There was no question in her tone, so Ada just watched her shoes as she swung her legs under the chair's edge. "Stop fidgeting child." The Home Mother sighed then began to orate, her words emphasised by lightly beating the side of her hand on her desk, fingers curved into the shape of a "C". "This is what happens when biological mothers defy the state uptake. By the time we get the girls, they are already too far behind..." The Home Mother continued on in this vein to an invisible audience, very specifically not Ada King.

It was rumoured between the girls that her name was Esmerelda, but no one ever called her that. She was the Home Mother. She wore a utilitarian grey suit as did all the other educators, but with the addition of a silver lapel pin in the shape of a sword, and in winter, a woollen tank top to protect her toast-rack ribs from the cold. When she had finished, she slumped with a defeated posture, gently rocking the tilting chair-back and squinting at her from the corner of one crows-footed eye. Ada still could find nothing to say. "Look," the Home Mother began on a new tack, "I know we don't have all the facilities we could have. The Middle Bloc has ensured we barely have enough for bread and milk, let alone holoscenes, computers, fancy this and fancy that. Our education is raw, basic. But it is fundamentally just as good for all that, perhaps even better because... don't you see? – " She leaned forward, excited now "– it's purer! You girls don't have pampered brains and you have to work hard." She squared her hands in front of her, calming slightly and sniffing. "The state approves this as a method, but it's not magic. You have to put in the effort, girl. The world doesn't owe you a living." Ada had never asked it to, and thought it a strange thing to say.

"You have been here for three months now and unless you start to take the responsibility to learn, there is only one outcome." The Home Mother leaned forward ominously. "You will become a Left-behind." Ada stiffened. Left-behinds were commonly understood to be pushed into the school incinerator rather than become a blot the home's academic record. "Do you understand?" Ada nodded, terrified. "Good. Now go play." Ada walked quickly out of the office, attempting to do so without her knees parting, hoping that no-one else would see her before she had a chance to deal with the growing dark stain on her uniform trousers.

A forest of knees surrounded Ada as she huddled against her locker in the dormitory. She distracted herself from her growing dread by judging them on a scale of beauty. Butterfly lighted on each as she looked around, eyes barely above her own knees. The scale went: knobbly, bruised, cross-eyed, smooth, perfectly round. Genevieve's were at the better end of the scale, of course – Genevieve with her almost white blonde hair and grey eyes, standing over her with a discordantly ugly expression twisting her perfect face. "I said–" Genevieve poked her "–you're a Middler, aren't you?"

"No, I'm not," replied Ada wearily. She had played this game with them before. The more vigorously you denied it, the more it proved what they said. The more you sarcastically agreed with them, the more it proved what they said. There was no way out. A person from the Middle Bloc was the worst you could be: greedy, grabbing, an animal.

"Look at you," Genevieve continued, "your hair and eyes are the colour of shit. Shit-eyes," she added for effect. *Shit-eyes, Shit-eyes,* was the chant, uniting the girls into a group. It was true that Ada King was darker than the average for the state, but not the darkest. She tried reason, although she knew it for the futile plan it was.

"Sister Ida has darker hair than..."

"I think Shit-eyes must be a Middler spy," Genevieve said, drowning out Ada with a malicious note of triumph.

"Why would I bother spying on you? You're just a stupid girl!" Ada blurted out before she could stop herself. Genevieve's face lit up with triumphant vindication as she bent down and grabbed a handful of hair. Pain blistered across Ada's scalp. She began to panic and yelp which made the tiny mob of eight-year olds around her begin to cheer.

"What did you say, Shit-eyes?" her persecutor demanded, dragging her half-upright. Although her chest and lungs were heaving, Ada felt like no air was going in.

Blue spots began to form before her eyes and the dormitory began to reel. In amongst the confusion of legs and arms that spun like a zoetrope, a dog passed by. Her eyes fixed and the room stopped swinging and she saw that it was standing by her side. What was it doing here?

The dog's hackles were raised in a vertex of hairs down its spine and its teeth were bared as it growled like an engine. It barked, once and gathered its legs beneath it to spring. Ada understood what it was trying to tell her. Her hand flung out and slapped Genevieve on the face. As her attacker fell back in shock she let go of the hair and Ada jumped on her, flattening her on the floor between the beds and began scratching, biting, hitting, whatever she could do. Genevieve screamed but did nothing to defend herself except feebly cover herself with her hands. As adrenalin pumped through her, Ada realised that the mob was now shouting and howling, but not on anyone's side. They just seemed delighted that fighting was happening. As this occurred to her, a hand reached in and pulled her straight up in the air by the collar. Home Sister Dolores set her down abruptly. Another Home Sister rushed in to tend to Genevieve who had several long but shallow scratches on her face. "Ada King," Dolores yelled, "why am I not surprised?" Ada burst into adrenaline-fuelled tears.

The Home Mother sat for a long time in silence, fingers in a tent before her mouth. She looked at Ada, who passed the baton of that look to her shoes, as was customary. After several minutes of nothing happening, Ada thought she had best take responsibility for beginning. "She called me a Middler spy," she began. A dam of fury was building behind the Home Mother's eyes so she thought she had better ask while she still could, "Am I?"

Strangely, the fury seemed to dissipate, without the flood Ada had expected. "No child," the Home Mother said carefully, slowly. "You are almost as far from that as is possible." She did not continue and explain, but Ada sensed she had narrowly avoided a lot of trouble, so she did not push it. The Home Mother was clearly pretending to rearrange her papers as she considered what next to say. "When we are here," she said after this long pause, "we use our words, not our fists to fight for us." She launched into a long spiel about community and working together, how Ada had a right to defend herself but not at the cost of hurting another student, how if it were to happen again she should consult a teacher immediately and how she must understand it was in no way appropriate to take matters into her own hands again. To Ada's disbelief, she was punished only mildly with the withdrawal of reading in bed for a period of one month and let out of the office. She walked slowly, slightly stunned, down the corridor. The dog, whom she had not mentioned at all, padded after her with its claws clicking on the floor. She looked at it. The dog looked at her. They continued walking.

***

Outside of the range of the witricity mast, on the other side of the island, Ikatere had set up camp on the beach. Torch and phone didn't work here, but that was kind of the point. After just a few seconds looking away from his fire, he could see well enough in the starlight. He slept right there on the sand, listening to the waves.

Early light woke him and found that the sandy point he fell asleep on had become a rocky ridge of basalt that pushed out into the sea with a shape like the hindquarters and tail of a rat. The gap in the rocks that he had sheltered in was almost cut off by the waves that were splashing brown arcs into the yellow shell-and-coral sand. Ikatere did some dragnet fishing, up to his chest in water, watching for stingray. When he had selected the best and discarded the tiddlers, he bundled up his catch and slung it over his shoulder. He walked along the spine of the ridge, dripping dry and picking his way along the sharp young rock with caution. Small but hardy plants were colonising the crevices. They were fluttering in the onshore breeze and he wondered if it would keep his net of fish cool enough or if they would start to stink before he got home. At one point, one of his flip-flop's toe-posts popped out and he had to balance with the one bare foot on top of the other while he reinserted it.

The dormant Phalanx beach buggy greeted his sandy footsteps by about ten o'clock. Ikatere hung his net of fish in the back from the roll bars to wind-cool before opening the door and releasing the hand brake. With a hand on the steering wheel and the other on the door arch, he started slowly to turn the vehicle around. He stopped once, to remove his flip-flops and chuck them in the passenger side. Bare feet dug in with better purchase on the sandy track. He had pushed nearly fifty metres up before a binging noise told him that he was back in witricity broadcast range. He jumped in, banging the door shut. Next time the car cut out he would not let it coast so far. He decided he'd be back soon.

He sang as he drove with the windows down back to the Smoke. Birds called in the trees as the Phalanx whirred its way up the track and the sunlight left blue puddles of shade in the sand beneath mangrove, pandanus, fig, tea tree, palm, boxwood and ash. Flying foxes were roosting, making chattering sounds and hanging like pendulous black fruit. They stretched their membranous wings to show off rusty waistcoats. A goanna plodded across the road, unconcerned by Ikatere's sudden swerve around him, a dragon in its own personal myth. The buggy wound around the coast – it was impossible for roads to be in a straight line on the island – and shook and rattled through potholes and creek crossings. The sand turned to red volcanic earth at the foot of Mt. Pupuni and he wound the car up through the saddle. Passing a homestead in the next bay with its semi-feral dogs trying to bite his tyres, he looked up to see an old fella sitting on the porch, drinking his first beer already. Ikatere waved to him and the old fella raised a finger of salute in return but there was something dull and staring beneath the bushy, knitted eyebrows. Well, whatever it was, it was hard for Ikatere to share the feeling after last night's escape.

As the Phalanx rose again to cross the next buttress of the central range, he glanced out into the serene blue of the ocean. It was hard to believe that there was a city out there, somewhere beneath the waves. He parked up in a lay-by for a moment and called up his car's HUD. Feeling slightly self-conscious for all that he was alone, he requested a location marker be overlaid. On the passenger side window, a star mapped out where Marisenal was supposed to be, far out past the island shelf's escarpment, into the deep.

Fishermen had told him that it was a graveyard now, abandoned by the Totalists who had found out that man was not meant to live under the water. It seemed a shame. It wasn't the first time that Ikatere resolved to get the cash together for an expedition there. To explore, maybe salvage. If he got the right contacts, he could even make a documentary. *Interest in the Middle Bloc about the horrors of totalitarian states*, he mused, *kind of outrage porn*. But Marisenal had started out with good intentions. They were going to farm the deeps, seek out new mining resources and help combat overpopulation and climate problems. At least they had tried. *Nobody bloody tries anymore.*

He looked at the time. 11:51. He considered Faipa, waiting by the *Bessu*, pissed off. He would fish him some abalone when they went out as a peace offering. Faipa loved it barbecued with chunks of chilli and lime and if Ikatere shined him up some good shell, he would probably forgive him, especially if he explained why he needed to get away for one night. He began to word his excuse.

Galvanised chain-link snaked out of the tree line to form a promontory then back into the thickness of forest. He was close to the boundary of the missile base. Ikatere's father had been somewhat apocalyptic when Ikatere was a kid and the base was installed. He had cursed the island's council who had decided to sway towards the Middle Bloc as "weak" and "short-sighted". He had warned family, neighbours, shopkeepers and anyone who came in range that the island should not pick sides in the ever-increasing consolidation of states. Ikatere particularly remembered one day, he was picking at a rotten custard apple in the long grass in their front yard while his father spoke angrily to a representative of the council. "Have you ever met them?" he had demanded. "These Middle Blockers, have you ever shaken their hand? Looked 'em in the eye? How can you tell a man's intentions if you don't look him in the eye?"

"Jeez," Ikatere had whispered to himself, cringing inside. He'd pulled his tshirt up over his nose and turtled his neck in, crouching where he was until after his father had marched up the steps and slammed the front door behind him. The council rep had left too, saying bad words under his breath. Neither of them had noticed the small boy, crouching in the long grass.

Ikatere shook off the memory and called up the HUD again to start making a To Do list for the rest of his day. He would get back at about 12:30 or so. Faipa should still be able to catch the tide and they would go free diving for abalone, sponge, shellfish. They would get back at maybe three or four. He could go home and catch a shower, spend a few minutes talking on the Middlenet to Priya from Chennai then catch up on his sociology studies before helping mum make the dinner. She'd be pleased he got a couple of snapper in his dragnet but his little brother would not. He made faces like he was going to throw up every time they had snapper. He added, 'Put fish in boat cooler,' to the list and downloaded it to his phone. He was tempted to get Priya online now, but she would probably still be asleep. He liked how impressed she was that he lived on an island in the middle of the Pacific in a town that didn't even have a scene plaza. He thought about putting some music on, but switched off the HUD again and wound the windows down. He smiled as the breeze ruffled his hair and tried not to think about Faipa waiting by the boat anymore until he had to.

The missile base fence was looming out of the trees again and he rounded a corner of it while checking his messages on his phone. He looked up and reflexively slammed on the brakes, nearly ploughing into the road block that covered the track. Men in strange uniforms stood with guns as his heart pounded in his ears. He followed officious signals from one of them and pulled over to the side of the road and switched off. As the soldier came up to the window, Ikatere asked, "What's going on?" and the man shouted something at him. "What, man?" Ikatere asked, confused. The soldier barked louder at him. "Fuck, I don't know what you're saying," Ikatere mumbled and reached for his keys which prompted the soldier to raise his rifle and shout louder. Ikatere raised his hands quickly. "I don't understand you, fella," he tried, a hint of desperation creeping in to his voice. The soldier pointed to the ground next to him. Ikatere understood that well enough. He slid out of the car and got down on his knees with his hands on his head. He'd seen enough outrage dramas to know where this was going but still grunted with surprise when the booted foot hit him in the middle of the back and put him on his face in the gravel.

The soldier yanked his arms behind his back painfully and tied his wrists together with something tight and cutting. "Oww, I want a lawyer or something," Ikatere tried but got a gun barrel to the cheek. He was hauled to his feet by his bound hands and was surprised when his shoulders didn't pop out of their sockets. The soldier and some of his mates frogmarched him into the gates of the missile base.

The room they put him in to cool off looked like a utility cupboard, but there was nothing he could use to try to escape, just shelves. The brackets might have sharp edges or something, but impossible to get to with his hands still tied. It became very crowded when two of the military types came in to question him. One of them held a mobile phone while the other held a gun pointed at him. The phone guy spoke into it. Jerky sounds came out of it. "This is a translator," it said.

"Why did you do this?" Ikatere asked, but the man ignored him.

"You are a citizen of Corporation of Attorney States, why do you no speak Experana?" the mobile phone asked. It didn't quite have the same demanding tone as the man who had spoken into it. It almost sounded reasonable. He did not. Ikatere wondered how the island could have gone from Middle Bloc to Corporated States in one night without him noticing anything. He had heard no guns, no bombs. But then he considered. The island didn't have anything to stop them, just an agreement with the Middle Bloc that they would help if anyone tried to attack. Clearly, they hadn't thought it was worth their trouble to uphold that.

Ikatere looked at the man and waited. He stabbed a few buttons and held up the phone to Ikatere's face. For a moment, Ikatere's tongue froze.

"I... didn't... know I was now a citizen." He said haltingly, trying to be as reasonable as possible.

"Why did you no know? We sent out broadcasts as we take island all night. We told you speak Experana. Ling and other language is forbidden."

"I didn't hear. I was on the other side of the island. No witricity," he added for clarity. Ikatere could only speak Ling and a few words of marketplace pidgin.

"Ignorance of the law is no excuse."

"You can't just learn a language overnight, man. If I knew about it, I'd want to obey your law, but how is it possible?"

"Then why you did try to run?"

"I beg your pardon?"

"If you want to obey our law, when our roadblock

stopped of you, why you did try to run?"

"I didn't," was all Ikatere could think to say, somewhat more indignantly than he should have.

"We have a video." The man stabbed a few more touch-screen buttons and showed a disorienting helmet cam video of Ikatere reaching for the keys.

"I was not trying to run; I was trying to turn on my HUD. To get a translator. Just like this one." He jutted his chin at the phone. He felt clever as he added, "So I can obey the law, speak Experana with you," then immediately regretted it. How could he have wanted to speak Experana when he'd just told them he didn't know about the take over?

The man held the phone to his chest for a moment and had a whispered conversation with his friend. Sweat began to tickle Ikatere's face as he watched his captors. The translator programme made some random squeaks as it sensed the muffled sounds. The talker turned back to Ikatere, finally. "We do not believe," was all he said.

Ikatere made a small sound in the back of his throat with frustration and growing panic. The soldier held up the phone to his face again. "No, I wasn't... Look, I can show you my HUD. I can take you out to the place I was and you will see witricity doesn't go there. The mountain stops the signal. It's a bloody volcano, it's got a lot of radioactive rock and shit. It really fucks up your witric signal..." Ikatere paused so the translation could catch up. At the end, the second soldier appeared outraged and raised his gun. His friend made calming motions and he lowered it again.

"Please do not swear," he said. "Does not translate good."

"Sorry," Ikatere mumbled. The translator was raised again. "Sorry," he enunciated into it clearly. He was getting sick of this and they still hadn't untied his wrists. "Look, please call Faipa; he can verify what I say. You'll need a translator because I can guarantee he can't speak Experana either."

"Then he will pay fine too," the translator spat out. "To defray translation costs."

They left him in the cupboard while they went off, presumably to check his Phalanx out, look up his net footprint. Ikatere assumed he would never hear from Priya from Chennai again. The island would be put onto whatever equivalent of the Middlenet that the Corporated States used. The two systems were not even linked. His sociology course, net friends and probably every show he watched would be wiped out, like they never existed. Ikatere began to feel very low.

They left him for many hours in the cupboard. He crouched down, trying to rest his legs, but his arms behind him would not let him sit nicely so he ended up squatting and standing alternately. He began to really need both a pee and a drink of water. He tried to tell his bladder to reabsorb some fluid. He'd never really been sure if that worked or if it was his imagination that this was possible. Either way, he wasn't really having any success. The door was opened and he was summoned out by curt gestures. Ikatere was surprised it was still daylight outside. The translator guard cut his wrist ties. As it fell to the floor Ikatere saw it was a bit of plastic that looked no stronger than a bread bag tie, but it had felt like steel. They grasped Ikatere's elbows and steered him out as he tried to roll some life back in to his wrists. He was put back into his car. As he was about to reach for the keys, the translator was raised once more. "You are a young man. The Corporation of Attorney States requires that its citizens are useful. What you intend to do with your life?"

Ikatere was slightly flummoxed by the question. A careers advisory? A veiled threat? He pursed his lips. "I'm going to live under the sea and grow seaweed," he said before winding up his window and driving off. The Corporation soldier's face was a picture that Ikatere savoured for a long while after.

***

Dog jumped up and snapped at Butterfly then wove back and forth between the legs of the girls as they stood for formal assembly. It made Ada smile. At the front of the hall on the little stage was that rarest of beasts, a man. He was old, dressed stuffily and did not look like he wanted to be here. He spoke about the great work the education home was doing for the Corporation of Attorney States, in particular the Attorney State of Western Citizens. He spoke about the gratitude that their parents would feel in giving the burden of their children to the state so that they could continue working for all their shared dreams. He spoke about the duty for each of them to find a role; that even the most humble child was an indispensible cog in the state machine. It was stirring, patriotic and bore the marks of incessant repetition. Other men lingered at the side of the hall apparently indifferent to the speech as they stared into space.

Ada was distracted by the reaction of her peers. They spent most of their time whispering to each other and giggling. Somehow, despite a lack of contact, the concept of male genitalia had made its way around the girls who hid disgusted, gleeful smirks re the trousers of these state men.

Ada was beginning to get fidgety during the second half-hour of his speech. Dog and Butterfly had disappeared somewhere and the girls were shuffling their weight from one foot to another after standing so long. Checking over her shoulder discreetly for the direction of the Home Sisters' gazes, she quickly ducked down to see if she could spot Dog through the crowd. There was a huge pop, a sudden breeze and later she would swear she saw the line of all the skirts in front of her jump up. The girl on her left, Laeva, decided to duck down too. She instinctively turned to look and saw that Laeva was not ducking but folding up under gravity. Half her face was missing. The lines of girls around her prevented her from completing her fall and so Laeva was held, kneeling in some gross parody of prayer. The ringing in Ada's ears began to clear and she could hear the screaming and began to notice the devastation further over from her. Glass was shattered around them. A big piece of metal was lying on some girls. One of those girls was making noises that sounded like they came from an animal. The metal was plinking and cooling. Home Sisters were flurrying around, alternatively herding girls out and insisting they stay inside. Looking out the hall's high windows, Ada saw a black spider of cloud moving slowly across the grey of the sky.

Eventually they were told to sit on the floor and stay away from windows. Poor Laeva and the other girls were taken to the curtained-off area behind the stage in an attempt to erase what had already been seen. The state men seemed to have disappeared sometime during the hurly-burly. It was lucky for them. The cries of those who were still alive rubbed a rasp down Ada's nerves as the Sisters did who knew what to them.

As Ada sat with Dog curled up in her crossed legs, she watched the Home Mother stride purposefully down the side aisle while Sister Dolores hurried behind like a helpless hen. "It couldn't be because of..." The Home mother halted sharply and Dolores's face turned towards Ada. They locked eyes for a while in a paralysed stare. "Don't be ridiculous," the Home Mother snapped and Dolores shook herself and turned to bustle off somewhere else.

Later they would be told that there had been an accident in a factory nearby that had sent shards of metal hundreds of metres to crash into their hall and that it was sad that some of their friends had died but the important thing was that the state man had been immediately evacuated and was safe and they should be grateful for that. Ada was only ten but her jaw clenched and her teeth ground as she listened to this, and she stared and stared and stared.

At last, at the end of a fractured evening, the exhausted

girls were allowed to return to the dormitory but a rumour began its rounds that in fact the metallic spearhead had come from the Middlers. The rumour grew legs and eventually it was stated with hushed and solemn reverence that they had decided to end the world and that they were going to throw the switch at midnight. Some girls even began to say their whispered goodbyes to each other. Ada didn't believe this either. She had it worked out in her head. If the Middlers threw the switch then they would blow themselves up as well and that would be just stupid. Also, what was this switch attached to anyway? Bombs? How many bombs would they need? They would have to go right around the world and probably through its middle. She thought someone might have noticed them setting all this up. Nevertheless, an intellectual cowardice she could not shake kept her awake until midnight safely passed.

Ada swore as she pricked her finger again. The Sewing for Victory Bee was painful. They were constantly reminded that security of state was built on the blood of the men and women who fought in this glorious and just cause. Ada also believed that a great many blankets and jackets made for the cause were built on the blood from her fingers.

The state man never returned, but some less important Colleagues of the State had turned up to tell them about the war, about how the Middle Bloc had made craven attacks upon civilian targets and how it was the duty of every girl to contribute to the brave efforts of their military to protect, defend... staunchly, valiantly... brave, honour, unity... Ada felt a strange mixture of boredom, fear and hatred of the enemy stirring around in her stomach with every speech.

In fact, the education home went on much as it always had, with the exception that they were given ridiculous tasks such as sewing one epaulette on each of a hundred shirts per day, precision marching formations which made Dog bark and bark, they were often tired and they had much less to eat. For all the reports of battles and incursions, it seemed that everything was happening on the other side of the world. Holoscene recorders often came to their school with journalists who would commend the girl's patriotism and support for the troops. Ada wondered why they would find that extraordinary, considering they had no choice in the matter. But the reports would always end on a sombre note that it was here in this very home that the first blow in this terrible war had been struck by the cowards in Middle Bloc. So why had they been told it was a factory blowing up? Ada decided not to trust what adults said, ever again.

After a few months of this war, they were informed that it was all over and the Middlers had been beaten back and would not be trying that again for a long time since they had learned their lesson. The girls celebrated with a victory party. There was bunting. Then life resumed as normal.

The careers advisor set up the small, foamy pads on the walls of the assembly hall, describing a rectangular volume of space at the front of the stage. Ada noticed that the shirt rode up on the back of the woman as she reached for the correct height, showing her waist. She was young, with a constant white-toothed smile, so different from the Home Sisters and especially the Home Mother who was looking at the advisor with a slightly down-turned mouth. Ada wondered if she worried that the paint would peel off when the pads came down, or if all young people were distasteful when you were as old as the Home Mother. The young woman began her presentation, standing in the centre of the rectangular space.

"Hello girls, my name is Colleague Fabia, and I'm here to talk about something very exciting," she began. "But it's such a big topic I'm going to need an assistant." Ada wondered if they were supposed to volunteer and considered for a fraction of a second putting her hand up. To her relief, the woman went on before she could humiliate herself, "So I'm going to ask my friend, Figgy to join me. Figgy? Figgy? Are you here?" She made theatrical attempts to find her 'friend'. As she was looking one way, a cartoonish clown head appeared to float behind her, winking at the children and wiggling his white-painted nose. Ada jumped a little then began to smile. The smaller tots at the front called on Fabia to find him, pointing and shouting. She turned and the head vanished, only to reappear behind her on the other side. After much pantomime, the cartoon man revealed himself properly.

"Oh, *there* you are, Figgy," she said. "It's about time. We have a very important job to do, Figgy."

"Yes, we're here to talk to you all about your future in the Corporated States," said Figgy, talking now to the children in a silly voice. Ada decided she didn't like the clown at this point, but she couldn't have defined why.

Fabia and Figgy turned so they were back to back and walked to either end of the space. "When you receive your marks for your school work, you'll be placed on a graph." A scroll of colour began to pour from their feet, bunching up and spreading into a curve that expanded in their wake. Fabia began to walk back to the centre, her face green behind the curve's transparency. The cartoon clown walked in front of the curve. "Now most of your marks will come into this part of the graph. Figgy if you please." The clown's arms began to stretch inhumanly to show a wide section of the graph, including its belly. "People who fit into this part are what we call Adequates," she further explained. They worked their way up the graph, carving out smaller and smaller portions. The Adequates were superseded by the Satisfactories. The top of the graph was a tiny portion given to the Excellents.

"Now let's watch this presentation on the role all these types of grades will play in society," Fabia smiled. "Figgy, you pay attention too," she admonished with a shake of her finger and a smile.

"S'uh, of course Fabia," he replied and sat cross-legged on the floor, giving a choppy little soldier's salute. He somehow managed to fall over in a seated position and rolled himself back up again without a pause. The girls burst into laughter.

The giggles settled down as pictures and voices played across the space. A truck pulled up at an impressive building and smiling workers got out. "The term Adequates might give you the impression that your grade is not important," an authoritative voice intoned. "Nothing could be further from the truth. Adequates are the lifeblood of our Corporated States. Without them, there would be no industry and industry is what drives our economy. There are many exciting opportunities within food production, mining, manufacturing, power generation..." The presentation continued to show many positive and hearty-looking folk with clipboards and hardhats or worker's overalls and a shovel. All of them smiled as they went about their work. "Another role for our Adequates is as brave military personnel, defending our way of life against the tyranny of our enemies..." Determined smiles and smart uniforms, cleft rugged chins and broad shoulders dominated this segment.

Satisfactories, the next category, would be given jobs in the state's government, or supervisory roles in industry. "Satisfactories ensure our way of life functions smoothly. They make the trains run on time, make sure bread is distributed to even the tiniest and remotest of our member states, New Alba."

"The smallest number of you will become the Excellents. Excellents are the leaders of their fields. They are sent to University. When they graduate, they become scientists, logicians, doctors, political theorists..." The presentation showed a young adult woman sitting on a bed, studying in her room. "Excellents enjoy the best facilities that the state has to offer, as they will be the ones with the most responsibility on their shoulders to fulfil the manifest destiny of our glorious Corporation. Excellents can travel freely throughout our member states and, unlike other blocs, they will be guaranteed a job no matter how specialised their study choices because, unlike other blocs, the Corporation of Attorney States cares about knowledge and is not driven purely by greed. Excellents and the highest grade of Satisfactories will become Colleagues, the men and women tirelessly working for your future in the glorious Corporation of Attorney States."

The presentation ended with some rather disappointingly low-level fireworks. Maybe if Colleague Fabia had used a ladder, Ada thought vaguely.

"Are there any questions?" Fabia asked as she looked around the hall. "Yes, little girl with the lovely curls," Fabia said as she pointed at Ada's hesitantly raised hand. "Yes, you."

"What about those who get grades on the other side of the graph?"

"They are the Left-behinds, honey, of course. Are there any more questions?"

"What happens to them?" Ada persisted.

"That is something that I'm sure will never happen to anyone here," Fabia said with a sympathetic shrug.

"But what if it did?"

Fabia began to look uncomfortable. "That's a question you should really be speaking about with your home educators," Fabia evaded. "And that's the end of the show, girls, bye-bye! Say bye-bye Figgy!" The clown waved and did a backflip before flapping his hands and flying out of the top of the space. Fabia waved, smiled and abruptly walked out of the hall, leaving the foam pads where they hung.

Ada looked carefully at the question again. She read each word carefully. "What is the shortest distance between point A and point B?" it asked. The A and the B were two dots given on a Cartesian plane. Ada was just beginning to count tick marks along the axes when Butterfly landed on the page and began to sun herself. Her wings opened and closed rhythmically. Ada was annoyed but she was becoming used to Butterfly's acts of sabotage and merely sighed and waited. She noticed how the eye spots on the wings almost exactly covered the dots on the plane then disappeared as the wings folded together. A flash of inspiration lit up her world and suddenly she saw the clever trap they had put inside the question. *Zero*, she wrote carefully. There was a little more space left on the line, so she wrote *No distance*, for clarity. She put down her pen and drummed her fingers with nervousness for a moment. She picked up the pen again tentatively and underlined *No distance* twice and put the pen down again, folding her hands over the completed paper. She had determined she would become an Excellent.

The Home Mother, whose name might have been Esmerelda, sat with a ramrod straight back and a frown. Ada sat with her characteristic reticence and waited. "You have been brought in here again to discuss your test results," the Home Mother began. "At first, we believed you might have a genetic anomaly, your results were so bad." Ada snorted softly and looked away. "So we sent them to the state, to see what we should do with you. And now there is a man to see you. Mr Mull?" the Home Mother raised her voice to call to someone from her anteroom.

A tall man with large hands and a receding gingerish hairline entered the room and Ada began to grip the side of her chair until it hurt her fingers. The Home Mother introduced him and he perched, without speaking, on the edge of the desk near Ada's left side and studied her for a moment. He breathed in like he was about to begin speaking but then let it out again. He did this a couple of times as if he was suffering some kind of fit. Ada's eyes darted up uncertainly to his face for a moment. She did not know what to make of him.

"Hello, Ada," he finally said in a surprisingly light voice, "It's a pleasure to meet you." Ada was unsure if anyone had ever been pleasured by meeting her before. Why would he be, if he was about to drag her off to wherever Left-behinds went?

"Ada, don't be rude," the Home Mother prodded, *sotto voce*.

"It's a pleasure to meet you too, Mr Mull," Ada responded tonelessly.

"Perhaps you've been a little worried about your test scores," Mr Mull said. He laid a hand heartily on her head, nearly making her jump off her seat. The ridiculous thought that raced through her head was that she could wear her shoulders for earmuffs. "Well, I am here to tell you that you needn't worry. In fact, you should be happy." Ada's face wrinkled, confused. "Yes, we have seen your test results and your answers are often wrong for these tests. But our team spend a long time looking for students who make these particular errors. You see, it turns out that these answers are wrong because your educators have been giving you the wrong type of tests." As he said this, he flicked his eyes with a grin at the Home Mother's who suddenly looked extremely uncomfortable. He stood up and began pacing about the office, pausing here and there to apparently examine certificates upon the wall, or pick up an object and put it down again.

"You see, there is a particular narrowness in the way of thinking of our run-of-the-mill education homes. Don't get me wrong, for the vast majority of students who come through these doors, these tests are perfectly... *adequate*." The Home Mother's eyebrows went down in the middle. "But every now and then, a brain that can't be confined within these parameters comes along and that is where my department steps in."

He turned to face her. "Ada, we would like to take you to our special unit to give you the right tests, and give you the support you need to prove if we are right or wrong. You will come with us and we will begin working your brain correctly and see whether or not you are what we think you are."

"An Excellent?" she shyly proposed.

He leaned forward and rested his hands on his knees. "No, no, Ada, much more than that."

"But... but what if you're wrong?" she asked in an ever-smaller voice.

Mr Mull stood up again and gave her a confident smile. "Then you will become a Left-behind. But if you don't try, you will become a Left-behind for sure, here, with her." He jerked his chin at the Home Mother. "Come on, Ada, what do you have to lose?"

***

Typhoon Canute was a memory but its effects were not. All around were the pieces of his life. Agung stooped and picked up a small plastic shoe. It looked like it had been chewed by a dog. He bit back the temptation to cry. They were alive and many of his neighbours could not say the same. He lifted his eyes, looked down to the sea. His house had never had a sea view before. Of course, now he didn't have a house either. The beach had been carved into a new shape and debris formed little mountain ranges along the front.

Canute had been the second cyclone of the season. The first, Boudicca, had already devastated his community and Canute had struck just as they were beginning to try to pull their lives back together. The frame of their small home lay scattered – a petulant child had smashed it. Agung's wife was starting a smoky, smouldering cook fire under the corrugated iron lean-to they had built. But they had nothing to cook. She had found a metal bucket with some rainwater in it and was edging it closer to the coals with her toes, trying not to slop any water and put out what little fire she had.

Agung looked up behind his town to the skyscrapers of the city, relatively unscathed. The buildings had been coming closer year after year, squeezing the fishers into a narrow margin of shoreline. Cheap flat blocks backed onto their bungalows, troublemakers would come down to the town with their drugs and illegal tech. The city would be giving the fisher town no help in their time of need. They were on their own. His attention returned to the lean-to. They had nothing. His boat had been washed away and the fishing grounds were fouled for miles in every direction. He could not even catch his family some supper without a boat.

"I'm going for a walk," he said to his wife. Her chin was on her knee and her eye-whites made large crescent moons beneath the olive green of her irises. She said nothing. There was nothing for her to say. His son sat in his nappy and stacked things into piles, ignoring all of them; perhaps he was the only one content. Agung turned and began to pick his way through the forest of rubbish down towards the sea.

Large breakers churned around the dead jetty and gnawed away at the shoreline some more. Every now and then Agung saw a cake of sand slowly collapse into the waves. He hadn't managed to scavenge anything useful yet. There was nothing useful left, just parts. His heart lifted when he saw a tin can sticking out of the ground, but as soon as he touched it he realised it was empty, just some trash filled with sand, like everything else.

Other figures could be seen picking around the carnage of boats, uprooted palm trees, broken glass louvres, perished plastic containers. He had lived all his life in the town but could not recognise any of them from the distance he was keeping. *People change in circumstances like this*, he thought. *Who knows how?*

He sat for some time on an old tyre. He could not go back to that lean-to, that sullen excuse of a fire, not without something to show for his trip. But there was nothing here to find. He felt like screaming at the sea. But it was not the sea's fault. Or the wind's. Or his. Somehow, it did not make him feel any better to know it. Perhaps one of the Affiliate states would send aid. Perhaps the city... he looked towards it to see a group of people coming down from the top of the dunes to the north. He instinctively moved behind the hulk of a yacht and knelt down in the sand to look out under the point of the bow. They were leading someone, a woman. On the wind, he could hear sounds. Piggy sounds. They were the woman's squeals. He watched them throw her on the sand. He swallowed, his throat suddenly sore and dry.

There were about eight of them and they fell on her, ripping her sari, smacking her face. Eight of them. He could not help this woman. He began to back away, keeping low so the yacht sheltered him. He dropped down to the line of the surf and half-waded his way back towards home. His bare foot sunk into the sand and he fell, biting his tongue so he didn't shout as blood came from his punctured sole. Something sharp. After he had got control over the pain and the tremors from the salt water sting, he got to his knees and dug a little in the wet sand. He pulled out a rod of metal, the type to reinforce concrete, broken and rusted. It felt heavy in his hand.

Agung hurried home, walking on his heel on the injured foot and did not speak to his wife as she bathed it in tepid bucket water and wrapped some rags around it. He sat watch all night, however, his found metal club in hand.

2. THE CROUCHING MAN

Dog was up on the long table. His head was between his paws, his rear in the air and he was snuffling suspiciously. He growled and whined at the small paper cup of brown, gruel-like substance. Its box-pleated sides were gathered up into a neat rolled rim and its contents were beginning to leach through in a greasy stain. *Put it off long enough*, Ada thought. Dog heard her and looked up with a questioning whine. She picked up the cup and drained it, trying not to gag and spit it back up again as the contents clung to the sides. *Toasted oats, poo and a hint of battery acid today*, she surmised, a connoisseur.

Dog sat down on Ada's plate and wagged his tail, panting with a dog smile. Ignoring him, she picked up the breakfast dishes and cutlery and balanced the small cup on top to take it to the hatch. She walked past her fellow students. There weren't many of them, only three long tables in the dining hall. Each of them had a cup similar to hers and she saw a few that remained untouched. She put her plates up then came back and sat down next to Beagan, facing out on the bench while he faced in, studying his plate morosely.

"You know you have to drink it," she said, referring to his ignored cup of supplement.

"It tastes like shite," he said, without turning around. Butterfly landed on his head and beat her wings slowly.

She had first seen him in the unit's reception, hair plastered flat from the evening rain, holding a battered case in one hand and staring around at the bland linoleum, magnolia and woodchip of the former military barracks. He'd had an expression that Ada recognised from her own feelings when entering that place. He was wondering if he could ever call somewhere this dead 'home'.

"It'll build you up, shrimp," she said confidently. "We're the future of the Corporated States, you know. Take a run up at it." She picked up the supplement and placed it in front of him. He sighed with the whole of his small frame and then drank it quickly. He put the cup down with a hand clamped over his mouth. He had such a face on that Ada laughed a little, especially with Butterfly still clinging to his hair.

"Why do you care anyway?" he asked miserably after he managed to swallow.

"I don't," she said automatically and stood up to leave him to it. The hell if she would admit that. Perhaps it was too hard to say why this small, unthreatening boy made her feel protective. It was what it was. It was just hard to get close to anyone without those connections becoming a liability. Perhaps she should avoid his friendship. She didn't know. People could start talking and implying they were boyfriend and girlfriend. She would probably have to commit suicide if that happened.

The classrooms of the unit were very different to what Ada'd had before. There were so many gadgets and devices at their disposal that she'd become blasé enough to toss a paperslate back into the pile once she'd finished with it, eliciting a scolding when she was caught. Schoolwork here was hard, always she felt like she was being pushed which filled her with a mixture of anxiety and exhilaration but she'd been amazed at what she'd discovered she could *do*.

Her favourite preoccupation while she was thinking was to stare out the window of the classroom down the hill at the town that was laid out beneath its looming, fortified black rock. The scene was often misted with rain and low cloud and Ada thought it was the most beautiful view she would ever see.

She was staring out this window while Butterfly was doing her best to turn into a Klein bottle for her. Her shape deformed and revolved until the manifold appeared. Butterfly was looking somewhat weird and fuzzy as she tried to represent four dimensions. Still, at least she was more helpful with schoolwork these days. It had taken a force of will on Ada's part and much silent chiding, but it was beginning to work out. Dog mostly slept curled up next to the radiator.

It was after this class, she would later recall, that they were directed to go to their rooms and take a nap in preparation for the trip to the observatory that night. Ada opened her clattery and old-fashioned door to the room to discover a cup of some supplement beside her bed. A note underneath it half-stuck to the cup with a wet circle explained mandatory consumption for all students. She sniffed it. It smelled different from what they had been given so far but was lumpy and thick as always. She grimaced but drank it anyway. When she had first arrived, Mr Mull had taken many pains to explain to her that the special unit was in the business of making their students stronger and smarter and as such she would have to repay their troubles by taking the supplements and doing the exercises exactly as prescribed or she would be sent back to the home sharpish. She believed there would probably be some room for manoeuvre but life was much simpler if you just did was asked of you. They were so firmly polite. And such tools. She lay down on her bed and Dog jumped up to nestle and nose his way under her arm. Butterfly flew in graceful arcs to take up position on the curtain rod, her usual roost. Ada began to drift off.

Suddenly a feeling of eating apples too green hit her stomach and her mouth began to water. She rushed to the basin and threw up. After she'd spat and blown her nose, she realised the basin contained chunks of her lunch that would not go down the plughole. She rinsed the vomit best she could and, with a feeling of bone-deep disgust, scooped out the chunks with her hand and put them in the bin. After washing her hands probably an unnecessary amount of times, cleaning her teeth and blowing her nose again she lay back on her bed. She hoped none of the students in neighbouring rooms had heard her vomit but her head felt strangely heavy and she began to blink, long and longer. As she was just closing her eyes, a crouched man appeared by her bed. She started awake in fright.

She was no longer in her room. A bright light dazzled her and people were standing over her, masked people. She was unable to move her head. It was clamped somehow. There was a screeching, mechanical sound coming from somewhere out of sight. "Shit, she's awake," one of them said. "For fuck's sake, turn it up. Quickly!" And she began to panic, pawing and grasping at the sheets over her body. The room fuzzed as the gasps she was taking started to smell strongly of chemicals. The last thing she remembered was the face of the man who leaned over her. He was wearing a cap and a greenish mask looped over his ears, then blackness descended again.

She woke after dreams of trying to run for an infinity from a nameless terror but her legs were slow, useless things. She was on her bed, but under the covers. Her mouth was dry and she had a sore throat. She could not see Dog or Butterfly. When she realised that, she sat up in shock. The crouched man was in the corner of her room. He was gaunt, round-headed to the point of deformation, with straggly brown hair that hung in strings about his piggy face. She began to shake and scoot back in her bed.

He shook his round head slowly then disappeared. Butterfly flitted up into view from behind the foot of her bed and Dog sprang onto her lap. She almost cried with relief.

She put a hand up to her head and began to feel around gingerly. She could feel nothing specifically wrong but a section of her scalp just behind her left ear felt inexplicably raw, and the pang of a deep headache was beginning to take hold. She bit her lip and began to wonder what she could do. The masked man who had leaned over her had been Mr Mull.

***

One day Agung began to drag the timbers of his smashed home down towards the waterline. "What are you doing?" His wife asked.

"You'll see," he replied. He had attached a rope to the largest beam and was attempting to lift one end off the foundation pad.

"You'll give yourself a hernia," his wife said. "Here, I will help." Despite his protests, she took a strand of his rope bridle and put it on her own shoulder. She was not a fragile woman, and her name was Sakti. She smiled at him and he shrugged as they began to shift the large beam. Their son, Topan, sat under the lean-to and gave them the slightly upset look that only a two year old can give.

When they had dragged several of the beams down to the beach right next to the new high tide mark, Agung began to tie them together with rope and bunched up fishing nets. After some time and further scavenging, they had a platform. Around the edges of the platform Agung began to tie objects of all sorts – plastic bottles, fishing floats, bamboo poles, diesel barrels, lifejackets, oil containers and polystyrene. He went to the smashed yacht and took its smallest mast. He had already scavenged the sails as a shade cloth for the shelter and he set these up too. He put a smaller version of their lean-to near the back to complete it. He stood back and looked at Sakti, expectantly.

She looked from him to the raft and back again. "You will not take me or my baby on this thing," she said flatly and turned to march back to the lean-to.

"I'll make it better, sweetheart," he cried as he ran after her. "Sweetheart!"

One of Agung's neighbours, Obrolan, came wandering down from his makeshift shelter to see what the fuss was all about. "What's going on, Agung?" he asked.

"We need a house," Agung said. "We need food. Why on earth should we not do both at once?" He gestured back at the raft.

"She's right," Obrolan said with a look at the raft. "You're crazy."

"I'll make a better one tomorrow!" Agung spat and headed off down the beach into the setting sun to look for more salvage.

The next morning, Agung returned to his raft to see that it was in ruins. Scavengers had scavenged most of what he'd scavenged. Some of it was still there, though. He began to pull his gear together in a dejected sort of way when a person came quietly down to stand next to him.

"Brother, good morning," said the small man politely.

Agung vaguely recognised him. "What do you want?" he asked miserably. "Can't you see I'm busy?"

"Yes," he said. "That is what I wanted to talk to you about. I want to help you build your floating home." It appeared that Obrolan had been talking.

"Why?" Agung asked suspiciously.

"So you can help me build mine," the small man said with a shy smile. "Maybe together we can build better ones than if we are alone?"

Agung could not really afford to reject the help. "Okay," he said, but he would be keeping an eye on this man, to see if he was a trickster.

"My name is Dwi," the small man said, nodding courteously.

"Agung," Agung said rather stiffly.

The next day more fishermen had come down to watch. Some began to shout advice. "No, you should attach that to the front or it will tip over!" and so on.

"Why don't you make your own, then," Agung would shout back angrily, "and stop interrupting hard-working people!" But he would secretly consider their advice, and when he thought no-one was looking, he would amend his craft accordingly. It was beginning to shape up. All down the shoreline, other rafts and boats were being built under the heat of the sun. It was hard and hungry work, but strangely, most people didn't seem to mind. It was as if they were just pleased to have something to do.

Sakti had come around to the new look of the raft. It seemed sturdier, more like a houseboat that could handle the open sea. He had added many outriggers and pontoons to it as he went, to make it wider than it was high in terms of solid compartments. A couple of masts protruded but they were the tallest parts. It would not be long before they could set off and not before time. Agung was starting to lose his strength. Aid packages had arrived and been divvied out in what resembled an angry rugby scrum, but they were dwindling.

One evening a deputation of villagers approached the raft and began to speak. "Agung, what is your plan for getting water?", "Agung, how are we supposed to steer these things?" Agung this and Agung that.

"Why are you asking me?" he said at the start, angrily. But the questions persisted. He wanted them to go away. Quite a little crowd was forming. He stood up on his deck and shouted, "Shut up!" He looked at them angrily until they shut up. "That's better. How am I supposed to answer everyone at once? You, you asked about water. I'm going to make an evaporation still, and catch as much rainwater as I can, but I guess we'll have to come back into shore if we need more. You, why don't you have a rudder?

It's quite simple, I'm astounded you didn't think of it," and so on. It was almost dark by the time they all went away and he sat down on the back of his raft, tired.

Dwi came up and sat next to him. "You know, that was very good," he said in his quiet voice. "You could be a very good leader if you wanted."

"But I don't want it," Agung said despairingly. "I only wanted my family... I never asked anyone to follow me."

"But they need someone. And things need to happen before the next typhoon comes in." He looked across at Agung. "It's coming soon."

The coastguard patrol boat circled them menacingly. "Return to shore immediately." The words came out with a whine of feedback from the trumpet attached to the boat's wheelhouse.

Agung stood on the front of his raft and shouted – he had no tannoy – "We're not causing any problems! We're going away!" The speedboat had already passed and there was very little chance his voice would have carried over its engine in any case. The boat continued to attempt to herd the flock of rafts into a clump.

From the far side of the group the guard's voice was taken away by the wind but it soon came around to Agung again. He heard: "Your vessels are not licensed under law. They pose a risk to health and safety. Return to shore immediately or we will open fire."

Agung tried to make sense of that whilst waving his arms. Sakti shouted, "Make them go away, they're upsetting Topan," who was indeed crying so hard Agung could see his uvula. The boat passed on again, relentlessly. Dwi's raft was close by with its washing lines that were always full. He was always washing his clothes, relentlessly fussy about their cleanliness. He could see Dwi watching him, waiting, his linens flapping around his head, which gave Agung an idea. He grabbed a handful of the slack sail that flumped over the roof of his own cabin and pulled it down to the deck. He began waving it and doing a desperate dance as he shouted, "We surrender!" at the top of his voice when the speedboat turned towards the front of the flotilla again.

The coastguard seemed to pick up his signal as they swerved the boat suddenly. But they must have been going too fast. The boat punched up into the air, flipping over and falling back to the waves upside down and in several pieces. Agung gaped. He watched to see if any of the guards would resurface. The ocean around the boat began to bubble and it sank, disturbingly quickly. "But I..." Agung stammered. Suddenly he was finding it hard to breathe.

Sakti walked up to the front of the raft with Topan on her hip. She surveyed the patch of rainbow-sheened water where the boat had once been. "Good," she said brusquely and returned to the cabin.

Agung looked over to Dwi who was just as shocked, staring at the spot the boat had sank. He thought he saw him mumble the sentence, "What have we done?" but it could just as well have been, "What has he done?"

"There's nothing for it," Agung said firmly to the circle of faces sitting around his round charcoal brazier that smoked gently in the wind. "We will have to make a run for it."

"But where?" Arto asked.

"I've been thinking," Agung said as he picked at a patch of dried skin on his foot. "International waters. No one state has any jurisdiction there. They can't get us there."

A clamour of objections filled the air. "How will we get there? We don't know where international waters are!"

"They will call us murderers for the lives of the guards! They won't care that it was a freak accident!"

"We were supposed to go back to land soon!" and so on.

Sakti chose that moment to bring out fish soup and gave each of the raft owners' council members a bowl. *The woman is a political genius*, Agung concluded, as they could not do anything except politely accept the bowl without causing great offence. And besides, despite Sakti's lack of ingredients, she was a resourceful cook. It smelled good. They wouldn't risk missing out. *The politics of stomachs*, Agung mused. Perhaps it there was a science to it.

Into the silence that was broken only by slurps, Agung put forward his plan. "We go east," he said softly. "It will be easy to see by the sun which way, at least to begin with. We look for other boats to trade with, fish things from the sea where we can and when we can, we will send parties to shore to get whatever else we need. Fast – in, out. We won't need money if we have things to trade. There have to be other communities that were smashed up in the typhoon. Maybe we can find them and trade there. As long as we're quiet and don't cause any trouble there is no reason why they should come after us. Yes, apart from the accident," he said to the ones who were breaking contact with their soup. "But you know, it's a big ocean. Finding a small boat at the bottom of it will be difficult. And if they had any proof, wouldn't they be here by now? And another thing," – keep talking, that was the key. "I want us to try to sail a lot closer together. It takes a long time to get you all here in Kolek's dinghy and communication and sharing is hard..."

Agung spoke long into the proliferating darkness around the little brazier of coals. He spoke about sharing, community, freedom and hardship, about water and sanitation, recycling and fishing until the stars began to sleep into the purple velvet of the dawn sky.

The wave broke in an angry scud of whitewater over his legs. Sakti screamed a little, involuntarily. Agung looked back. His wife and child were both covered with their improvised flotation devices. She wore several shopping bags full of polystyrene and strapped together with duct tape. Topan wore water wings on his arms and legs and the pillow from a lilo strapped to his stomach. They were both tethered by ropes to the deck but Sakti held her son on her hip as always. Lightning struck the ocean worryingly close. "Don't be scared," Agung screamed, but his words were stripped away by the wind and the rain.

The flotilla was becoming ragged, driven further and further apart by the violence of the ocean. Some of their own raft's lashings were looking disturbingly loose. Agung watched as they crested the next giant of green, sensing the muscles of the ocean beneath his feet. Through the curtain of grey that spread from horizon to horizon, he saw a shape. It was comparatively white, angular. Big. "Look, there!" he cried. "There!"

When the storm had passed they were fewer, but the waves had brought them a gift to make up for their petulance. A ship. Big enough to anchor a community, perhaps.

***

Beagan stood beside the smashed glass. His emaciated chest heaved up and down as the blood dripped from his arm and his teeth were bared in an inhuman snarl. Ada stood in shock. She took a step towards him but he pulled a wicked, queasy piece of glass from the frame of the window and held it like a knife. "You're hurt," she said as the sound of racing footsteps approached from behind her. Beagan's eyes were wild and his pupils were bullet holes. White puffs of cuckoo spit were forming at the corners of his mouth. He was flicking the glass shiv in a nervous, digging motion, taking up an unholy fighter's stance.

"Ada, get back," a voice said at her shoulder, low and edgy. Mr Mull. The corridor of the hut that they were having their music lesson was narrow. Ada was bundled behind the adults who had appeared. They were making calming gestures at Beagan. She glanced down at Dog, who was in a defensive hunch at her side. *What do we do?* she asked him silently. Dog worked his way up the side of the people, scraping past the classroom door frames. Ada bobbed side to side to see where he was going. He had taken up a stance just behind Beagan and barked, once. Ada nodded and headed the opposite way.

She exited the hut by its splintering wooden steps and ran around to the rear of the building where a window was open just above her. Dog's head appeared out as he dangled his paws over the sill. Butterfly skimmed out to watch. Ada hoiked up her pants and took a good grip on the sill. She ran her feet up the wall, leaving muddy marks and tried to pull herself in. Her grip failed and she dropped back down, painfully turning a fingernail inside out. Dog barked louder as she swore under her breath, clutching her nail. She took five paces back and after a few moments of vacillation, flung herself at the wall. Through sheer momentum, she just managed to get her stomach over the sill, severely winding herself in the process. She hauled and flailed her legs in the air until she tumbled into the room headfirst.

She opened the door quietly, hoping the thump of her body hitting the ground had gone unnoticed. Beagan was still holding them off, making stiff little movements at the teachers. Ada stepped on one heel and then the other to pull off her shoes and made her way towards Beagan's back in her socked feet. *What if he stabs me?* she asked Dog. It was an important question. *He could get me in the eye*, she thought. Dog merely made a gruff wheeze of doggy contempt, somehow managing to communicate a world of meaning. *If you're in my head, how come you have such bad breath?* she had time to think but they were nearly on Beagan and Dog was slinking forward with intensity in every sinew. They were within touching distance and Ada saw the panic in the teachers' "O" shaped mouths. She would have to act before they gave her away. But what to do?

Butterfly touched down and clung to the back of

Beagan's collar. Ada took the hint and reached for it. "Don't," Mr Mull began to say as she yanked, hard. Beagan landed on his back and the teachers seized the opportunity to restrain him, kneeling on his arms and laying their body across his legs which had soon started to kick. Mr Mull looked up. He looked angry at her. "Don't you ever try something like that again," he said in a tight voice. Beagan's wrist had been cut when he'd tried to put his hand through the window. It was seeping into the beige of Mr Mull's trouser-knee.

It was one of those friendly meetings. Mr Mull would speak to her while they sat on a sofa. He was turned towards her and had one elbow up on the back, foot tucked into the crook of the opposite knee. "You must have some questions," he prompted. He was referring to the recent demise of the special unit.

Ada thought. "I can't stay here," she stated. It was a practical fact. She was the only one left. Beagan and all the other schoolmates had gone. She was the last one. Beagan's was not the only psychotic meltdown that she had witnessed, but it had been the only one that she'd been directly involved in. The rest were subdued and whisked away more efficiently. She never found out where they went, but none had come back. She herself had experienced splitting headaches and severe acne ever since she awoke on that operating table, but it seemed she'd got off lightly by comparison.

"No, you can't," Mr Mull replied. Ada could sense an unvoiced 'but'. *But you've seen too much. But you have been surgically altered.* Those were facts that he would never acknowledge but they were both aware of the truth. She was becoming worried, even more so when Fred leaned forward from behind Mr Mull's back. Fred was the name she had given the crouching man to try and humanise him. He still menaced her but she knew he was a companion in the same way as Dog and Butterfly were. He was just not a pleasant one.

Go away Fred, she thought. *You're not helping.* Fred merely gurned at her, poking out his tongue and apparently finding it all very funny.

"The department still has a few contacts," Mr Mull was saying. "And I've managed to pull a few strings. I've managed to get you into the University. You're just about old enough anyway. You'll have to study what they tell you to, but..." He did not have to say, *but at least you will not be a Left-behind.* He leaned forward and rested his elbows on his knees, head down. Ada wondered what was wrong with Mr Mull.

Ada had no clothes of her own that were not a uniform, so the special unit had supplied her with some. Practical shoes. Blue, hardwearing jeans for casual, black trousers for formal, several tops and, embarrassingly, a range of underwear. She felt the constructivist underwiring in the bra and shuddered with suppressed revulsion. Butterfly landed on a cable-knit sweater. Ada decided she could get away without the torturous bra for a while, at least while it was still winter. Dog was chasing his own tail inside the boxy trunk they had given her.

She packed. The new clothes and other meagre possessions filled only the bottom quarter of the trunk's volume. Dog curled up on top of them, and she closed the lid. She picked up the handle at one end to put it onto its wheels and heard everything fall down into a heap under gravity. Dog grunted a few times, but then fell silent.

She looked around her room one last time then closed the door with the strangest feeling of inertia. She pulled her trunk along the squeaking linoleum up to the foyer and put it down. She turned to the unit office to say goodbye to Mr Mull. Fred was leaning on the wall by the door. He poked his tongue out and gurned at her again, making horrid hissing noises at her. A sense of foreboding crawled over her with fingers of cold. She steeled herself and turned the door handle. The door squealed as it opened to her gentle push.

To a light fitting, above his desk, Mr Mull had tied a rope. From the bottom of that rope, in a loop of it, Mr Mull poked out his tongue. His face was a purplish-brown.

3. THE HAND THAT FEEDS

Ada wormed her way back through the crowd towards the centre of the square. The front had been exhilarating but the violence on her comrades' faces as they threw their half-bricks and the evil satisfaction the police had taken in tasering them into boneless sacks of meat had made her feel sick. She checked her scarf was in place across her nose and mouth as drone cameras swooped through the crowd. The claws of a headache were creeping up the base of her skull, digging hooks towards her forehead and her disguise was making stinging runnels of sweat seep into her eyes.

She passed by some homeless men who were huddled in the doorways, caught up in the kettling just the same as anyone else. Fred leaned out from their ranks and gave her a grin, rocking and laughing as he squatted there, trousers around ankles. She walked away from him, disgusted, as Dog and Butterfly kept pace. *I hate him*, she thought. Dog looked up. Always, always, there was empathy in his eyes. Not for the first time Ada wondered how it would feel being alone.

She skirted around an incursion of policemen who had made a breakthrough at the back line. A woman was bravely trying to hit an armoured cop with a sign that said "Attorney States lead to hate, let me live my own life," as she chanted the same words by herself. *A solo chant is one of the saddest things in the world*, Ada thought. The woman was tackled and cruelly contorted into a roast chicken trussed with cable-tie handcuffs. She was still gamely trying her chant. Ada kept walking and over her shoulder heard a yelp that cut off the words.

The police were beginning to get the upper hand. Ada seriously doubted they would arrest the entire protest crowd, but her stupidity at being here was becoming more and more apparent. She would risk her place at the University after only one year. She wasn't as worried about Left-behinds as she had been – from the information she had gained from student agitators, it appeared they were merely taken to re-education centres – but it was still not something she wanted for herself. It seemed that re-education was accomplished mainly through hard manual labour in the Corporated States. *Stupid girl*, she thought with the vehemence of a curse.

She caught sight of Dara, a classmate. He was beckoning her with a whisper to a doorway. "It's not barricaded," he said to her and let her in discreetly. The house was a still, dark cavern after the noise of the square.

Ada thanked him and asked, "Whose is this?" gesturing round at the concrete, dank carpeting and tired decor. Fred had already taken up post in the shadows beneath the stairs.

"Andy's squatting here," Dara replied diffidently. "He's a friend. You'll like him."

That evening, as the police continued their mean harvest, Ada and her new friends smoked weed, drank cheap cider and listened to music. Ada leaned her head against Dara's shoulder with one leg over the arm of a mouldy sofa and – while the others argued about politics and the correct way to combat the evil of the Corporation of Attorney States – she told him about her companions, that ever since she was a baby, she'd seen things no-one else could see. She turned to look at him, gauge his reaction to her frankly crazy confession.

"You know, you're pretty," he said with a fuzzy voice, and that was the last they spoke of it.

Ada woke up the next morning under a hairy and scratchy blanket on the same sofa. Her headache had returned but had brought friends. By a process of tentative explorations, she discovered that her top was rucked up, her jeans nowhere to be found and she was lying next to a snoring Dara. Apparently, apple-eating badgers had been making their ablutions in her mouth. She edged out, saw her jeans in a heap on the floor and after she had put them back on, wandered around looking for something to drink that was most definitely not cider. She ended up sticking her head in the sink to catch water from the bathroom's basin tap. Half of it went down the side of her face, but this was actually okay. After this, there was the gauntlet of the mirror: a fright wig, bloodhound eyes, and every pore on her face standing out like a pointillist had gone to town while she was asleep. Just over her shoulder, she saw Fred was standing behind her. He showed her his missing teeth and rotting gums. Dog began to bark continuously.

"Shh," she told them and then looked for her shoes among the sleeping piles of humans on the living room floor. As she was pulling them on, Butterfly flew straight into her face, palpating her with her wings, blinding her. Flapping a hand in front of her face, she turned instinctively to the path of least resistance. There was a back door that led from the squat to somewhere else, so she decided to try being somewhere else. It might be somewhere to be sick that was not a basin. As she opened it, the front door was smashed in. She just had time to get out and close up.

She desperately tried to take in her surroundings. There was a large courtyard square with stubby trees and a patchy-looking lawn. She began to run to a diagonally opposite side. Blood pounded into her brain, building up for the aneurysm she was definitely going to give herself. As she ran, a rectangle of white stood out from the looming buildings. She changed course and pelted for the passageway. On the other side was a normal street in the town. She stopped running for a second and tried to hold her breath. She looked around the corner, quickly. A black helmeted figure had come out the back door of the squat and was looking around, but did not seem to be immediately ready to sprint across the courtyard at her, so she waited and learned how to breathe again. After a while, she gathered herself and walked as normally as she could down the street to the bottom of the hill. She would have to take the long way back to the student halls.

***

The crown of circling seabirds, wings flashing light then dark where there should be clear sky, gave it away. It looked like a floating scrapheap from a distance, but through his binoculars Ikatere could pick out structure, coloured cloth in the wind, glimpses of movement and even the sound of laughter as he approached the baroque monster of Raft City. The white, elegantly-planed cruise liner was a centrepiece while pontoons, boats and yachts, catamarans, outriggers and even what looked like a jet ski were laced into a kind of living mat. When he focused on one part, an individual unit, the fact that it was out here in the open ocean was crazy but when he looked at the whole, it was an organic leviathan, a man-made island and it made perfect sense.

He had heard about it on Statenet, officially advertised as a hive of murderers, thieves, anarchists, gypsies, pirates, Middlers and gangsters but Ikatere had managed to winnow out a few fringe media thoughts on it that had set a burning feeling inside his belly.

After Faipa had passed on, with the lack of any alternatives, Ikatere had taken over the fishing boat *Bessu*. She had a seawater cracker in the rear, housed in an ugly bum of carbon fibre over the props. She had a catch hold, kept cold by some arcane system of heat exchangers and an engine made by Frankenstein. There was a cabin below but the wheelhouse was Ikatere's second home. He couldn't count the number of hours he had lain on the orange plasticised cushions of the benches and stared at the oscilloscope of sunlit waves reflecting on the ceiling while the slosh of water poured back and forth along the grooves between the floor grips.

She also had some sheets of mechanical sandwich that compressed and released with the bobbing waves along her keel, but these were imperfectly installed and supplied only a fraction of the power they should. Ikatere had been going to fix them but the Statenet only allowed access to that information via a convoluted chain of engineering course modules that he had not got around to applying for. Business had been terrible since the Corporated States had taken over the island and it had got to the stage where he was working all the hours he could just to pay off the tax. His family were noticing the pinch, his mother making up for the lack of money with a desperately cheerful bustle about the house and his father just sitting there, listlessly, on his verandah, looking small in his clothes, his face slowly caving in on itself.

Ikatere had regretted his moment of whimsy in declaring his future intent to his inquisitors the day after they took over the island. When Statenet had been booted up, he had been automatically assigned a course in oceanography and marine engineering. So much sociology. Nothing he'd done before counted as credit and he'd had to start again from scratch. Most of the rest of the net was in a locked down state – no porn, only educative programming (and propaganda and brainwashing), and very little in the way of independent news reporting. One of the fleeting noises he heard before that voice was clamped down was that perhaps the Rafters could be traded with, and that the nomadic city was going to be coming close to his area. It was the spur he had needed, so at one o'clock the night before he had quietly churned his way out of the harbour in *Bessu* with her hold filled with as much seafood and gear as he could lay his hands on. Now it was mid-afternoon and he was still hesitating. It was hard to tell from here if they were a threat or not. He was taking his family's fate in his hands and the burning feeling turned into a hot, leaden rock in his stomach.

He pushed the throttle forward. He would just get within shouting distance. As the black, protruding pontoon dock neared, a couple of kids appeared, running to the end of it like colts. They started waving. He pulled his trucker's cap down, almost to his eyebrows and slowed up. The kids waved some more but soon stopped and stared as he dithered. One of them shook the other's shoulder and pointed and they both dived into the sea. He checked his depth gauge. The bottom was more than a kilometre beneath them. He hissed between his teeth.

They surfaced in an eruption of bubbles and laughter, holding up something orange. Ikatere swung the boat in closer with a kind of unconscious curiosity. They had just fished out a semi-deflated basketball. They kicked themselves back up onto the dock and stood waiting for him, a girl of about seven and a boy of about four or maybe five, dripping glassy maps of water onto the black surface. Ikatere pulled up to a berth almost before he knew what he was doing. He sat there a while, and, strangely embarrassed by the children's frank gazes, turned off his motor.

He jumped out and tied up, realising that the surface of the dock was made from the treads of tyres, maybe hundreds of them. "Have you come to trade with us?" the girl asked in Ling. He was a little fazed by this. He'd expected some foreign babble.

"Yes," he said with a certain feeling of reserve. He hadn't spoken Ling for years, since Experana was forced upon him. It was weird.

"Come and meet Uncle Agung," the little girl said plaintively and put her hand into his to pull him along.

"Um," he said looking back at his boat.

"It's okay, nobody's allowed to steal things here," she said and the little boy took his other hand with a look of supreme trust.

"My name is Vam," the boy said matter-of-factly.

"I'm Zika," the girl quickly cried, jealous of her companion's initiative. "Hello."

"Hello, hello," Vam sang to him.

"Hello. I'm Ikatere," he replied and in a dream, he walked with them, a lopsided chevron of three, into the floating town.

"We used to have just a few rafts," Zika said proprietarily as she guided him around. "But now there are lots of people who want to live with us. Uncle Agung says it's alright as long as they are a good. Are you a good, Ikatere?"

"I like to think so," he responded modestly as he began to pass some locals. There seemed to be a bewilderment of different ethnic groups here. Saris passed jeans, passed saffron, passed drainpipes, passed stovepipes, passed tshirts, passed tail-coats, passed epaulettes, passed palmleaf hats, passed south seas fishers, passed red sea pirate, passed ghost-white niqabs, passed expanded earlobe, passed tattoos of pinups, passed marines with shock guns, passed merchants with cloth bolts, passed mechanical droids, passed purveyors of shellfish, passed hawkers of electronics.

"Does anyone *else* think so?" Zika asked.

"Sorry?" he murmured in a daze.

"Does anyone else think you are a good?"

"Well... yes."

"Lots and lots of people?"

"Look, what's that over there?" he pointed with the

hand that still held the little boy's to shorten the inquisition.

"That's the council barge," she said proudly. "That's where Agung goes to meet his friends and decide all the sorts of things you decide when you're boss."

The council barge was a flat, shallow-draft boat with an open-sided pagoda. The roof was decorated with carved wood and painted red and gold. Images of lotus blossoms, monkeys, cranes, turtles, dragons, demon warriors, water snakes, vines and leaves covered its structure, but other than that, it was spartan inside – just a few cushions and a couple of low tables were scattered about.

"But they're not in there just now." Ikatere could see that for himself. "They have special times that they meet and talk and talk... and talk and talk..." Ikatere wondered if Zika would make a council member one day.

They wove through a bustling marketplace. The smells of food from the myriad vendor stalls were a little overwhelming and Ikatere was reminded he hadn't eaten. He looked around to distract the pangs and saw that the curving hull of a large junk had been converted into a block of residences behind the main strip. Colourful banners streamed down its sides, ruffling like a mane in the wind. Beyond that were some lower buildings of canvas and girders with multi-coloured stockings of rope tying it all together. To Ikatere's shock, he recognised the snake-entwined rod painted on its side – it was a health care building. He silently chided himself for his surprise. There was no reason why these people shouldn't have a hospital. A precarious scaffolding of bamboo surrounded a large mast that topped another vessel and workers swarmed over it with simian ease. His mind was brought back to sea level when a heated argument broke out between two neighbouring vendors. The children deftly redirected their path to go around. Raft City was loud and busy. Ikatere smiled.

The three of them roamed up a gangplank onto a

broad punt that had a garden planted on it. Fruit trees
rustled and palms with monkey nuts sieved the sea breeze
through their bristling fronds; taro, ginger and sugarcane
grew in heterogeneous clumps; clover leaves and broad
blade grass brushed his toes over the edge of his flipflops
as they walked down the central lawn. Between the trees,
he could see a bustle of foot traffic. At the far end of the
garden was a large square platform covered in seaweed and
dotted with men, women and children who were somehow
processing the plants. Some were feeding it into
contraptions made with tubing and letting off some water
vapour from tiny chimneys. Some were turning the
seaweed over with rakes. Others were bringing large crates
in and out.

"What are they doing there?" he asked the children.

"Umm, they're making the seaweed into things that we
need. Every time some seaweed gets stuck on our rafts, we
pick it up and it goes here. We use it for lots of things."
Ikatere resolved to make some more enquiries with a taller
human being.

After a few more turns and gangplanks, pontoons and
precarious rope bridges, they stopped in front of a large
floating shack. "We're here," the little boy Vam
announced. "This is Uncle Agung's house." The children
released his hand and left him staring at a doorway that
was barely covered by a hessian flap. He tried to look into
the darkness of the gaps around this doorway, craning his
neck this way and that, when a man stepped out, preceded
by a chicken.

"Hello," said the man. Ikatere suddenly woke from the
dreamlike state he had entered with the children. Here was
the man whose face was usually captioned with words like
"modern day mafia don" or "murderer". He had bare feet,
Ikatere noticed. The man was waiting for a response.
Ikatere opened his mouth but not much was happening
there. The man rolled his eyes.

"Come in when you are ready," Agung said and went

back inside, the hessian flap falling shut behind him. Ikatere looked at the rolling deck beneath his feet. Its planks were silvering. His foot moved to the threshold.

More children ran in a gaggle through the houseboat, shouting and laughing. Agung moved his cup of tea out of their path while a yellow, fat puppy squirmed over his lap. "My sons," he said in passing. Their shouting grew fainter as they left to take their adventure elsewhere. "And this is my daughter Putri," he said dotingly to the baby who sat in a crèche improvised from a clothes horse. The baby wore a nappy and some drool. She looked at Ikatere with sober seriousness.

Ikatere found his manners. "Lovely," he said politely. "It's a little different than I expected here," he said slowly, trying not to offend.

"What did you expect?" Agung asked with an honest note of enquiry in his voice. Now Ikatere was stuck with how to word it diplomatically.

"We get told a lot of things by official channels. It seems the Corporation of Attorney States has got a real chip on their shoulder about you. They say you are bad people." Agung's lips pressed together and he nodded for some moments.

"You know at first I was a Middle Blocker then the Affiliates of Solidarity took us over in some kind of concession deal. No-one asked us about it. One day we were just a different state with a different government." Ikatere nodded, feelingly. "At one point we got hit by two super-typhoons within about two weeks of each other, and we were left with nothing. I mean, nothing. And nobody would help us. What are you supposed to do when you used emergency funds to rebuild your house and it gets knocked down in the next typhoon? At some point the handouts stop. I got sick of it and I decided to leave. So we came out here. The Affiliates didn't like it one bit. They don't like it when people leave them," he said. "But the

Corporated States liked it even less. Call us a 'rogue state'. We're just some people!" Agung shook his head, amazed. "They think it's a bad example when folk try to set up on their own. Probably give their citizens some ideas. And nobody likes the undeclared, the unknown quantity. They want you to pick a side. When you don't, they give you names, like 'Gomorrah'. And they make up stories. Anyhow, I imagine I'm on all of their shit lists," he concluded.

The puppy began biting Agung's fingers and mock-growling. Agung wiggled the little dog's head back and forth by its jaw's grip. "Shh," he told it. A woman was humming a simple song somewhere in the background. "Sakti," Agung called with a long and lilting familiarity. She came out, chewing something and wiping her hands on her apron.

"What?" she said with no trace of reverence.

"Can you get our guest some food?" he asked meekly.

"What did your last slave die of?"

"Please, sweetheart, we're talking."

Sakti looked at Ikatere directly. "Don't let him gasbag you to death," she said and marched out. Seconds later the sounds of pots and pans clanging made Agung smile.

"She loves me, you know," he said confidentially. "Now, what were we talking about?"

"The Corporated States. How they don't like you."

"Oh, yes. They're not the only ones, of course. The Middle Blockers and the Affiliates would have you believe they were liberals, but they don't like us either. People come to us, you see, and use our neutrality to do things they couldn't do in their own borders." Ikatere tensed a little at this. *Illegal drug deals? Black market trafficking?* Agung noticed his discomfort and began to stroke his beard. "Did you see our liner?" Ikatere nodded. The great white ship was hard to miss. "How do you think we got that, stole it?"

Ikatere shrugged as innocently as possible. "When we

were coming out here, we had to pass through the ocean's gyre. It's like a conveyor belt for storms, these days." Ikatere knew that fact well, but he just nodded politely. It was part of a story. "We got our asses kicked quite a few times getting through to the calmer parts of the ocean. A lot of us died on the way." Ikatere blinked. "One day I saw her, coming out of the storm like an iceberg. I thought to myself, it's a sign. Not from god or any of that stuff, but that maybe the universe was agreeing with us, that humans should be free. And that ship was a life-saver. We didn't even have GPS before that, can you believe it?" He chuckled. "I look back and wonder how we ever managed. The liner has state-of-the-art technology and it was left in the middle of the ocean. And why? We looked that up just as soon as we could. We were worried that someone would come to take it back. But they won't. Because its owners know the insurance payments for it are worth more than running it or scrapping it. So they abandoned it, lost mysteriously at sea." Agung shook his head. "How a people can believe that this type of thinking will sustain us is beyond me. Of course, now they're suing us for salvaging without license." He sighed.

Ikatere struggled with his chopsticks. "Have you thought about making your own side of the story more public?" he asked while his fingers and thumb wrestled each other.

"How do you mean?" Agung asked with a noncommittal tone.

"Well, I mean, like getting a life curator." At Agung's frown he explained, "Someone to document your life story, to make holoscenes about it, net programmes, hell, they'll even do songs about you."

"I don't know," Agung said doubtfully, "It sounds terrible. And besides, who would want to look at this ugly mug," he said with a backwards jerk of his thumb.

"I could help you. All I'd ask in return is to be able to

trade with your city." Agung regarded him with suspicion. "Honestly." Agung sucked some seaweed from his soup bowl as he looked at Ikatere in a slightly strange manner. Ikatere was suddenly reminded of Agung's reputation and felt a slight chill to his stomach.

"What about farming the seaweed?" Ikatere said over their ices. Agung raised an eyebrow. "You could make floating mats around the city; it would act as a resource and a kind of defensive barrier. Also, maybe you could let it be known that you were doing it for carbon capture. Make it an environmental issue. If people thought you were trying to save the planet, they would probably be more on your side."

"I like you, you've got big ideas," Agung said suddenly. "Why don't you come work for me?"

"Ah. I'd love to but I can't," Ikatere said, dissolving into embarrassed smiles. He was overwhelmed by Agung's abruptness. "I have to look after my family."

"Bring them here," Agung replied.

Ikatere was taken aback. "It's not that simple. I..."

"Why not?" Agung said with a very direct look. Ikatere felt himself recoiling slightly from its force.

"I... Listen, thank you, I'm flattered but I'd need to, you know..." Agung merely grunted at this stumbling excuse and Ikatere felt some of the contact drop away from between them. With a sinking feeling, he saw that he should make a quick exit. "Is it okay if I trade?" he asked as he put his flipflops back on. "I've come a long way..." Agung merely flapped his hand as either a dismissal or permission. "Please say thank you to your wife for the delicious food," he said lamely and left.

Ikatere idly swivelled the new fish detector between two fingers as he walked from the jetty up the sandy hill. Palm trees contained chattering birds and the sun was beginning to heat the pavement between their shade even this early in the day. He had traded his entire catch for the detector and was wondering if he had made a wise decision when he noticed his house was shut up and quiet. His father wasn't sitting under the porch awning. The scent of garlic and lemongrass wasn't spilling from the kitchen windows. His little brother Tu-te wasn't playing touch football in the yard with his smelly, loudmouth teenage friends.

He climbed the steps to the front door but it was locked. He pulled on it a few times fruitlessly then went back down and around the perimeter of the garden. Ponciana trees with their fiery petals swept boughs down to near the lawn and mango and papaya trees huddled near the back, but their tropical exuberance seemed muted by the silence, somehow. He walked up the back steps and entered. The house was ghostly still. He checked the Statenet and all the phones he could. He even stopped to check the fridge for a handwritten note. Nothing.

He went next door and was greeted almost as soon as he came into their garden by a woman hurrying towards him. "Oh, Ikatere, it's terrible," she cried.

"Calm down, Mrs Kiore. What's happened?" Mrs Kiore had burst into heavy sobs and was frustratingly incoherent. Ikatere suppressed the urge to shake her furiously. "Please, Mrs Kiore," he urged.

Mrs Kiore wiped the back of her hand across her nose. With red-rimmed eyes she said, "It's your brother. They took him. The state. They took him." Ikatere felt his bowels lurch. "They said he had been seditious, but we all know it was just some talk." Ikatere dropped his grip on Mrs Kiore's shoulders and began to run. "He's just a baby," Mrs Kiore wailed after him. "I never meant..."

Ikatere's lungs were fit to burst by the time he made it to the state outpost's headquarters. He ran into the reception area. The ever-present security guards began to cover his entrance as a threat so he slowed and caught his breath. The official behind the desk moved back from his computer terminal and looked squarely at the new arrival. "My name is Ikatere... Punga," he said, still gasping.

"Ah, I see. Take a seat, Mr Punga, they'll be out shortly." The official pointed with a pen to a bench.

"But..." The official stonily pointed again to the bench and Ikatere helplessly went to sit. After aeons had passed and he had fossilised, been dug up and put in a museum, his mother came out with a strange look on her face, holding his father's hand. She was escorted by two burly guards with shock guns and full riot armour, ridiculous against his parents' diminutive frames. Ikatere's body shot him into a standing position without his brain's consultation. "Where's Tu-te?" he asked urgently. "What happened?"

"Mr and Mrs Punga," the official called from his desk. "You have to sign for custody." Ikatere's father was suffering from some sort of catatonia, so his mother approached the reception desk. The official pulled out a small, plastic box and some forms for her to sign. "There, and there," he pointed and she made some desultory marks on the forms. She took the box and, customs satisfied, was allowed to leave. She turned back to her menfolk.

"Mum, where's Tu-te?" Ikatere asked hopelessly.

"Where were you?" was her only verbal reply. She shoved the box into his hands. It was small, just covering his two palms but very heavy. It was labelled, 'Punga, Tu-te-wehiwehi.' An advisory notice cautioned, 'Human remains, dispose of in accordance to environmental directive 5.3.1.' Underneath that, in block capitals it was stamped with one word, 'SEDITION'. Ikatere looked up and the guards around him raised their shock guns. He turned to follow the remnants of his family. The battle was over before he had even known it existed.

The nighttime harbour was a syncopation of buoys beating against hulls, cables ticking against masts and waves slapping and slurping around the docks. Ikatere grabbed his mothers arm to steady her as she made her way on board. "Just stay quiet, Mum," he said with a voice gauged to weave into the sea breeze. She nearly fell but he fielded her and delivered her into the cabin to sit, holding a bag on her knee. She perched on the orange vinyl of the bench cushions with the immovable calm of a carved deity; the cheap carpet bag with imitation bamboo handles just a part of the regular habiliment of a bodhisattva or saint. He watched her in the half-light for a moment before continuing his clandestine preparations.

He began to cast off. Chains rattled on their windlasses and ropes rubbed loud enough to be heard in prehistory. His mother began mumbling from inside the cabin, soon becoming a loud argument with an invisible opponent. He hurried back inside. "I don't like leaving your father," she said defensively as he made shushing motions. He knelt at her feet.

"I know, Mum," he said desperately, "me neither. But he's at peace there." A small mound of sandy earth near the foot of Mt Pupuni was where his father took his rest now. Lilies and orchids were planted on it and would hide it eventually. "We've got to go now. There's no choice," he said with a whisper and a kiss on the cheek. She lost her brief spark and stared at the opposite bench dully. Ikatere fended off from the dock as hard as he could. Sirens began to ring out from the island.

He took the wheel and pressed the starter for the props with some trepidation, lowest possible power, but it was no use. They would have to make some noise if they were going to get underway, and hopefully the state would be too distracted to notice. Looking over his shoulder often, he was disappointed not to see any flames. He had expected them to leap high, an avenging inferno. But trees screened off the main outpost headquarters. *Still*, Ikatere thought grimly, *they're going to burn just the same.*

***

Ada stared at the screen and thought about a dog. Not her Dog, not one with intelligent, liquid eyes and a warm smell, no. Just a fluffy, stupid member of the family canidae. Nothing happened. She paired that thought of a dog with one of a moth, grey scales dusting off its wings. Nothing happened. Then she thought of her companions, Dog and Butterfly, or more accurately, watched them. Dog was sitting on one side of the desk; Butterfly was perched on the top of the screen. The display changed and a message flashed up: Login Successful.

A slow handclap began. "Well done," Colleague Oswald drawled. "I am impressed. And can I do this too?"

"Of course, Colleague. I'll setup the imprint process." She tapped a few keys then vacated her seat.

Colleague Oswald sat in front of the screen and nodded with an uneasy smile at the four witric accumulators that were pointing at his brain, reaching their delicate fingers of wireless electricity into his thoughts. His steel-and-carbon hair was sculpted into a series of well-defined contours and his suit was impeccable, even for a Colleague. He turned to her. "And what should I be thinking of?"

"Any strong and familiar impression. A loved one's face, your favourite room in your house, that kind of thing."

"Okay, I have one," he said, sitting up straighter and smoothing down his shirtfront with a hand that ran down his chest. Ada leaned over to click the final button. Colleague Oswald's eyes wandered a little and she realised her breasts were quite close to his face and straightened up with alacrity.

"Should I be feeling anything?" he asked innocently.

"No, there should be no sensations. Wait a moment," she replied, then leaned across to press the button again, but with her other hand so that her back was to him. "We'll have to start again. Please think only of your login key." He nodded and sat more rigidly, eyes goggling somewhat. "We have it now. I'll lock the machine and you can try to login to it using what you were just imagining."

The lockscreen appeared and Colleague Oswald strained at it a few seconds. Nothing happened. His cheeks began to crease with the effort and he began to shudder a little. He broke off with a heavy exhalation then spoke, quickly back to his politician's smooth veneer. "I think that you were better at this than me," he said with a wry grin.

"I've just had more practice," Ada said just as easily, although this was a lie. She had only managed to get the prototype working after a fraught all-nighter. It was a lot easier to visualise something you could actually see. Dog wagged his tail and it thumped on the desk. "Try relaxing your mind and emptying it. A lot of extraneous thoughts can hinder your efforts, such as performance anxiety." He glanced sharply at her and she shone an insincere smile at him. He relaxed back in the chair and stared at the screen, a couch potato in a well-tailored suit.

'Login successful' flashed up and the computer went to its home screen. Colleague Oswald pealed with delight. "Isn't it amazing what we can do with witricity these days," he said and turned towards her, draping an arm over the back of the chair and hoisting one ankle up to the opposite knee, showing off a perfect shoeshine.

"I suppose it would be very difficult for someone to force you to think these thoughts and unlock the system with this method?"

"Impossible, really. Apart from anything else, you have to be in the same emotional state in order for this to work. There are so many layers of information relating to an image. Let's say that you and I had the same login key – which we call a shibboleth – say a sailboat, for example. But your sailboat might have a blue hull, where mine is white. Yours might be on the sea, mine in a harbour. Is it a sunny sea? Which one? Is it a modern boat, or a boat from the last century? Did your education home take you for a trip on this boat? Were you happy? Were you sad? There is an entire landscape of emotions and cross-referencing facts that you're hardly even conscious of. If you were in a stress-state, your patterns would be different. In these ways, this kind of encryption is far superior to retinal or fingerprint kinds as these can be detached from you or faked by another person. With this you must be whole, sound, and most importantly, *you*."

"So can you, as administrator, tell what my shib..."

"Shibboleth."

"... thank you, what my shibboleth was by looking into this system?"

"No." Ada detected a quirk of satisfaction from Oswald. *Something dirty then.* "All encryption software is anonymous by design, generally speaking, but even if it wasn't, our system doesn't look for what the thoughts were, rather it merely detects the neurons that were firing at the time you set it and matches the shape of that pattern. Here, you can see what your neurons look like." She brought to the screen a diagram that held a glowing, three-dimensional network of purple lines. It was a frozen firework, a dandelion seed puff. Certain areas were very bright, others nearly black. "You see, it bears no resemblance to anything in particular, it's just a map of your brain. This mapping would be different on each person, and each person would think of their own particular shibboleth, so it would be practically impossible to guess what it was. You would have to map each person's thoughts for years to be able to do that."

"So it is possible to read someone's thoughts, then?" he asked, casually. He began chewing on one fingernail.

Ada frowned. "Perhaps, but only if they told you each and every thought they had as they were having it, and even then by the act of making them record it, you might change things. It's somewhat like Heisenberg's uncertainty principle in that respect. And apart from all that, the brain is a living, growing thing. Each time you think the same thought, you make that neural pathway more permanent.

Each time you hit your head, some neurons die off and things have to be rerouted. So as I said, *practically* impossible."

"Technically correct! Very good, Ada, that is the kind of exactitude I like to hear from our science graduates." He smiled broadly. "Are there any dangers to the system, any chance that someone could receive a shock?"

"No, Colleague. I know we're all still used to the old lightning bolt icon of electricity, but if you imagine this is a more subtle power source, more like magnetic resonance than current, you'll see it's perfectly safe."

"Could it be changed to be painful?" Oswald asked abruptly, his tone changing. "To perhaps deliver a resonance that is not so comfortable for the human brain or indeed body?"

Ada thinned her lips. "Possibly," she said. "It would require some work to even discover first principles..."

"Good, good," Oswald said breezily. "That is all I wanted to know... about that." He stood up and straightened out his jacket. Fred appeared in the corner of the room and gave Ada that sinking feeling.

"You know, I think you and I might be a good match, genetically speaking. I might just go speak to the Fertility Board today." Ada's head whipped up. "Oh, it's nothing to worry about. It will just mean a few weeks away from work while you recover after the birth. You can treat it as a holiday." His eyes dropped to her chest. "You know, you really should start to wear a bra once your pregnancy begins. You're young enough to get away with it now, but saggy breasts are so... unappealing, don't you agree?" He met her eyes again. "But since you're young – what, twenty? – I think it's the best time to have a child, decreases the chance of genetic deficiencies. I think we should even conceive the old-fashioned way. Much more chance of a normal pregnancy and of course, much more – " he inhaled sharply and closed his eyes for a second, as if savouring a thought, "– bracing. What do you think?"

"I... I'll have to think about it," she said, smiling with a sickly feeling. She picked up a folder as casually as possible and held it in her folded arms across her chest, wincing at Fred's disgustingly dirty laughter. She felt sure he was dropping his pants again but ignored him as best she could.

"Good. Good," Oswald said as if it were all resolved. "I'll speak to the Board this afternoon. I have a few friends. I'm sure we can arrange things easily. You know there can be such a mess of red tape with these things, but I'm sure you'll agree we are exactly the type of people who should be passing on our genetic superiority." She nodded, feeling faint. "Anyway, I'm sure we'll speak again soon, Ada. Bye-bye." He raised his hand and waggled his fingers at her, pursing his lips a little.

"Err, bye," Ada said awkwardly and stood stiffly as she watched Colleague Oswald exit her workroom and make his way down the corridor. Dog made gargoyle faces at his back, a tangible hatred in his growl. As soon as Oswald was out of earshot, she slammed the door. Fred was laughing so hard tears were coming and he was slapping his naked thighs. She had never particularly wanted to touch Fred before but now the thought of kicking him to death crossed her mind.

She sat down and chewed on bitter thoughts. *If only I had been an Adequate.* Butterfly fluttered serenely into her field of vision and settled on her shoulder, brushing her cheek with her soft wings. "Stop trying to cheer me up," she said out loud, then closed her eyes and dropped her head painfully onto the chair back.

The bra was uncomfortable, but currently it was having the psychological effect of a metal breastplate, shielding her from the world's gaze and in particular, its male inhabitants, one of whom was currently in front of her. She shifted, trying subtly to move the point of an underwire from poking her painfully as she sat in front of the impersonal office desk. The doctor was currently looking down at a folder of notes while he explained her results. "The good news, Miss King, is that you are completely healthy and Colleague Oswald is too. All gamete counts are regular and there is no physical reason why the two of you might not be a match for the programme." She breathed strongly through her nose to try to keep her gorge from rising. The phrase 'gamete counts' was particularly retch-worthy. The doctor looked over his spectacles at her. "But, Miss King – Ada – I am not made of stone. I can see you are not enthusiastic about this match."

"You can say that again," she muttered. The doctor continued as if he hadn't heard.

"It is very common in girls your age to balk at the thought of being pregnant, not at all unusual. So you will be relieved to hear that the Fertility Board has denied the application." Ada was unsure she heard him correctly.

"Pardon?"

"Nothing to do with your compatibility, but apparently word has come from on high that you are to be off the list indefinitely."

"What? Why?" Ada was not keen to have a child with Colleague Oswald, but 'indefinitely' had a ring to it very much like 'forever'.

"I don't know, Ada. They don't share their reasons with the likes of me, I can assure you. Perhaps your work is too important right now. Pregnancy hormones can play havoc with the reasoning facilities and I understand you are quite well considered in scientific circles." He smiled. "Rumour has it you might even become a Colleague yourself one day. You should be proud at such a young age."

"Thank you," she said faintly, mouth on autopilot, head still spinning around other thoughts.

"Of course there could be many other reasons they blocked the application but I think the best thing is to not let it bother you too much. You'll be back to normal in no time," he threw the folder of notes to one side with a flick of his wrist and smiled, "with no more uncomfortable prodding and probing." He folded his hands and smiled paternally. "Consider it a blessing for now. Things change, Miss Ada King, and I'm sure it will all work out for the best. You'll see."

She chased Stackareman down the corridor. "Wait up," she called. He looked over his shoulder to see her trot up and slowed his pace but barely. She overtook him and backpedalled, keeping up to his long, spare strides with many smaller ones of her own. "Did you have a chance to, umm –?"

"Not here," he said with a look of annoyance. "Let's –" he turned her by the elbow and guided her over to a fire door that had been propped open with an extinguisher. They exited into the small rain of a dull autumn. Leaves on the quadrangle trees glowed an eerie lemon and the sun was a mere superstition behind leaden clouds. Stackareman steered them to a spinney surrounded by yellow stalks and red berries where Dog and Butterfly immediately began to get lost in the shrubbery. Fred was probably in there somewhere as well. She began to ask again but he cut her off. "I've looked and there's nothing," he said plainly.

"Nothing?" Her tone was disbelieving.

"Nothing," he confirmed with a shrug and an inspection of his pocket contents. "Which is, in itself, interesting. No one has nothing on them, Ada. Not even the lowliest cowpoke from the former Pomeralian substrate has no file..."

"So why don't I have one?" she concluded for him.

"Exactissimo. Now, about that favour..." he asked, leadingly.

"I'll leave it in under the houseplant again," she said with a feeling of deep dissatisfaction. Through a Byzantine series of favours and secrets, she had managed to find the only drug addict with access to the state system that surveilled their own people, and yet it had led to only frustration. She turned on her heel and her companions were dragged from the bushes in her wake.

She entered her rooms on the sixth floor of the Schlusser Building. A cold wind was going down her neck from the open balcony walkway that connected all the flats. As she was turning the key with white-tipped fingers, she looked over to notice Dara who was entering his place at the same time. Ada smiled but it faltered as he resolutely focussed on turning his key with a hurried motion and she winced as he slammed his door behind him. She sighed and continued in to her own flat.

Clothes and crockery, bags and books lay everywhere, on the floor, sofa, bed, even on the kitchenette table. It wasn't that she was a slob, just that almost anything seemed more important than cleaning and after the years of enforced domestic regularity at the education home she felt like she could live without. She took out a bottle of white wine from her tiny fridge. An advert for a state-sponsored alcohol addiction clinic appeared on its door. She threw a towel over it. *It won't be long until my toilet starts giving me ads for laxatives*, she grumped. Frustrations had been building up recently and as she poured herself a glass, she tried to think about something else, anything. A life away from this one on a desert island would be a start.

She awoke later on the sofa with a scientific journal draped over her nose. Fred was squatting by her feet, like a demon from a Boschian nightmare, sans horns. A groggy recollection that a loud noise had woken her provoked her into standing up. When the room stopped spinning, she took in her surroundings. Dog was asleep at her feet. Butterfly was a thorn-shaped statue. Only Fred was with her. There was nothing in her tiny rooms, but soon the sound of a scuffle brought her over to her door's peephole. She saw a number of black-clad and armoured bodies outside. They were hustling a man past who was silently uncooperative. When the group had gone, she opened her door cautiously.

Feeling unwise, she leaned out into the hallway. After some moments, she managed to convince her hands to let go of the doorframe and tiptoed three doors down. Dara's door was fettered with yellow and black tape. As chills came up from her bare feet on the polished concrete of the floor, answering coldness rippled down her spine, causing her bodyhair to spike like a porcupine. "Property of the Corporation of Attorney States" was emblazoned across it.

4. HUMANITY

Vam was calling his name from at least two rafts away. Then, "Ikatere, Ikatere, you have to go see Agung," he shouted as he clattered his way up the bridge to the decks around the *Bessu*.

"Excuse me, Mum," he said gently and put her foot down. He had been painting her feet with manuka honey for weeks to treat the tropical fungal infection that had made them blister and weep. He opened the curtain they used as a door and waited while the puffing Vam gathered himself.

"It's very exciting, you have to go to the liner right now," he said and began to turn and run back the way he came.

"I'll be there just now," Ikatere shouted at his back. Vam turned and ran a few paces in reverse to wave an acknowledgement before resuming his pell-mell course.

Ikatere calmly finished his ministrations, bandaging his mother's feet with reverence. "I'm such a burden to you," her croaking throat wheezed.

"Shut up, you are not," he refuted, unruffled. She said this nearly every day. "Do you have everything?" he asked at the door. She waved one creped wrist to shoo him out and he rotated through the curtain. Their home was on the outside of the tangle of Raft City with an unimpeded view of the vastness of the sea. His mother had initially been phobic of the view, almost cowering from its enormity. She had never really gone out with them on the boats. "I'm an island girl," she had said ritually as she refused invitations to come out for a jaunt with the fishers, but since the cancer had taken hold, she seemed resigned to anything.

He walked along the perimeter of rafts and boats. Most were someone's home, but also part of a way to cross the city. Rafter manners had grown up to deal with this duality. Ikatere waved at those who waved at him, and ignored those who ignored him. Four rafts in, three over, he hit a thoroughfare barge and shortcut his way to the marketplace. His senses were assaulted with cooking smells, heated plastic, seaweed derivatives, cloned birds of paradise on perches, children laughing and barging by, the taste of salt on the breeze and the architecture of the waxed moustaches of the Raft City dandies.

At the end of the row of stalls, he had to backtrack to a different gangway as they were opening the city to introduce a newcomer's craft to the fold. Shouts and waves from the workers were relayed to neighbouring rafts, who relayed them to their neighbours and so on in an expanding wave so that they would all move a little bit over. A gap of slightly scummy water was widening into a trench to the open sea where the long vessel – that looked for all the world like a canal boat – would slot in and be sealed up into the fabric of the ever-changing city.

After his detour, he continued to the permanence of the ocean liner. Many routes in, both orthodox and improvised, lashed the ship down, Gulliver to the Rafters' Lilliputians. Ikatere looped one foot in a dangling cable and turned over a lever that had been welded to the hull. He rose into the air until he was level with the bridge deck and swung onto a toehold. He opened the gate, incongruously a white picket one, and strolled to the bridge. Agung had no time for secretaries, bodyguards, officials or generals but had managed to accumulate a cloud of general purpose hangers-on, one of whom, Dwi, waved him in impatiently with a scolding look. "Where were you?" he said. Ikatere chose to ignore him.

Agung was leaning by the ship's wheel, holding onto a spoke and swaying his hips unselfconsciously. Ikatere presumed his back was troubling him again. He stood beside Agung and waited, quietly. Eventually Agung, as if continuing a conversation they had just broken off, pointed to the small screen to his right. "Well, anyway, you'll find this interesting." Ikatere stepped over to examine it. Strips of false colour showed the profile of the seafloor beneath them. Most of the strips were deeper blues, indicating depths of over two kilometres. The strips moved in a timelapse to show tranches of seabed in succession. A three dimensional image was building up into a long cigar shape down there. There were maybe a few distortions, but there was no mistaking its general significance.

"Submarine?" Ikatere said quietly in wonder.

Agung looked out of the corner of his eye and nodded. "I think so."

"It could be old. Pre-treaty even."

"Maybe."

"That means it could be dangerous. Even to be in its general area could be dangerous for the city."

"I know. That's why we've been monitoring things, but looks like the background biote count is no higher than it ever is."

Ikatere began to breathe faster. "Are we going to...?"

"No," Agung replied. He turned to look directly at Ikatere. "*You* are going to go down there and see if it can be used."

"How?" It was a deep trench. It wasn't as if he could free dive down there.

"You wanted to go to Marisenal, to exploit the riches of the sea, go where the Totalists failed." Ikatere stung at the words. He'd shared his idiotic dreams with Agung in a moment of home-brew confession, and now they were being flung in his face. "You wanted to explore the deep. Well..." Agung pointed out of the bridge windows to the newcomer, the canal boat-like craft that was still being sewn up into the city. A large panel of water was being left by its side. "We have a gift for you." The sting of shame was lost in a heartbeat. The roof of the canal boat was splitting along its centreline and a yellow set of deck cranes began to unpack themselves. A small but heavy object was being raised by those cranes. "I've been told it can go about five kilometres deep," Agung said with satisfaction in his voice. "Should be enough." The miniature sub was swung over the panel of water by the side of the boat, ready to be deployed.

"I... thanks," Ikatere breathed.

"Don't crash it."

The floodlights stabbed white blades of light in front of the small observation port of tempered glass. This was the only real aperture in the sub's hull; the majority of the views of the exterior were via cameras and displays that gave a three hundred and sixty degree field of vision. Ikatere's sweat was beginning to get chillier as they descended further from the tropical heat. He had taken a crash course in sub handling from the city's pirate feeds into the Middlenet and after a few agonising moments when he thought he would crunch into the hull of the sub's mothership, he had taken them down below the waves.

Two other men had volunteered to come with him. One was named Luis and the other Dan. They had armed themselves with cutting and breathing equipment but both of them were currently looking upwards, sending prayers to the surface world. Occasionally, bubbles of air would escape from the bottom of the sub – intercessory messengers. Ikatere was looking outwards at the panoramic blue. He had hoped to see some sea life, but once they had past the sunlit pelagic zones, there were fewer and fewer shapes nearby. He had hoped to see an angler fish, a sperm whale or colossal squid but the ocean was vast and very, very empty.

They descended towards the maritime trench and the view became inkier and inkier until it was night. Not the velvety, star-and-fairy-lights night of the city above, but Night the Destroyer who haunts all newborns. Ikatere became very conscious of the possibility of failure of the floodlights. He tried to stay calm but each and every pressure clank of the mini sub's hull made Luis and Dan jump and some hardwired trait of herd mentality made him flinch along in time.

When the trench began to narrow until the floodlights could pick out a rock face in front of them, Ikatere could feel the tightness of his chest that he hadn't realised was there until it began to relax in response to sensing something concrete. Soon the downwards cameras picked out the shapes of tiny fumaroles. Their infrared signatures materialised onto the instrument HUD, no longer dissipated into the enormous heat sink of the ocean and the sub's handling began to react to the rising water. He swooped the mini-sub along the white boneyard of albino crabs and tube worms' chitinous furls that clustered around the little volcanoes of life at the bottom of the trench. After a few hundred metres' turbulent glide, they came to the black bulge of the abandoned submarine. It lay like a dead whale, its towering fin ploughed into the side of the trench. Marine life had attempted to gain a foothold here, too. White carbuncles and corals pustulated their ways up the side. It could be a problem, Ikatere decided. If the animals and plants had found footholds in the hull, it might not be sound.

"From its design I would say it was late Secessionist,"

Ikatere said, clearing his suddenly dry throat. His assistants just grunted their interest. Using the inbuilt sensors, he took readings from every possible angle in every possible variant. Using infrared, he looked for hull breaches. In ultrasound, he looked for internal fracturing. He looked for radiation leakage, he looked for hydrocarbon traces. He constantly checked the nanobiote levels. He could find no name or designation on the boat. Nothing was conclusive and they were nearing the return point for their air by the time he'd finished.

"We should probably go back," he murmured. His assistants mumbled some acquiescence, not entirely convincingly. They were here now.

"Right, we'll latch on and probe it. But quickly," Ikatere said impulsively and manoeuvred the little sub over to the larger one, attaching the bottom of their craft on like the foot of a limpet, pushing out all the water until they were sealed tightly to it. Luis opened the floor hatch at the rear of the craft while Dan prepared a delicate piece of equipment. It was a drone that would drill its way through the hull then seal up behind itself in case there was only water inside. Ikatere was proud of finding that bit of tech. It used a trick pioneered in explorations of Europa, Jupiter's icebound moon.

Ikatere kept watch on their air gauges from the corner of his eye while the others set the drone up, hooking insectile legs into the matte surface of their prey. At a command from Dan, the legs of the drone began to flex and the hooked feet contracted, digging small scores along the sub's skin as they gained purchase. The beak of the drill dipped and it had begun. The harsh screeching of its drill drowned out the monotonous hum of the air filters that were straining in response to the heat and fumes of the process. Ikatere was starting to worry that they would be overwhelmed by it when abruptly the sound of its passage became muffled as it sealed up behind itself. Dan monitored the drone's progress on a handheld readout.

The sounds became harder and harder to detect until they were the merest of vibrations, then stopped. They were through. Ikatere looked over his shoulder impatiently. "Water or air?" he asked.

"Give it a second," Dan replied steadily. "Right... right... that's it."

"Well?" Ikatere nearly exploded.

"Air," said Dan. "Looks like there's at least one compartment that's airtight still. Didn't pick up any problems. We can probably refresh our air with theirs. Want to go in?"

Ikatere gave a toothy grin. "Where's the nearest hatch?"

He stared down at the foot of the ladder, some metres below the hatch. He would have to go feet first, of course, despite the fact that their angle that made the ladder almost diagonal. Ikatere tried to dispel all thoughts of being dragged off by unseen enemies attacking feet that would be blindly poking down into the hole, and steeled himself. He had put on a bulky breather suit with the facemask undone just as some kind of protection for an unknown environment. The breather mask would help if there was a problem with the air, but would not make an iota of difference if the ocean decided to equalise its pressure suddenly. At this depth, it would probably bludgeon them to death before it drowned them. His booted feet sounded loud and hollow on the treads.

He landed on the sloping floor with both feet and looked around. The interior was covered by a sheer plastic moulding, smooth and white. He reached one hand out to touch it, but couldn't feel it through the gloves. "Is it alright?" Luis shouted from above. He looked up the ladder well again and gave a thumbs-up. As the others clanked down, Ikatere pushed further into the interior. It was a narrow space, as with most submarines, mostly made up of bulkheads. "Hey it's kind of soft," called out Dan behind him. He had taken his gloves off and was stroking the wall like it was a kitten.

"Don't touch it," Ikatere warned. "It could have the plague for all you know!" The man snatched his hand back from the inviting white wall.

"It looks clean," he said doubtfully.

"You can't see the plague, dumbass," Luis said sardonically. "That's why it's called the nano-plague." Dan put back on his glove, looking slightly pale and sheepish.

They came to a pressure door. "Do we have another drone?" Ikatere asked. The men shook their heads. A slap-pad with a small screen above it was mounted on the wall beside the door and there was a central wheel in the middle of it. Ikatere considered the possibilities. "Hold onto that," he pointed to the door wheel. Luis took hold of it and braced himself. Ikatere touched the liquid crystal of the small screen. Nothing happened. He sighed and hit the slap-pad. The wheel-lock began to turn and Luis groaned.

"It's too strong, I can't stop it," Luis cried as the handles started to drag his heels across the floor.

"Go! Run back to the sub," Ikatere shouted. The other two ran towards the ladder. Ikatere lifted his mask and latched it on. He tried to grab the wheel and pull down with all his weight, to slow it and give them time to escape, but it was inexorable. He let it go. It was no use. He looked at the small screen above the slap-pad. An image was slowly forming. The liquid crystal was cracked and colour-spread but something was coming through. It was showing what was on the other side of the door, a ghost of the future. The door swung itself open.

The woman wore a white outfit that fell in lines so clean they almost hurt the eyes and she glowed with an unearthly radiance. Her blonde hair was laser straight and her eyes were violet; not the sort of bluish colour for eyes often described as violet, but actually closer to purple. Her hands were clasped neutrally, neatly in front of her. "Who are you?" she asked, sounding politely curious.

"My name is Ikatere," he responded, slowly. His mind began many calculations. The sub had been here for probably fifty years, maybe up to a hundred. "And you are...?" He made cautious movements as he entered the room. It was configured with command chairs and large instrument panels. A bridge, then.

"I am *Liberty Via Force*," the woman answered. "For whom do you fight?" she asked, tilting her head slightly to the side. Ikatere began to breathe a little faster.

"There is no fighting anymore," he answered, holding up his hands, placating. "At least, not for the people you're thinking about. Things have changed. Access your comms and you will see I'm telling the truth." The woman frowned, a little puzzle of lines crinkling her forehead in an appealing way. She closed her eyes for a moment, then opened them and nodded.

"I cannot access my base. I was put on dark protocol. It has been a long time," she said thoughtfully. "It seems that things have changed. I conclude you are truthful." She lifted her chin and it was then that Ikatere heard the descending buzz of some system powering down. He forced his chest to let out his breath. "But of course, there is still the matter of your trespass on Secessionist property." His breath deserted again as the system buzzed and spun up again. This time he noticed little ports opening with some wicked machinery behind. He began to talk, fast.

"The government you fought for no longer exists. You don't belong to anyone anymore!"

Liberty Via Force tilted her head once more, clearly intrigued by this concept. "And do you wish to make me your property?" she asked, gun ports still open. "Perhaps salvage me?"

"I don't think I could," Ikatere answered honestly. "Can we just try to be friends?"

"Friends," she said dreamily, as if testing the word in her mouth. "Perhaps."

As Ikatere and his crew walked the interior of the *Liberty Via Force* submarine with her avatar of the same name, he explained the history and troubles they were having above, on the surface world. She walked beside him, measured tread and hands clasped behind her back as she listened to the human interpretation of events. Luis and Dan walked behind, attempting nonchalance. "And you mentioned that there was a treaty regarding the use of nanobiota that would affect vessels like myself?" she asked gravely.

"Yes, technically you are illegal. There was a problem with the way some nanobiotes worked... and, well, it wasn't great for us humans." Ikatere looked around uneasily at his surroundings. Wouldn't the plague have manifested itself by now it lurked here? Wouldn't he start to feel it? "So all nano-tech was made illegal. If you were found by one of the established states, they would have to destroy you or face being attacked by the other members of the treaty."

"But you are not a member of the 'established' states." Ikatere nodded to confirm. "And so, not subject to this treaty."

"We are more or less outside the system. But of course, I'm not sure that the established states would recognise our sovereignty and so would probably still strongly suggest the treaty applies. That is part of the problem we are facing now with our day-to-day functioning anyway. The three super-states have been trying to foist their laws on us. It's all very tricky."

"But you think that your leaders would not attempt to destroy me."

"Our leader sent us to find you in the first place. I very strongly believe he would never destroy you. We have far too few resources. In truth, we are weak." He changed the subject. "What was the last thing that happened before you went dark?"

"My crew, who were Secessionists, guided me to this trench. They ordered me to sever all comms with the outside world, disable my location beacon and left."

"Did they say they would come back for you?"

She frowned. "They did not. I did not ask. I somewhat presumed..."

"Do you think that truthfully, they intended to retrieve you someday? Why do you think they did not turn you in for decommissioning?"

She snorted, a quite unexpected sound from a holographic projection. "Decommissioning," she spat derisively. "I was something new, something they had never tried before. Perhaps they did not want to waste their efforts." She seemed almost angry, a stiffness in her posture.

"Perhaps they did not want to kill something that seems so... alive." Ikatere said gently. "I have not seen anything like you, even today. You are perhaps unique in all the world." Ikatere glimpsed a vast loneliness in her eyes for a moment before she recomposed herself.

"In any case, if what you say is true about the treaty, I will have many difficulties. And so will your people if you associate with me. After all, if they wish to destroy a vessel just for having nanobiote capabilities, what will they feel about my arsenal?" Ikatere stopped in his tracks, nearly colliding with Luis and Dan. *Liberty Via Force* spoke over her shoulder. "Did you not hear my name clearly?" She continued to pace, leaving them to catch up. "And so, to be associated with your rogue state may be dangerous for both our existences." They stopped in front of a new bulkhead through which she showed them a small room. "This is where some of my crew rested when they were inside of me." Ikatere winced a little at the terminology. "You may rest yourselves here before returning if you wish."

Ikatere lay on the perfectly crisp, dustless bedsheets

and began to think about what they could possibly do next as the others excitedly reviewed the day's discoveries. He could not bring the sub back to the city, at least, not for any length of time, without the danger of detection by one or more of the states and subsequent attack. On the other hand, it would be foolish to give up a potential weapon of such strength. But then, the sub seemed to have a mind of its own and with a start, he realised that this was possibly quite literally true. He mulled the many possibilities over in his mind and began to doze. He woke himself up several times as he was falling into the depths of sleep with snores and murmurs. The final time he did so, he sat bolt upright. "Marisenal!" he shouted, frightening Luis and Dan awake.

As they approached the deepwater city, *Liberty Via Force* displayed her enhanced imagery on the bridge. It felt like they were flying through the water. Marisenal itself looked somewhat like an Aztec temple complex that had been reclaimed by the jungle. That, crossed with a hamster run that had an absurdity of tubes and junctions. The outer surface was covered in algal growths, sponges and corals and thanks to the false colour spectrum supplied by the submarine, it was a gem studded reliquary too. Oranges and pinks glowed within the greens, whites, and blues of the growth. Fringes of marine plants waved gently in the current. The silvery ripples of the seabed flowed over the city's multitude of anchoring stilts and made the darkness of the depths a moonlit desert.

To their port side, a dump site of machinery and equipment was gently corroding on the salt currents. Marisenal had been conceived as a mining settlement that would reap the wealth of minerals on the seafloor and even electrolyse gold from the seawater itself. But for the amount of wealth it returned, and the hardship and energy cost of living with hundreds of metres of seawater over their heads, humans had left this place, much as they had given up their mining of the moon. Grand dreams built grand piles. Behind the city, at the top of the seamount, was the gigantic tower of an Ocean Thermal Energy Converter, its top half lost in the haze of water overhead. The OTEC tower used the difference in sea temperatures to boil and cool a volatile chemical, probably ammonia, to turn turbines and drive the city's energy. Large fish were treating the tower like an extension of the mount, circling in a timeless dance.

The sub nosedived in a hawk-like swoop to emerge in a moon pool, shedding a waterfall as it rose. *Liberty Via Force* stretched her arms and arched back her head in a very human posture. She inhaled like a yogi. After exhaling, she said, "The air is good enough in here for you. But take your breathing equipment just in case you hit some pockets of carbon monoxide. Or other gasses that might be toxic to you." She gave Ikatere a look that made him think, *puny humans.*

"We'll just take a look around. See if we could use this place." He was beginning to become a little dizzy. Marisenal! He wished he'd brought a holocam. What a film it would make, the first person to step inside the abandoned city... the discoverer of an A.I. submarine... But of course, the story could never be known. He would even have to be careful who knew about this place among the Rafters.

"I hope you do like it," *Liberty Via Force* said sweetly, "since I have taken the trouble to come here. While you are away, I will do my best to restore some power to the place. It may not be possible without some longer intervention." He assumed she would use her nanobiotes to inspect the OTEC tower. If the ammonia had seeped away, she would have difficulty.

Ikatere and his team began to prepare. They put on their breather suits and shuffled towards the ladder in the fin tower. He made the awkward ascent to open up the hatch and poked his head into the atmosphere of Marisenal. It may have been breathable air, but it wasn't exactly sweet. To say the air smelled of damp was to say that sashimi was a bit fishy. He switched on his headtorch and shone it out over the darkness. The docking facility was a huge rectangular moon pool inside a warehouse-proportioned bay that his torch beam barely illuminated. Ikatere hooked his legs onto the tower's exterior ladder and began his descent. Halfway down a smile appeared on his face and he jumped his feet on to the handrails and slid the rest of the way down. "Always wanted to do that," he said to himself.

Up above Luis and Dan were arguing a point. "I'm just saying," Dan just said, "why doesn't the water come up into here?"

"And I'm just saying, because of air pressure, dummy." Luis replied.

"So why did we have to worry about it when we were going to open up the sub?"

"If you don't understand, I'm not going to waste my time explaining it."

"You'd better stop talking to me like that."

"Fucking giggleheads," Ikatere muttered under his breath.

He crossed to the side. The mini-sub was still attached to the hatch on the foredeck like a carbuncle. As Ikatere passed it to approach the edge, looking for a way to get to the dock dryshod, an organic rippling motion like knuckles pressing beneath a rubber sheet rippled the hull. A bulge began to deform the side of the sub in the wet darkness, reaching and probing upwards. It hardened and ossified into a small ramp.

"This thing is not right," Luis moaned.

"This *thing*," Ikatere said as he ascended the surprisingly grippy slope, "can probably hear what you're saying. So, you know, don't be an arse." Luis promptly shut up.

They quickly surveyed the dock. There were a few other rusted yellow craft, some half-submerged, others removed from the water by the hulking, silent dinosaurs of cranes. Nothing looked particularly operational, which was a shame. It would have made setting up here a lot easier.

They exited the docking shed though a small pressurised lock and Ikatere felt an immediate change in their surroundings. The air pressure was much lower and they found themselves in a tubular corridor. "Hold on a second," Ikatere said. "Turn out your lights for a moment." The head torches that were creating a mirrored reflection on the corridors snapped off one by one and the darkness fell.

"Why are we doing this?" Dan complained.

"Shh," Ikatere merely replied. As their eyes adjusted to the gloom, they noticed shadows gliding above their heads.

"What the fuck is that?" Luis said, panicked.

"Sharks." Ikatere smiled. A long and familiar silhouette blocked the meagre light from the surface above them.

"Fucking great," Luis said as he turned his head torch back on, making Ikatere's eyes hurt with the sudden change. "Just what we need." Ikatere watched him stomp off up the corridor. Dan turned his torch on too and curled up his lips. Ikatere looked up. The beautiful ballet of shapes above his head had disappeared and he shook his head as he followed.

At the head of the corridor was another pressure door. Ikatere inspected it as the others worked out if it would be safe to open, arguing the exact wording that the *Liberty Via Force* had used. He ran a hand over the surface. It was surprisingly rough. "It looks like these have been grown, rather than built," he said wonderingly. The others seemed indifferent to this. "They would have to stretch a skeleton out then encourage the biorock material to grow in the right pattern to make a solid fill. It's actually a way of mimicking nature. We're standing in a giant, living thing."

Luis seemed to react to that. "Would rather people built it," he said glumly. "Can't trust nature. Always turns around and bites you."

They finally decided to unfasten the pressure door and

the view opened out until their headtorches only vaguely lit the farthest surface. There was a musty, stale smell and a lot of indistinguishable shapes. "It's big," Dan said, his voice skipping away into the vastness of the space. A metallic bang sounded in the darkness as the echoes died away. Something large and thumping made its way towards them – had it detected their movement and was bounding closer to them? Something alive, down here in the darkness? An automated defence system? The thumps came inexorably nearer and nearer. They backed quickly, instinctively towards the door, torch beams going in all directions trying to detect what was coming, seeing nothing but blurs and shapes swinging in the panicked stabs of light. Ikatere stumbled into the others when they couldn't get out of his way fast enough and he thought he would trip and fall but abruptly the hall flooded with painful illumination. He stopped the undignified retreat while he forced his eyes to unsquint. There was a lot of mess, but nothing living or moving could be seen. "Libby's come through with the p-power," Dan said with a grateful stutter. *Libby*, Ikatere thought dizzily. *I wonder if she'd like that.* "It must have been some old machinery reactivating," he said aloud. The others were bent over, panting, looking like they'd just finished a footrace. Luis was giving him a baleful glare, but Ikatere ignored it and began to take in their surroundings, now lit. He turned off his headtorch and stared in amazement.

The great hall at Marisenal was a grandiose affair. Balconies were draped with mildew-tattered hangings. A central botanic space had grown rotten and dank in the darkness without power. Fronds of plants had rotted beyond decay and into some sort of mummification. Cells open to the main space lined walkways along each wall. They had apparently been attempting to compensate for the grimness of undersea mining with a leisure arcade. On a protrusion at the end of the hall, a statue of a woman with upswept wings overlooked the destruction below.

Piles of wrecked furniture were lying about as if the previous inhabitants had been building bonfires they had never lit. Twin tracks of a tramway encircled the hall and disappeared into a tunnel at the far end, beneath the statue.

"I think Agung would like us to bring him that," Dan breathed, neck craned back. Dangling from a broken housing, the railgun looked thuggish, muscular, brutal. "He's always going on about lack of defensive capabilities."

"I think you could be right," Ikatere said with glee. He pounded Dan on the shoulder.

"I'm not so sure about this," Dan complained as they mounted the steep ramp of the maintenance tube. He was taking point, gingerly feeling his way along in the orange glow of the bulkhead lights. Luis was bringing up the rear, and Ikatere was stuck in the crossfire of their bickering.

"I couldn't see any other way to get up there. Could you?" Luis replied.

"No, it's just that it feels a bit, well, thin and..."

"It can't be that thin, Dan," Luis interrupted. "It's been here how many years without flooding? Why would it start now?"

"I'm just telling you my opinion. What do you think, Ikatere? You're the engineer."

Not really, he thought, but now was not the time to discuss credits and course modules. "It does feel slightly brittle. I imagine these kinds of things would be not as robust as public areas. Less traffic and so on. I'm not sure if we shouldn't go back and try the tram tunnel. There might be a kind of service shaft off that." As he finished talking, a crunching sound came from beneath Dan's boot.

"Yeah, let's go back," Luis said, and with this reversal, started back to the bottom of the tube.

A horrendous crack allowed a thin jet of water into the tube. It hissed past Ikatere's face with skin-piercing speed, making him jerk back and fall onto Luis who barely kept his feet. Dan scuttled away above the crack, inching his way up the tube on his backside. A jagged breach in the structure began to widen and soon the jet became a torrent of freezing water that fountained in, surging around their legs, nearly taking their feet from underneath them. Dan shouted something that they could hardly hear. A depth of water was beginning to rise at the bottom of the tube, against the lower edge of the pressure door that sealed it. "Quick, get that open," Ikatere shouted at Luis. They hurled themselves at the central wheel and began to strain. Ikatere felt something distinctly pop in his side but he ignored it.

It was no good; the pressure door was not budging. Some kind of override in the presence of seawater must have sealed it. Ikatere looked up to Dan who was still gazing hopelessly at them above the crack which was now a hydrant. "Go up," he shouted. "Try the other end." Dan cupped a hand to his ear. "Go up, go up! Luis, put your breathing mask on." It wouldn't help if the water reached equal pressure with the crushing depths of ocean outside, but it was something to do. The water was now at waist level and was so painfully cold, it felt like battery acid. Dan seemed to understand but respond in slow motion. *Go faster!* Ikatere willed.

The crack widened, opening a trench between Dan's feet. Ikatere was beginning to lose feeling in every limb. He was shivering uncontrollably, working his way to the side of the tube. There was almost no grip as he tried to kick himself up the flume without falling into the gap.

What if I could swim out? Ikatere thought to himself. *Would I make it any distance before being crushed?* A bizarre thought that perhaps he would be alright made him begin the process of hyperventilating as he would before his free diving fishing trips, but it was hard to take the air from the breather mask in when the cold was taking his breath away.

The pounding surge of the water suddenly began to

sound fainter. *I'm passing out*, he thought. It was true that blue spots were appearing in front of his eyes, but the water sound did actually seem to be lessening. He looked across at the gash in the tube. Unsure if he could trust what he was seeing, it seemed ice was forming at the edges of the tube. Frost-like formations that should have been washed away were growing and crystallising across the gap, closing it. As he watched the process, it sped up, and the ice became whiter, less translucent. The tube appeared to be sealing itself.

"I think," said Luis, panting, "We're going to be alright." Disbelief. Relief.

The level of water at the bottom of the tube began to sink, defying its normal behaviour and being somehow dragged out of the hole. Dan was cautiously descending. Ikatere began to shake even harder as the water evaporated from his skin. Tiny drips were being flicked from his hair with every spasm. His side was a dull agony now.

The sound seemed to shimmer out of the air. "Do not worry." Libby's voice seemed to come from everywhere at once with a buzzing, vibrating sound. "My nanobiotes have ensured this structure's own growth patterns are repairing this conduit. I will now attempt to undo some of the damage done to you. Do not panic."

The buzzing came closer. Sudden warmth began to steal into his purple-and-white blotched fingers and so into his core, his marrow. The pain subsided in his abdomen and when he pressed his hand there, he could almost feel the small knot of the hernia suck back inside. He began to feel distinctly hot. Panic surfaced. The nano-plague had supposedly felt like this. Humans just burning up from the inside. "Libby," he moaned. "Libby." He could barely speak.

The heat subsided into a normal temperature. He felt neither hot nor cold. *Liberty Via Force*'s cloud of nanobiotes vibrated again to speak for her. "Do not panic, Ikatere. Your fears are unfounded." *Are they?*

He spoke to the air, to nothing. "How did you know to come and help us?"

"My nanobiotes just happened to be inspecting that part of the city for structural integrity when they noticed the breach. It is simple, Ikatere."

"Yeah, sure," he said gruffly. He stood up and coughed a few times. "I guess we had better go back," he said, addressing Luis and Dan. "We'll just have to leave it, I think."

"Leave what?" The nanobiotes asked innocently.

"There's a railgun we were going to retrieve."

"There are no problems, Ikatere," the cloud buzzed. "The gun will be retrieved. Although why you would want such a primitive machine is beyond me."

"I imagine it is," he said sourly and turned to the pressure door at the tube's bottom, which opened at a touch of his hand.

Ikatere watched from the deck of the liner as the mini-sub was winched back into its mothership. The railgun inside it was heavy and the deck cranes' motivators could be heard whining even from here. The bustle of Raft City's usual activity seemed somehow smaller now that he had returned. "I can't help but notice you were gone an awful long time. We had given up on your return. But most of all, I can't help noticing you've brought me nothing back," Agung said mildly.

"Don't worry," Ikatere responded, still thinking a little dazedly about the submarine's avatar, wondering if it had been programmed to be so alluring, or if it had chosen its own face. "I've brought you back quite a bit." He scowled around at the collective hangers-on. "But they'll need to leave before I can tell you about it." Agung waved them away casually and turned back to Ikatere. He enjoyed the looks on their faces as they reluctantly left the bridge of the liner.

"I brought you a sub, a gun and a city," he said. "Is

that enough?"

***

The liner's fog horn sounded and over the deep thrum of the engines, the clatter of a thousand smaller boats starting up could just be heard. Agung used binoculars to sweep the city for problems or incidents. A spout of water in the first quarter and some shaken fists indicated that even the jet ski had been started successfully, although perhaps not to its neighbour's delight. All hands were on deck as they began the migration.

Over the many days of its somnolence, the city would drift and change and after a while, it would have to be moved. Agung had also found that moving through different zones would attract a different set of clientele, vital to keeping the economy churning over. Different markets would open up and visitors and refugees would come when the city was within about a day's journey by water. People escaping the scrutiny of their state would do business in the relative reclusion. Agung was sure that some of the deals and meetings were not exactly clean but his policy was that the city was neutral territory and that all business of a violent nature must be carried out elsewhere or the offenders would be floating home.

The taste and smell of the city would change subtly with each slow circumnavigation of the ocean's all-encompassing embrace. Different spices would waft from the markets and the canny food trader would alter their offerings to fit the palate of the newcomers. Different fabrics would emerge like the shiny grey suit of the slicked-back gangster, the formless wrappings of the political refugee, even envoys dressed in obvious disguise – steel grey coiffure and silk's shimmer would be hidden beneath headdresses and hempen sleeves. Harder-edged or more guttural speech and skin tone would change the cadences and chiaroscuro of the city. Today they would be heading north to cruise beside the sovereign waters of an archipelago that was a member of the Corporated States.

It was not an easy task to move this disjointed mass of floating units. A concerted effort of all the citizens who were capable was needed to redirect the rafts in symphony. Other citizens who could not help were brought into the liner's ballrooms and restaurants to wait. Picnics and a fete-like atmosphere usually pervaded these gatherings as the elderly and the young tended to the infirm and played pinochle, quoits or charades. Down below in the city, young, strong backs disassembled bridges, untied hawsers and fended off until separate components were freely floating where possible, and GPS coordinates were piped to each major vessel indicating the way to go. The floating grids of kelp farms had to be towed to the back to follow along like dog trailers and the city became more like a maritime comet, trailing its tail across the seas.

The fog horn sounded twice and Agung secretively watched Dwi as he pushed the liner's accelerator slowly. "Careful," he hissed from behind his shoulder, and the man's hand snatched away from the lever.

"It's on the lowest setting," Dwi hissed back. "I wish you would let me do this by myself."

Agung did not answer but raised the binoculars again. It was a difficult and tense time for him, watching his city break apart. He had to hope that it would come back together again as successfully this time as it had in the past. They were under way.

The sun was high above by the time they were arriving at the agreed stopping point. "We're a little near the Corporated States border," Dwi said, looking at the map readout.

"Just as long as we don't cross it," Agung replied confidently, "we're in international waters. Nothing they can do. Well, we're here, let's tie back up."

The foghorn sounded twice again and the flotilla of smaller vessels prepared to stop. The liner reversed its engines and any boats behind had to do the same quickly, or risk collision – or worse. They came to a relative stop and cut the engines. Bodies swarmed over to the side rails and cables were thrown down to the crafts and rafts below. Agung ran an expert eye over the patchwork quilt as the city quickly joined back together. The smaller rafts found it a quick process as they only had to tie up with their neighbours and throw back down any planks and bridges they'd taken up. The longer process was getting the kelp apron back around. Motorised junks and jetboats towed the light frames back gently to reduce damage to the sea plants. He surmised that the city was almost exactly as it had been before the move. Perhaps one or two boats had taken the opportunity to swap places, but for the most part, business could recommence.

"Ah," he said with satisfaction. "Our first customers." He took out his binoculars again and squinted towards the smudge of grey on the horizon. It was big, whatever it was. There might even have been more than one.

Dwi's voice broke in. "We're getting a warning from the coastguard. They are telling us we are ten kilometres within their waters and if we don't move off, they will fire!"

Agung dropped the binoculars away from his eyes. "What happened?"

"I don't know! The GPS still says we're in international waters."

"Quick, change the GPS feed. Get some readings from the other instruments! I'll organise getting us out of here." He raced away from the bridge. "Sound the fog horn, and keep sounding it," he shouted to the men who were just finishing tying off the liner's largest gangway. "We have to go. Now!" The man was stunned, so Agung pushed him a little and he seemed to recover.

"We're going to reverse engines," he bawled down to the rafts at the stern of the liner. "Ready your engines." His words were drowned by the basso groan of the fog horn firing off quick-paced blasts. Faces from the city below turned up to look in confusion. He desperately jabbed a hand at the horizon back the way they came and had to hope they would understand.

He pelted back to the bridge. The ships were alarmingly much closer. "Dwi, start up the engines again."

"Agung, it's dangerous!"

"I know, but we don't have a choice," he snapped. "Do as I say." Dwi unwillingly turned the large sets of keys and pressed the buttons that started up the powerful propellers of the liner.

"What now, Agung?"

"We're going to haul them with us. Reverse all."

"But it'll never..."

"Get out of the way, Dwi!" Agung shoved the slender man from his hometown across the bridge and took control of the lever. He slowly edged the ship into full reverse. He would just have to hope. Dwi dashed out of the cabin. Agung could see the hawsers at the front of the ship getting taut. Still he increased the acceleration. He heard a crashing, splintering sound and felt the ship judder. He'd hoped it wouldn't be this bad, but the floating kelp mats and smaller boats behind the liner must be rucking and piling up on each other. He hoped the propellers would not pull them under.

The coastguard cutters were fast and were gaining on them when part of their bulk detached and hovered up into the air. They were sending helos. The aircraft gained with alarming velocity. There was no way to evade them.

The helos came right up to the city and one hovered so close to Agung he could see the pilot's face. "Raft City," boomed out from some hidden speakers, "you are violating the sovereign territories of the Corporation of Attorney States. This is an act of aggression and piracy. If you do not remove yourselves we will fire upon you."

"What do you think I'm trying to do?" Agung shouted at the helo.

Suddenly there was a pop and a hot smell of metal and plastic burning. They'd fired on one of the rafts! "You bastards!" Agung screamed. "Dwi! Dwi! Where are you?" He forsook the bridge long enough to call in one of the men to keep the ship under course and swung up the side to the observation post at the very top of the liner faster than he'd ever ascended before.

Dwi was there, calmly loading large cylinders into the belly of the railgun "We can't shoot them down," said Dwi with angelic patience as Agung flustered, trying to speed him up. "But we can fire a few warning shots, make them retreat. It might give us enough time." Agung could see the raft on fire from here, a wallowing old tub that housed some of their copra supply. As it was burning and foundering, the neighbouring craft were rescuing its crew and pouring water whilst trying to keep up with the direction of the big ship. Some of the craft weren't able to handle this reversal, and were being dragged by their connecting lines. Some were nearly being swamped and he could see people bailing, desperately fighting to hang on. He glanced aft and saw that the destruction was worse than he'd imagined, great swathes of raft and kelp rucked up into concertinas. It reminded him all too depressingly of the typhoon.

He looked away again to witness Dwi pushing a few buttons then pulling the clunky lever that fired off a canister, magnetically accelerating the metal to speeds that set the air around it on fire. There was a deafening boom as the canister detonated safely away from the helos but made them wobble in the shockwave. After a few seconds, the aircraft backed away. "That went well," Agung said uncertainly.

"The trouble is that they don't have to leave us alone as soon as we get back to international waters," Dwi said glumly. They were both shouting a little loudly after the firing.

"What? Why not?"

"Hot pursuit," Dwi explained. "Because we drifted into their territory, they can chase us into international waters if they want."

The helos began to fire again, white exhaust clouds marking their missiles' trails. "Shit, intercept, intercept!" Dwi punched the buttons again, then fired off continuous rounds that exploded chaff and flack to confuse the incoming rounds. Agung clapped his hands to his ears. A few of the attacking missiles wobbled off course and exploded above the sea but two streaked towards the city. One exploded midair in an orange flower and another nearly shook Agung and Dwi off the roof as it struck the liner. Agung ran to the edge and flattened himself on his belly to peer over. "I think it's above the waterline. Anyway, keep intercepting. Do not fire on the helos or ships, alright?"

Dwi gave a thumbs up and continued his grim work. Agung slid down a small antenna to land with a backwards lurch on the deck. He ran back into the bridge. "Have we been able to get a proper fix?" He shouted. One of the men poring over the GPS console nodded. "Where are we?" He pointed to the map readout and Agung shouldered him out of the way to have a closer look. They were still miles from International Waters and if what Dwi said was true, it wouldn't make any difference. He shut his eyes and thought for a few seconds, mentally remonstrating with himself for lack of brains.

Suddenly he opened his eyes and stabbed a finger at the map. "North," he said to the man at the wheel, bellowing over the explosions of more chaff rounds from Dwi.

"But that's away from International Waters," he protested.

"I know, but it's Affiliates territory. And it's closer. Now do it!"

If they could last just long enough to get inside the Affiliates of Solidarity's borders, the Corporated States could not follow without declaring war. And from there, they would try to limp back into International Waters before the Affiliates could muster a response.

Agung tugged on his beard, thinking on the strangeness of how the GPS had misdirected them here and the coastguard had shown up so quickly. He would have to try to find out how that happened, if they survived. Firing went on above his head as Dwi took out a few more enemy shots, but for each wave one or two were getting through. He hoped they would survive long enough to hang out the bastards who did this for the seagulls. □

5. SYMPATHY

There was a lot of hauling to be done. The constant beep of loaders reversing filled the main hall of Marisenal. Ikatere was inspecting the progress of the supply stores. They were beginning to rip out and refit some of the arcade's cell-like shops on the ground floor and had finally forced a few pressure doors to spread out on the upper galleries. The huge piles of furniture and debris that they had found left abandoned by the former inhabitants were being sifted through by workers with gloves and boots for anything worth recycling. Most of it appeared to be useless, rotted by years of damp. The smells of refuse, glue and sawdust were all-pervading.

He walked to the shop halfway along the parade that was being used as a tea room. Luis was inside, boiling some water by heating a pan with a small blow torch. "Hey," he called cheerfully as he noticed Ikatere come in. "Are you setting off soon?" Ikatere nodded and pulled up a rusted wire-frame chair that had been scavenged from the heaps. Its style was so comedically retro that he felt ridiculous sitting in it, like they were in a period drama or something.

"Am I going to be okay leaving you two in charge?"

Ikatere asked, folding his arms and rocking a little in the chair. It made some alarming sounds so he stopped. Luis looked offended.

"I know Dan isn't the sharpest knife in the box, but he's a hard worker..."

"I meant you as well. How are you managing?"

"There's nothing really difficult to do. Sort through the junk, continue cleaning the atmosphere scrubbers, clear out the things that are rotten..." Ikatere nodded, chewing his bottom lip thoughtfully. "It's easy. Just a bit of hard graft."

"How is the crew?" Luis' face dropped a little, and he turned back to the boiling water, which was beginning to bubble and steam.

"Well, you know how it is. New surroundings, little spooky down here. Plus there's your cloak-and-dagger routine." Ikatere had put the crew on strict non-disclosure. Not even their families were to know what they were up to or where they were going, just that it was good for the City.

"So tell me what the stories are."

"Dunno what you mean."

"Come on, man. Who do you think I am?"

"Are you sure you want to hear?"

"I like a good laugh."

"Alright then," Luis said as he switched off the blowtorch and made them both a cup of tea. Ikatere allowed him to take his time, but tapped his foot a little nevertheless. "Here goes," he said, giving Ikatere a mug and sitting down next to him. "The statue is infected by the nano-plague and comes alive at night."

"That's a good one," Ikatere conceded, blowing on his tea.

"There are a swarm of nano-infected zombie Totalists who wander the halls in the places we haven't managed to restore power."

"Sure, sure. Go on."

Luis made a face. Ikatere guessed this one would be a difficult one. "The ceiling dome," he nodded towards the great hall outside, "is compromised and it will only be a matter of time until it breaks, killing everyone. Or, my favourite, Libby killed everyone here and then ran away and hid in the trench until we found her." Ikatere barked a short, disgusted laugh. "I know. Dan told me most of these and I don't know how many he made up himself," Luis said confidentially.

"What is it with people?" Ikatere said, throwing up his hands in frustration. The ceiling dome rumour was the most troubling in many ways. It was much harder to dismiss with laughter. He drank his tea. It was not properly boiled, disappointingly, and left a bitter aftertaste. He put the mug down when it was finished and stood up, slapping rust off his backside. "I'd better get back. I suppose I'd recommend keeping a lot of breather masks just sitting about. People like having some kind of security blanket there where they can see it. Even if it wouldn't really help if the shit hit the fan." Luis nodded up at him, not quite meeting his eye. Ikatere turned to leave, wondering how frayed Luis' nerves really were behind his bluster.

He returned along the row of shops where there was almost a coherent path between the piles of junk. Next time he visited, most of this stuff would be gone. He felt a strange feeling almost akin to regret tingling just at the back of his throat at the thought of it all being swept away.

Ikatere was roused from his bunk in the *Liberty Via Force*'s crew cabin by a chiming noise. "Sorry to wake you," he heard as he struggled out of his dreams. Libby's disembodied voice projected into the room. "There's been a bit of an issue," she said. "Come up to the bridge as soon as you can."

"Can't you tell me now?" he said groggily.

"Very well," she replied, a little snippily he thought, "I was only respecting your privacy." Libby manifested uncomfortably close to the bed and Ikatere was suddenly and irrationally reminded that he was only in his shorts. He sat up on his bunk. *She's only a submarine. The human body means nothing to her,* he thought as he stood up. However, he began pulling on his clothes just the same. "I've brought you to the drop off point you requested, but Raft City is not within range."

Ikatere stretched. "You took into account the city migration?"

"Of course," Libby said, and Ikatere was sure that if he examined each word microscopically he would not find a trace of offence taken.

"So where is it?"

The submarine's avatar folded her hands in front of her, demurely. "I have discreetly sent my nanobiotes out to see if we could relocate it. I have not yet been successful, but I did find some wreckage, consistent with Raft City architecture in the Corporation of Attorney States' waters."

"What?" he reacted loudly, raking his fingers through his hair, grasping it until it was painful. "What do you mean?"

"It was not a great deal of wreckage, certainly not enough to prove the entire deconstitutionalisation of the city. There is a chance we will find them mostly intact."

Despite her calm tone, his mind was not quelled. *Deconstitutionalisation?* It was a euphemism too far. Ikatere started to pace the cabin uselessly, looking for a direction to disgorge his anger and panic. "We have to contact Agung."

"I have tried," she said, almost timidly. "No reply via radio yet."

He dropped his hands to his side. "Let's start a search, then," he said, fists bunching to contain his anger. "If they were attacked, where would they go?"

"I've run some simulations. Here are my projections."

A map appeared in front of him, on the cabin wall: a

map with an intersection of boundaries, currents and prevailing winds appearing in a fine tracery over it. The ostensible location of the city, the site of the wreckage... Ikatere narrowed his eyes at it.

"Let's go north," he said. "Up here." He dabbled a finger in the hologram, describing an area just to the east of the borders.

"Why?"

Ikatere shrugged. "It's where I think Agung would go."

The view from the bridge screens of the *Liberty Via Force* showed the underside of Raft City on the surface, black shapes against the sky. It was a subverted aerial view of the city, showing the hulls and keels, parts most often unconsidered. Ikatere felt his heart fall at the number of gaps in the pattern. A trail of sunken objects had littered their path on the last part of their search for the city. The liner was still afloat, and it seemed the *Bessu* was too. But his mother...

"I'm going up," he told Libby and she nodded. There was an emulation of compassion on her face, at least. "You should get back to Marisenal. They might be watching this place pretty closely."

"I agree, Ikatere. I'm drawing my nanobiotes back from their search but I don't want the concentration to get too high until I am further away, with this likelihood of scrutiny. Indeed, I can sense there are a few helos and ocean-going vessels circling the city, but keeping their distance. Possibly they are merely observational. So I can't bring my nanobiotes in great concentration just yet. But leaving them out there makes me feel very vulnerable. So the best course of action would be for us to part company again. But you know how to call me back in case the observers become aggressors. I hasten to add this should be your last recourse."

Ikatere looked at her with a raised eyebrow. "Just out of curiosity, what would you do if we did get attacked and

I called you in?"

She pursed her lips a little. "I would do whatever was necessary," she replied openly and without telling him anything. "Good bye for now, Ikatere."

He left the bridge, feeling a little put out by her dismissal. He was beginning to wonder who was in charge.

Ikatere hurried to his mother's side. She was sitting with a view from a portal in the liner's state cabin, where many of the ill had been housed. "Oh Ikatere," she breathed, "it was terrible. Poor people." Her eyes wandered from his and back out to the view. "I'd like my dinner now," she said in a different voice, as if he was a nurse who had been mistreating her.

"You've just had lunch, Mum," Ikatere said gently. The dishes were still on the table in front of her.

"I don't care. Who are you to tell me when I should eat?" she said, turning back, her face twisted with disdain.

"Okay," he said, getting up. "It's okay, I'll go get you something to eat," he said sadly and walked out of the sickbay, shoulders slumped. No doubt she would forget about her dinner order as soon as he left.

He decided to find Agung and get more detail on what had happened. People he had met on his way to the liner had said something about an accident and helos opening fire and even Agung firing back. He walked along the liner's gallery deck past a small welding crew and men with hammers trying to patch the holes. The tang of heated metal hit his nostrils as the skittering static of welding met the clang of metal on metal. "Hey! Hey! Where is Agung?" he shouted down to the men.

One of them raised his mask and shouted up, "Try below. There was a leak in cargo fourteen, he was down there getting it patched."

It explained why he hadn't seen many people up here, but the word 'leak' made him worry about his mother again and when he descended the ladder into the cargo area he was more alarmed still. Great gouts of water appeared to be spurting in from all locations. He shivered with the parallel to Marisenal's broken service tube. Agung was up to nearly his waist in water as he directed a team of men to position a plug and brace while staccato flashes of light nearby indicated someone welding underwater. He was in a wet suit. The black rubber was not flattering, from the spindly shanks of his legs right up to the hood where his facial hair poked out at awkward angles.

Agung waved and waded over as soon as he caught sight of Ikatere and climbed partway up the ladder to meet him. "She will be sound again in no time," he said, a toothy smile lighting up his face. A smear of grease on his cheek was repelling drops of seawater from his skin.

"What happened?" Ikatere asked, unable to drag his eyes from the saline fountains frothing into the hold.

"Not here," Ikatere said, leaning in. "We'll discuss it later. In the meantime, can you get hold of those contacts you have in Middle Bloc? We'll need some other kinds of damage control. I think half the vultures circling the city are state surveillance, the other half reporters. We might be able to use them to our advantage this time."

***

"Agung, tell me, what happened?" the young man with the gentle manner softly asked. "What caused all this destruction?" He gestured to the wreckage of Raft City that spread around them as they sat on the edge of an ordinary pontoon. Agung cleared his throat. He still had some smoke inhalation problems.

"Someone in the world is trying to destroy us," he began, a little scratchily. "We have no idea who, but someone interfered with our GPS system and we were misguided into the Corporation of Attorney State's waters."

"And what did that mean for you?" the young man, Omote Ura, prompted.

"It meant that they assumed we were invading their

sovereign territories and sent a force to attack us."

"Wow," Omote said, "That must have been horrible."

"It was. A lot of people died," Agung said, trying to suppress his anger, "and a lot of my people's homes and properties were destroyed."

"Was there any attempt on the part of the Corporated States to talk to you, for you to explain your side of the story?"

Agung shook his head emphatically. "We were actually trying to leave when they fired on us, so in self-defence, we tried to intercept their missiles."

"So you didn't actually fire at the Corporated States personnel?"

"No, we sent off a couple of warning shots, but other than that, we just fired at their missiles. At no time did we fire directly at them. We are a peaceful bunch of people."

"Agung, how do you answer those who would say you shouldn't have these defensive capabilities –" the young man brushed his upper lip thoughtfully, "– that you shouldn't, in fact, be armed?"

"I would tell them to look around at my city and see what happened here. If we had not had weapons we would all be dead now, I strongly believe," he replied sadly. Omote nodded in sympathy.

There was a short pause then Omote Ura made a few curt, pulling motions with the fingers of his right hand. Small skeins of light could be seen coming from a thin bracelet on his wrist. It produced glowing lines and circles on his palm which he tapped or flicked with his fingers – a gestural command cuff. Agung admired it as Omote deactivated the hovering holocamera drones that surrounded them. They flew in – some from over the water – and stacked into a box neatly. As he closed the lid, he spoke, more prosaically than before. "I'll get some shots of crying children, that kind of thing. It'll be on Middlenet by tonight, and we'll try to get it over the wall to Statenet and Affilicom as soon as we can, although they're getting better at keeping us out all the time. It makes you wonder how their people can keep swallowing the state sponsored crap they constantly get fed without getting the shits." He grinned at an evidently well-practiced line.

Agung said nothing. He knew that Omote was somewhat blindsided by his loyalty to the Middle Bloc, but personally believed they were fed as much of a line as everyone else. "Thank you for coming," Agung said, standing and shaking the man's hand. "We'll get you a boat back to the mainland as soon as you're finished around here."

Omote Ura crossed the bridge from the pontoon to another raft and picked his way across the devastation of the city. "Huhuo," Agung called as soon as he was at a safe distance. A small, middle-aged woman came out of the cabin of a nearby boat and leaned her hip up against the gunwale. "What did you get?" he asked.

Huhuo had a cross-hatching of crowsfeet and freckles after years in Raft City. She wore a furry hat with fox ears although it wasn't cold, a ridiculously outdated style, presumably nostalgia for her youth. Despite this juvenalia, Agung paid close attention to her and waited for her to finish thinking. She squinted at Agung as her boat bobbed gently. "Seems legit," she said. "He's on plenty of feeds. Couldn't find any scent of stateware on him. I guess we'll just have to see how he spins it."

Agung picked up a small comms unit. "Okay, we can let him go," he said. A few clicks and squelches might have been an acknowledgement.

Huhuo crossed her arms. "What would you have done if he wasn't legit?"

Agung avoided her eye. "Nothing that you need to know. We can't afford to take any chances right now. Someone is out to get us. Did you find anything?"

Huhuo jumped over the gunwale and landed down on the platform. She settled, cross-legged on the floor next to Agung. "In order to fake GPS signals you'd normally need a microwave transmitter with some serious output that supplies the fake signal at a higher strength than the real signal. I've been able to look into the system's cache and see which satellites we were receiving transmissions from at the time. I managed to track it back until you could see a little jump in the positioning and ID numbers of the satellites. It happened just before we started to move the city. With all that activity, no-one would notice the switch, or if they did, they'd just think it was a glitch that rectified itself. It's been done cleverly. I can see that there's been a change, spot the fakes, but not tell you who did it."

Agung sucked a little at the bristles on his bottom lip. "We'll release the information anyhow," he said after a while. "It might help our cause a little if people can see we unintentionally went off course."

"The thing is, Agung, the GPS has been encrypted for so long now it is almost impossible to spoof it." Huhuo gazed out to sea as wisps of hair that had escaped from the furry hat fluttered around her face. "Our GPS receivers should have realised there was a spoof attack and at least given an error message." Agung waited for her to finish. Huhuo had a lot on her mind. "The only way I can think of how they would do this is by interfering directly with the actual satellites." She hesitated. "I think an entire state is gunning for us."

Ikatere, Dwi and Huhuo gathered, standing, around the table, waiting for Agung to stop his restless pacing. The wardroom of the liner was dark except for the pendulous lights above the long mess table. "The Corporated States – too obvious," he said to the room in general, running his hands through his hair. "The Affiliates of Solidarity have motive. We left them. But they've got no form for this. The Middle Blockers don't even have motive." He stopped and looked at Dwi. "Could they...? No, no." He shook his head and resumed pacing. The rest of the meeting attendees remained quiet.

Eventually, he stopped and put his hands on a chair back. "Any ideas, any at all?" he said tiredly.

"Huhuo was saying that the holoblogger was a great hit on Middlenet," Dwi proffered. "Got a lot of sympathy, especially among the Ling speakers of the world."

Agung groaned in frustration. "It's not enough! One blogger, two, a hundred, it will never be enough to change the fate of a persecuted group. In the past, so many people have been wiped out and all the others do is shake their heads and say, 'What a shame'. Sympathy is not enough!"

Ikatere stirred, the whites of his eyes bulging in the dim light. "So we need to give them something that they want, so they can't afford to persecute us."

"But what?" Agung threw up a hand and continued pacing. "We've given them trade, a neutral zone to meet, hell, we're carbon negative," he swiped his hand around as if to take in all the kelp farms that should have been there. "At least we were before they all got wrecked. So, what?"

"Something bigger," Ikatere said lamely. "Don't worry, boss, I'm sure that something will come up. We just have to keep an eye out for the opportunity."

Agung raised an eyebrow at him. "I'll start taking ideas tomorrow morning."

***

"The death of innocents and the destruction of property has long been the worst possible outcome of war." The speaker opened with a holoscene of wartime atrocities from the last few decades. Ada recognised some images that had been shown at her school by the propagandists who had visited from the state: images of stacks of bodies like cordwood; enemy soldiers standing with large smiles next to a pathetically small boy whose head leaked red into concrete... the usual. She doodled a picture of Butterfly in her notebook, glancing up occasionally to evaluate the reactions of her fellow prisoners of the state seminar. They looked uncomfortable at the speaker's bonhomie.

They had been ordered to attend this orientation seminar by the university's bureaucratic machinery. She was told she was now working with a new think tank in defence logistics. The Department of Struggle logo could be seen on all the paperwork, and as she had walked into the small, spartan conference room there were even a couple of guards at the door. She had signed form after form of disclaimers, confidentiality agreements and acknowledgements of her new status as a seconded employee of the department. At no point had she been asked if she wanted the transfer. And now this man from some defence contractor company was talking at them. Dog bumped her elbow and slumped against her chair.

"But what if we could prevent that bloodshed and chaos?" The speaker continued. His body language was motivational, as if he was sharing a great truth. He put his fingers up before his mouth. "What if," he continued, lowering them to speak in short snatches, "What if we could just neutralise the killers, the terrorists?" he asked trying to drive up the suspense.

"For many years we have sought the holy grail of targeted technology. Guided missiles, remote controlled drones, satellite strikes, micro-nukes. But the trouble has always been collateral damage. Even a bullet from point blank has the chance to hit someone else. But what if we could ensure our target was the only one to be neutralised? What if we could take out only the evil?"

A holoscene image of General Gonzalo, the de facto leader of the Middle Bloc appeared and slowly turned red. Ada shifted uncomfortably in her seat. She looked surreptitiously at her peers in the audience again. Most were looking down, at their feet or hands. In the front row, Fred turned around to glare at her over his shoulder. "What Parabellum Systems are proposing is research into using witricity as a means to this end. It's possible that in the very near future we could use varying levels of neutralisation and lethality to specifically target the enemies of our people and of course reduce destruction of private property to practically zero. And that is why you are here." The speaker opened his hands to the seminar audience. "Your work in the fields of witric engineering and science has demonstrated your abilities and the state has graciously seconded you to us in a mutual trust initiative to..."

Fred began to cackle and hoot, making Ada inhale sharply. She coughed, convulsively. The speaker paused politely. Fred jumped up on his chair and began to imitate Mr Mull's face again. Brownish purple, tongue out. Ada's cough got worse. She held up a hand. She stood up and walked to the door and past the two guards on either side. They watched her as she nearly stumbled, coughing around the corner to the ladies'. She pushed the door and let it swing open and shut, not moving, becoming silent. Dog sat by her feet, panting approvingly. Butterfly was already flapping down the stairwell opposite.

Ada watched her face, fifty metres tall as it was projected on the side of the black rock. The bowl of the municipal gardens had been turned into a scene plaza during the winter celebrations and this late in the day, it was packed with humans huddling with blankets and hot flasks. The holoscenes played by the castle-topped cliff all festival but at this moment the entertainment had been interrupted to show the face of the missing scientist, Ada King, who had probably defected. She shrugged into her shawl and blanket a little further, glad of the speed of winter sunsets, scarves and woolly hats. Dog curled up on her toes and butterfly alighted on the back of one of her gloves.

"The neuroscientist is wanted in connection with the theft of state secrets," the comforting but authoritative voice of the presenter spoke. "State colleagues have explained to the Voice of the People that the Middle Bloc have been ideologically attacking our young academics for years and tempting them away with promises – that they cannot possibly keep – of lives of luxury and pampering. It is likely that Ada King has now fled the country, but any citizen with knowledge of her whereabouts should remember that keeping this information hidden is a transgression against the state, punishable by re-education."

A man was edging his way along the benches, apologising and shuffling awkwardly along. He sat down next to Ada. "Your hair is different," Stackareman said casually.

"And it will be different again tomorrow," she said just as casually in return. Great long streaks of hair spec had turned her dark curls into a multicoloured and straight mop that covered half her face. She felt Stackareman's hand worming its way under her blanket. "Thank you," she said softly as she took the packet he had deposited on top of her thigh. Dog growled a bit, but she bumped his tummy with her toes, calming him.

They were silent for a few moments, just two friends watching the public scenings as the setting winter sun hit the black rock with its dying rays so the granite crystals sparkled. Now the holoscene was showing exciting and patriotic scenes of new territories acquired in the constant struggle to prevent Middle Bloc from perpetrating land grabs. Some of the new territories appeared to be on the other side of the world and had not been part of the Corporated States until now. "I never want to hear from you again," Stackareman said in a boring tone. "Or I will take you down with me. I don't even fucking care."

"I understand," she replied with a false note of cheeriness. "You won't." She had used her knowledge of his drug addiction to persuade him to supply some false credentials. She didn't know if it would be enough to get her out of the Corporated States, but she had to try. Guilt at the blackmail was tempered by the knowledge that Stackareman would probably betray her eventually. By the time he figured out that he might get immunity by turning her in, she would have used his fake line of credit and ID to get new ones and she would probably do that at least a few times to cover her trail.

He surprised her with a question. She had been expecting him to ask *Where will you go*, or *What will you do* next, some information that he could use to bargain with the authorities later, but instead he asked, "How does it feel?"

Her heart rose as the answer slipped from her lips with hardly an intervention from her brain. "Like I'm alive," she said to the evening air, watching the smoke of her breath drift into fascinating shapes, "for the first time." It was true. Ada was more ready for this than she had expected. She had taken to walking around with her lips pressed into each other and her nostrils flared. It was a horrible, cramping sensation after a few hours but it seemed to fool facial recognition on the hover drones and cameras for now. She had got in touch with Andy, the student squatter from her first year at the University and he had been shocked to see her at first, but offered sound, if terse, advice on who to speak to, where to go, pressing a few food bars into her hands before getting her out the door.

Stackareman rose and touched her shoulder lightly. "Be right back," he lied and shuffled again along the rows of seated people, apologising and lurching away. Ada narrowed her eyes at his back. *Probably two days*, she thought, rocking Dog's tummy again with her foot to comfort him. *Two days before he betrays us.*

Small hail ticked at her window, driven by gusts of wind. Ada sat up in bed with the dubious bedclothes over her knees and watched as the net curtains moved in the tiny draught around the window frame. It was afternoon. Patterns of damp on the wall reminded her of the coffee-stained paper they had made at the education home, in order to draw palm trees, dashed lines, tantalising Xs marking spots. Occasionally she would nod, sway, her hair would fall down over her face, but a creak of the old wooden house frame or a gust rattling at the windowpane would jerk her upright again.

She would not let herself dwell on it, but it would creep in at the edges of sleep: humane execution. She would not let herself dwell on it, but the thoughts would not go away, so she tried to confront the fear objectively. They would freeze her. Slow enough that she would feel her life ebbing, fast enough that it would take her breath away. Then they would shoot sonic vibrations at her, shivering her apart until she looked like animal feed, then sand, then dust. They would put some of her symbolically into a box and if her mother didn't come to collect her, which seemed likely given history, they would file her in a warehouse somewhere until the warehouse fell from age or disaster and she would be free to mix again with the world, drifting into the carbon of the grass or lifting into a sandstorm. Eventually, she might be present at the birth of a new star, perhaps some of her would remain material long enough to see the end of the universe. Of course, by then she might be pure energy, radiating into the infinite. Dog began to whine. It was a heartbroken sound.

The seaside guesthouse was ancient and had not been cared for. It was two storeys high with stucco, whitewashed walls and a dullness that some architect, back in the mists of time, had thought would really set off the sandy flats around it. She had been here for a few hours of snatched sleep, but Fred had made an appearance and she needed to think of somewhere else to go. She had fled the city and headed in an illogical direction to the shore, taking many weeks, reversing course occasionally and changing her appearance where she could. She had been wearing large-framed sunglasses outdoors but it was too noticeable now, the weather being the way it was. She had begun recently to chance her expeditions out only in the rain, which might foil security cameras and allow her an excuse to keep herself well-covered. She got up and looked into the mildew-spotted mirror above the room's basin and wondered if she could cross-dress successfully enough. She saw a strong jawline, a large nose. It was a possibility. Butterfly helpfully landed in her hair, ruining the vision.

She began to stuff her paltry belongings back into her rucksack. She sniffed a few items. They were beginning to smell now. There wasn't enough time even to wash things in the hand basin and then leave to dry. She smelled like the homeless men that she would sometimes ask for contacts. She would need to find a boat out soon. The coastal borders were well patrolled and the disincentives for those captured smuggling people out of the Corporation of Attorney States were as high as for those who wished to leave but she would have to find a way. They would find her sooner or later, no matter how devious she was. It would be a chance recognition or a suspicious landlord and that would be it. Over. Done. She would need a boat in the next day or two at least. Fred was beginning to get on her nerves as well. He wouldn't leave her alone, giggling and snorting for the last fortnight. His lank hair was looking particularly nauseating and he often sat right on her feet, making her involuntarily kick in her sleep. She tried not to look at him now, but he was imitating a gibbon, leaping and crouching and waving his arms with a nearly voiceless wheezing sound.

"I'm going, alright?" she muttered angrily. She lifted her jacket hood, hoisted her bag and opened the door to her room slowly. She paused at the head of the stairs to listen. She could only hear the wind. The other guests would be out for the day and the owner, a dowdy woman with a penchant for ponies according to the decor, was not in view. The stained glass door at the front entrance showed no shadows. Ada stole down and into the street.

The lonely arcade of out-of-season tourist shops was a sad and deserted huddle by the front. The hail had turned into intermittent stinging drops of rain and the sea was a turbid brown as the breakers spilled over the strand. Ada and her companions walked in a knot to the south end of the town where there was a harbour. They passed the vast and bulging terminus of the seawater cracker that had supposedly killed this town with its ugliness, whilst simultaneously promising a supply of cheap, clean power. The only trouble was that the power had not been even half as strong as promised and the terminus sat as a reminder of entropy and hubris. The zero-sum game of human energy needs had still not been fully solved, and Ada wondered if it ever would be possible.

She stopped staring at the cracker hub and a jolt strummed her nerves as she saw a man cutting across her path from the end of the arcade of shops. Fred went insane and Dog had already started to bolt. She followed him. "Wait," the man called after her, but she was not about to stop. A group of men began to run towards her from the south, right in front of her path so she vaulted the small wall to her right and felt a crunch of pain in her ankle as she landed on the stones that formed the sea defences. She strangled a cry, righted her balance and managed to scramble down to the sand. She made straight for the sea, getting to the easier running of the wet sand and mud and turning south again, but her attackers had not followed and merely paced her from the pavement. She made for the very furthest tip of the beach where the bay swung around and a barrier of rocks meant that the men would have to pick their way over it while she waded around the end.

The blackness of the razorback rocks stood like a grim warning. She hardly noticed that the waves were churning violently at the tip of the point as she kept looking over her left shoulder at the men, pacing her at a dog-trot from the hard surface. One appeared to have given up, was talking on a phone or a radio. Her lungs were not keeping up the pace, she was going into oxygen debt and wet sand was clinging to her shoes, flying in gobbets and setting her ankle on fire. The point was close, though. Dog had stopped and was barking, stupidly, at the waves. They looked like they would overwhelm her, but there was no choice, now. She started to wade into the water, shocked at the cold. *This is stupid*, part of her thought. *Humane execution,* another part thought. *At least my clothes are getting a wash,* thought a third part of her that had a sense of the ridiculous as the water reached up to her chest. Her shoes were coming loose as they began to expand in the water and the backpack was getting heavy and pulling her backwards. Suddenly she was swept off her feet and into the brown-green washing machine of a breaker. She flailed and something unyielding hit her head. A hand grabbed hers and she was jerked back upright, her arm nearly out of its socket. She burst into the painful air. "It's alright, honey," a voice said as she coughed and vomited up brine and sand. She felt arms around her, holding her. "I've got you." Butterfly moved in and out of a blur as she roosted on the shoulder of a man. Her head sank involuntarily on to a chest of black material. She smelled rubber and salt.

Her lungs and her forehead were killing her. That was her first thought. Her second was that she was in a tiny space, cramped but soft. A holding cell? She was lying on her stomach with one heavy arm dangling off the small bunk. She pushed herself up onto all fours then sat heavily on the edge of the bed, feeling the small bandage over a large egg-shaped swelling just above her right eye. Her eyes fluttered and she coughed, sending jarring lances through her head and chest. But the pain was irrelevant, really. She was going to be executed. Now that it was going to happen, she felt a kind of calm acceptance. Butterfly drifted down into view and sat on the back of a small chair in the corner. Dog came wriggling out of the bedclothes on his stomach, tail wagging. "Stupid mutt," she said with sad affection and patted his head. He sniffed her hand happily. "You've got no idea, do you?" she said and pulled softly on his ear.

She studied the room to see if Fred was hiding somewhere, ready to unnerve her but he wasn't. His absences were sometimes as jarring as his presence. She checked under the bed, a little self-consciously, but there was no space under there, just a solid bedframe that reached to the floor. As she looked up, she saw a woman sitting in the chair. Ada sat bolt upright.

Sensations flashed: *guilty, pants-down feeling of being unaware of observation. Anger, teeth clenching. Captor or rescuer? Benign? A new companion?*

"Ah, I see you are awake", the woman said conversationally. There was something cold to her tone though. "My name is *Liberty Via Force*." Ada frowned at her. The woman had a strange glow about her, a saint of cleanliness. "You are Ada King," she said in a matter-of-fact tone. Dog was still snuffling about, somehow oblivious. Fred was still in hiding. Butterfly could not be seen. Ada realised with confusion that Butterfly was probably still sitting on the back of the chair, behind the woman, out of sight.

"I am a state of the art submarine," the woman continued but then she paused, wistful. "Or at least, I was, if I am completely honest. Possibly still." A submarine? Ada thought. It explained the architecture, but not much else. "In any case, I am represented here by this holographic avatar."

"Are you AI?" Ada asked, suddenly interested. "Fully Turing compliant?"

Liberty Via Force made a face. "Turing was a little strange in what he classified as 'intelligence'," she said. "Let's just leave it at that. You will no doubt have questions, but," she lifted a hand as Ada made to speak, "I am not the one to answer them. I am merely here to point out the security features in this part of me. Here, here and here," she pointed professionally into some corners of the room, "are micro-turrets that fire highly frangible rounds at a rate of two hundred per second. The thing to note about frangible rounds is that although they are designed to break up easily, everything is relative," she said with a note of satisfaction. "The easy breakup means it will not cause any significant damage to my hull structure, but the downside of that, from your perspective, is that they tend not to go cleanly through the human body, but fragment quite a lot inside." She leaned forward in a way that reminded Ada of the Home Mother, Esmerelda. "This means it tends to damage your organs and soft tissues quite a bit."

Liberty Via Force stood up. "So please, for your sake, and the sake of my standards of cleanliness, don't try to leave this room. I have been told to inform you that you are in international waters. You are safe for now and that you can rest assured that if you co-operate no harm will come to you. There is a washroom in that alcove and someone will be along shortly to fill you in on the rest of it." The hologram of a woman abruptly vanished, leaving Ada with an afterimage that made her blink a few times before she could see Butterfly. She looked down at Dog. *International waters.* His tongue lolled out happily. She pulled him closer and began to cry into his shaggy neck fur

6. THE MINGLING OF THE WATERS

Ikatere leaned in the doorway. "Umm, Ada?" he said softly. He could see the girl in the dimmed cabin. *Liberty Via Force* had thought that evening spectrum light would be calming. Her eyes were red-rimmed and belligerent. He supposed he should have expected that. "Hi." He came into the room cautiously. "How's the head?" The dark shadow of a swelling where she had bounced off a submerged rock looked angry. It went well with the rest of her. "Do you remember me?" he asked gently. She shook her head, silent but still defensive. Her eyes flicked up to the mini-turrets not quite quickly enough for him to miss it. "I pulled you out," he prompted. "You know, when you ran into the sea?"

"Where are you taking me?" she asked with a curious wobble to her otherwise assertive voice. She looked and sounded like she had been crying into a pillow. He was a little taken aback by these signs of vulnerability after all the information the Statenet had pumped out about her. He knew they were full of it, but still part of him had expected a monster. She seemed like just another person. Youngish, frightened, maybe. Normal.

"We're taking you to our home. If you want, it can be

your home too. I know you don't have a place to go right now. Sorry for frightening you earlier. We'd have explained it all properly but you ran off and after you nearly drowned..." he shrugged.

"You mean those goons chasing me were your people?" She was outraged. "What the *fuck*? And what's with keeping guns on me? Who are you?"

Ikatere clasped his hands in a begging motion. "Please, Ada, we really want to be friends but if you did something silly we'll all be in trouble with the Corporated States and ...." He sighed. "Listen, I know we didn't get off on the right foot, but I used to be a citizen of the States too and I found a way out. I just want you to have the same thing." Her eyes gleamed in the half-light.

"How do I know this isn't a trick?" she asked slowly. "You could be a Colleague, just lulling me into telling you things before you freeze-dry me."

He thought for a few moments. "Well, there's Libby," he concluded. "I mean the *Liberty Via Force*. Don't tell her I called her that." He tried for some humour but received a stony silence in return. "I guess what I'm saying is, they don't have anything like her in the Corporation of Attorney States, do they?" She sniffed, a kind of concession to his argument.

"You still didn't answer me. Who are you? What state are you? Where are we going?"

He smiled; a wide grin. "I'm Ikatere and... Raft City answers the other two." She looked gratifyingly astonished. "But first we'll probably stop off at the lost city of Marisenal." He almost laughed. Her eyes were now those of an owl on amphetamines.

Ikatere allowed Ada a moment to stare around at the great hall of Marisenal. The mouldy banners and sigils of Totalist propaganda were long gone and the workers were finally in the process of replanting the park. Ikatere pointed at a gardener with a rotary hoe. "It'll be good to have the park up and running. It's useful for atmosphere control and people don't like living under the sea very much, so it's good for their minds too. Restful, looking at plants." She grunted, seeming uninterested in the technicalities of submarine city logistics. Her eyes were raised up to the statue of the winged woman. They had kept her despite her fascist symbolism but some wag had put a cleaning caution cone on her head like a hat. Ada seemed strangely fascinated by it.

He took her elbow in hand. She was still nominally in his custody though she seemed to have called a truce for now, and had agreed to cooperate in order to tour the city. He wasn't sure she wouldn't try something stupid, but there was nowhere really she could go. He steered a path down the arcade of cell-like shops. They were beginning to be used as quartermasters' stores and workers had started claiming some as private accommodation. The city was filling with activity, but it seemed somehow transient to Ikatere, as if it would be deserted again once the work was finished. The rota of staff taken from Raft City had to be run on a lottery basis as volunteers were scarce and these had been drawn from a small enough pool of security-cleared people to protect the city's secrecy. He would probably get hell from Agung for bringing her here, but since he was in charge of the project, he could do what he wanted for now.

A noise, a kind of groaning and creaking ran through the upper dome-like structure of the ceiling and almost everyone stopped what they were doing and looked up. Something settling, somewhere. Libby's nanobiotes had gone through the entire city for any compromised structure but somehow the men and women who worked here were still easily spooked. Ikatere frowned. People were supposed to be able to get used to anything. Why was he the only one who felt at home here?

"What's it like owning a city?" Ada asked abruptly.

"I'm not a... I don't own anything here," he protested,

surprised. He had never thought about it like that.

"Why not? I thought you found it?"

"Finders keepers, eh?"

She smirked a little sardonically. "Who does then? This Agung you're taking me to, allegedly?"

"Not allegedly. I am taking you, don't worry. It's just that it was easier to stop off here on the way. It's still a long way to Raft City. And no, he doesn't own it either. I don't think it's occurred to anybody to put their dibs on it. It's a city: lots of people coming together collectively. It sort of owns itself, I guess. Like Libby owns herself but she works with us for our mutual benefit."

"Yes. You seem to get a lot more benefit from her than she does from you, though."

Ikatere didn't reply to that. It was true that although they offered the *Liberty Via Force* the shelter of Marisenal she could probably cope on her own in any case. He changed the subject.

"What exactly made you want to abscond from the Corporated States?"

He noted a kind of tiredness about her posture at this question, a slumping of the shoulders, a dragging of the feet and he stopped walking to face her. "After I graduated," she began, sounding reluctant, "they gave me a job in the university cryptography department. I had done well in neuroscience. It has always fascinated me. I did enjoy it, at first. It was challenging. But they were pushing me towards using the technology to do things that I was not prepared to live with. It was either run or kill myself. I chose run." She jutted her chin out defiantly.

"What sort of things?" Ikatere noticed a sudden air of clamming up and a tension in her arm. "It's okay; you don't have to tell me. I know what they're like," he added bitterly. "We're very close to my old home, here. They took it over in a bloodless coup, but it was..." he sighed, remembering. "It was bloody awful."

"Yes," she said stiffly, "it is awful to be under someone

else's control." The icy levels of irony made him feel depressed. He gripped her arm a little more firmly than he intended as he pulled her along again. It was unnecessary. They both knew she had nowhere to go, and he kicked himself at his vindictiveness.

After a few minutes, he tried to brighten up and pointed out the tram that would soon be operational after the tracks were sand-blasted to remove the corrosion. "We've set up witricity broadcasters and it's just about working with the OTEC tower. It pulls power right from the sea, just with the difference in temperature between layers."

"What's the output?" she asked with a sudden professional intent.

"About a gigawatt."

"Oh," she responded, and the spark of interest dwindled.

"Well, it's enough for most things. Maybe it's time for us to get back to Libby. We've got a long trip ahead to get to Raft City." He spun them around and began to march back, causing her to stumble a few times catching up with his stride.

"You know, the reason I'm not worried about you sitting behind me is that if you hit me on the head, I'll release what we'll call a 'dead-man's handle'. It's not really that, but I don't want to give you any clues." Ikatere barely looked over his shoulder at Ada as he prepped the mini-sub for undocking from the *Liberty Via Force*'s upper deck hatch. "Once I let go control of the sub, it'll lose all power. No heat, no light, no buoyancy control. I know you're a scientist. That's why you're here." He heard a fidget or two from the young woman who was sitting, like he, in an undignified semi-straddle over the drive shaft in the cramped space. "But I don't think you'll figure out how to get control back before it hits the bottom and we're both turned into fishy pancakes." He allowed her to see a flash of his teeth before he punched the detachment sequence. There was, of course, no dead-man's handle. Even so, he didn't want her trying anything desperate. She would end up running out of air or steering it into a sea-mount and end up just as dead.

"Goodbye Libby," he murmured. "Safe trip." The *Liberty Via Force* was returning to Marisenal under her own recognisance. Not that Ikatere was under any illusions about human command of her. She had been taking a small risk shuttling the project workers this close to Raft City, but there wasn't much choice. Marisenal was deep; she would be hidden in its dock from most detection except perhaps another submarine coming right up next to her, but people had to come and go somehow. A flotilla of ships hanging around on the surface above the city to taxi people back and forth would be too obvious. They had decided, or rather, she had informed them that as long as she didn't linger and they took the mini-sub for the final stretch, she would be unlikely to be detected bringing them back to Raft City.

As the blackness in the mini-sub's screen moved from the metallic solidity of the submarine to an all-encompassing sea-black, he hit the flood-lights and two cones of white flared out into the gloom. Ada fidgeted more restlessly, as most people did when confronted with the deep for the first time. He thought he heard her make some sub-vocal sounds. "You know, you talk to yourself a lot," he said conversationally. The sudden stillness behind gave him a wry satisfaction. "It's okay," he said reassuringly. "Everybody does it sometimes. Especially if there's no-one more interesting to talk to." He laughed. "But don't worry. Plenty of interesting people up above."

"You still haven't really told me much about what Agung wants with me." Some petulance, he noted.

"I know, but all will be revealed. Patience, Ada King. I'm really just the delivery boy. I could tell you what I think he wants, but then I could be wrong. Agung never tells anyone the same story."

"So he's not trustworthy? He's a liar then?"

Ikatere laughed again. "I'd trust him with my life... and with your life, when it comes to it. And the life of my family..." He shook his head. "A lot of people put too much stock in what they think is 'truth'. After a while you find out it's all just another point of view." *Old man*, he chided himself a little. It was hard not to treat her like a child. The Corporated States education had a lot to be desired in terms of worldliness.

"Still, you're not giving me a great impression. He's a liar, he kidnaps people..."

This time Ikatere actually turned around and met her eye. "Kidnaps? You want me to take you back to the Corporated States?" *I'll turn this sub around, young lady.*

She pressed her lips together for a moment before answering, "No," grudgingly.

"Well, then." He turned back to the controls and they spent much of the rest of the journey in silence. After an hour or so, the view changed. The blackness lifted to blue. As the hull clanked and expanded, cables weighted with stones and rings of old wheel rims descended into the water. They grew silky fronds of khaki, olive, purple and orange. They rose into the small forest of kelp and other seaweeds. Ikatere turned off the lamps and let the surface light filter into the small cabin. Colourful small fish darted in and out among the hypnotically waving garden. "This is our seaweed farm," he said, tour guide voice. "Kombu, dulse, giant kelp." He pointed out. "You know we're capturing enough carbon here to get back to pre-nano levels within fifty years."

The nano-tech treaty had done more than control the plague. It had helped prevent the runaway levels of greenhouse gases from the deluge of nano robots that humanity had embraced fifty years previously. Advances in medicine, engineering and science had been abandoned in order to control the damage to the ecosystem. They were still dealing with the fallout. But nothing would have been done if it hadn't been for the plague. "That's very... *worthy*," Ada said.

"Yes it is, isn't it," Ikatere said, blithely ignoring any sarcasm. "Of course, we've been advertising the fact on the Middlenet and some guerrilla blogging on the Statenet and Affilicom, but it's hard with the Great Divide. That's what we call the disconnect between the three state comms nets around here. " They rose through the dense mass of green until a small portal of sunlight could just be seen above. "Everyone still thinks we're some kind of pirate savages without the moral compass of the state." He heard her snort in derision and allowed himself some hope. She probably had more reason to hate the Corporation of Attorney States than even he did. After all, she'd lived all her life in the industrial, steel-lined womb of their heartlands.

He presented Ada formally to Agung in his house. She looked a little fazed by the surroundings. "Please, please, sit," Agung said in his broken Experana as he cleared a space on a sofa between cables, kids' toys, cushions and crockery. His sleepy face wore its widest smile for their guest. She looked a little disgusted at the place, but Agung thumped it firmly a few times and said, "Sit," once again, leaving her little option. A small cat appeared from nowhere and jumped onto her lap, making her tense briefly, as if she had no idea what to do. Agung laughed at her and patted its head. "Good cat. No worries," he said comfortingly. She hesitantly began to stroke it, and it purred loudly.

Ikatere pulled over a cushion and sat on the floor. "My Experana bad," Agung said as he found himself some space, liberating a chair from beneath a pile of books. "So Ikatere..." he made a talky-talk motion with his hand. He then continued in a blistering string of Ling and watched Ada's face as it was translated.

"He says he is very happy to meet such a great scientist with such a grand reputation and welcomes you to his home and to Raft City." At this, Sakti bustled in with four cups of hot peppermint tea. Ada hesitantly took one thanks to an insistent burble of Ling that would have been incomprehensible to her, but presumably the motherly tone worked and she held the cup over the cat's head. Sakti took one for herself and hovered at the side of their conversation. Ikatere blew on his cup and watched Ada heroically swallowing the boiling hot tea with barely a twitch. He knew that it was currently scalding the entire inside of her mouth and throat and hid his amusement at her watering eyes. "His wife, Sakti, also welcomes you and hopes you're not tired or hungry. In fact, she insists that she will feed you up, very soon," Ikatere said with a smile. "She also says you are very pretty and that she could tell you were a genius and of genuine good character as soon as she looked at you." Ada's face and neck went very red immediately, but her shoulders began to retreat from her ears.

"Now to business," Ikatere translated on for Agung. "Where were you going to go?"

"What do you mean?"

"After you crossed your country's borders. Which state were you going to defect to?"

Ada looked at her feet. "I don't know," she said finally. "Any other state who would accept me, I suppose. I was more concerned about getting out than where I was going to."

"Agung asks if you think it is better in other states?"

"I don't know. They could hardly be worse. Maybe I just wanted to go to a place where you wouldn't be forced to work on abominations to humanity," she said with a defensive frown. Agung grunted at this.

"We heard many great things about you from your state Colleagues."

"How?" she interrupted, surprised and maybe a little

frightened.

"What they said about your defection on their news broadcasts, what they didn't say as well," Ikatere reassured with a hushing hand. "And from other sources. But what we heard made us wonder if you would work with us."

"Are you planning on making me develop new ways to interrogate, torture or murder people?" she asked bluntly.

"No, nothing like that. Ada, we want you to help us do the opposite. We want you to help us make peace. It's the only way we can survive."

"Peace through knowledge," Ikatere said, revising it when Agung grabbed his arm, "Peace through knowing each other." The peppermint tea in his beaker had long grown cold but he took a sip to help his throat. Agung had been talking ten to the dozen, often going off on tangents, often not waiting for him to catch up before moving onto the next long oration. He seemed to have finished now and was watching Ada for a reply, so Ikatere prompted her. "What do you think? Is it possible? Can you help us?"

She was looking at a small toy gorilla on the ground, thinking hard, perhaps a little overwhelmed. Ikatere wondered if that hadn't been Agung's intention. She moved to speak a few times then broke off. Finally, she tapped a forefinger on her lips as she said carefully, "I would need some guarantees." She had guts, Ikatere had to admit. "You will not be intending to use it to interrogate or pry into anybody's minds. Or torture anyone. Secondly, I will have ultimate control over the development project."

Ikatere simultaneously interpreted this and Agung waved his hands magnanimously. "No problem, no problem," he said directly in Experana.

"Obviously," she continued, "I'd want your full protection and a place here for life. I don't want to be thrown to the wolves as soon as I've given you what you want."

Agung looked pantomime-aghast. "Okay, no problem,"

he said clearly, patting his hand on his chest. He continued in Ling.

"We would never use it for the wrong reasons. We are not trying to interfere with our enemies; we are trying to change the world so that it can accept us." He looked off out the window, a rare pause. "People still do evil things. We used to have religion to explain why. We'd simply say, 'this one is possessed by demons' or similar and that would explain everything. But the truth is more complicated. For my children, I would kill you." He watched as Ada tensed up again somewhat. "I'd kill anyone if it was to protect my children. That is an evil deed. But any parent would do the same." Ada's glance dropped to the floor again. *Perhaps not any parent*, Ikatere guessed. "And then you extend the idea from your children to your family and friends, to your country... The evil deeds widen like ripples in the sea." Agung looked at her directly. "But what if we could speak to each other from the heart, and hear each other from the heart? I think we would find out one thing."

He broke into Experana thumping his chest almost savagely. "Everybody different, everybody same!" he said. "All people one!"

"Agung is explaining that the accommodation situation is a little complex here. Often we have to wait until we build or salvage a new craft..."

"You mean steal?" Ada said with a note of impishness in her voice.

"I'm not going to tell him you said that," Ikatere said with a warning look. "We don't steal. We reclaim what other people have thrown out. Most of the time they didn't even realise it was valuable until we make something of it. Then they suddenly accuse us of things," he said bitterly. "Anyway," he continued hurriedly as Agung had become interested in what he was saying, "he says you can stay with me until we find you something of your own. And my mother," he added hurriedly. "He says since we're both from the Corporated States we should have plenty in common."

Ada looked at him with new curiosity. "Yes, you said you were from there, but you don't seem like someone from the Corporated States. And mothers weren't allowed when I was..."

"I guess we'll have plenty to talk about then."

***

The sun was orange and rose as it sank beneath the horizon. "Sun sets quickly here," Ada observed as she sat with Ikatere on the edge of his deck. "Where I come from sunsets are a rarity. Too much rain." She was trying her hardest to be open and sharing like everyone else here seemed to be, but after everything that had happened, it was proving difficult to find the words. They sat together on some battered folding chairs on the deck which was attached to the side of a boat. The name *Bessu* could just be seen in faded black script. The boat had been converted with some uprights and awnings, some pontoons and decking into a rambling, floating villa. Ikatere had been apologetic for the room he had given her – a mattress on the floor in the depths of the hull where it smelled suspicious. There were no windows, so when the light was out it was an oppressive space but it had seemed solid, less ephemeral than the floating decks and awnings setup outside. Ada found it almost comforting.

They had spent the afternoon touring the city as preparation for the project. It seemed clear that Ikatere was in love with the place. He had looked upset when she had nearly gagged on the fishy-smelling delicacy he'd offered and had muttered something about getting used to it. He had frowned, too, when she had been reluctant to enter the crowds at the marketplace. She had never seen so many people with such different skin and hair and clothing before. The people spoke in a babble that did not include much Experana so it was a confusing and alien wall of people that she shied from.

So he had taken her back to his home at the edge of the city and Dog was currently hanging off the edge of the deck, barking into the water and Butterfly was become a firefly in the dusk. A metal bucket of ice and beers sat between them, condensation slowly peeling from it.

"I like rain," Ikatere said shyly. "Water is a problem here, sometimes," he said. "Because we mostly try to stay away from the currents that carry storms, it can get really dry. The seawater crackers in the boats and liner help a little bit with freshwater by-product, but they're not really enough for our population anymore. When we go through a shower all the little kids run out and dance in it," he smiled. "Me too, sometimes." It was hard not to smile in response.

"What's it like having a mother?" she said to the dimming blue of the dusken sky. She sensed, rather than saw, his glance towards his mother's bedroom which was more like to a sarcophagus, an air of ash, linen wraps and death. Ikatere had said that it wouldn't be long before she succumbed to the brain tumour.

"I'm beginning to forget." He stretched out his bare feet, browned by the sun with a rim of white sole. She looked at the small, curly black hairs that crept up his calf with a kind of benign curiosity. "I don't know, I guess that's not fair. She's just always been there. It's been nice. I wouldn't have wanted it different..." He glanced at her quickly from the corner of his eye. "What was it like not having parents?" he asked delicately.

"Oh, I had a mother for a time. But the Corporated States soon put a stop to that. No clue who my father was supposed to be. They don't tell you that kind of thing. Then I went into an education home to be tortured by other girls for eight years. Being a mother apparently took away time that could be better spent working for the state apparatus. The education homes were more *efficient*." She lingered wryly on the last word, tasting it.

"Did everyone in your country have to give up their

children?" She nodded. "I'd heard about it but... Seems a bit inhuman, really. I don't know if I ever actually believed it. I thought maybe they were making up stories. They never made us do any of that."

"They were probably more interested in your strategic value than turning you into model citizens. But yes, everyone where I lived had to give up their kids. It was shocking and somehow deeply... unfashionable to try to keep them. That's not quite the word I mean, but how can I say it? It just wasn't done. The ideal was to whip the baby off the mother's teat as soon as the colostrum had run out. Most children don't have memories of a mother, ergo, supposedly less trauma. But I was always different. Just lucky I guess," she said bitterly, looking askance at Dog, who was growling at some dark selachian forms that could only just be seen sliding under the mirrored blackness of the sea. She had been warned about the sharks. They followed the city. During the day, they turned on the system that repelled the creatures through their electrical sensitivity – so that seaweed could be harvested and children could swim. But at night, they would deliberately turn it off so the sharks would return and scavenge the waste of the city like rats. At night, she imagined it was a good time to push your rivals into the drink.

"So why did you run away from the almighty Corporation of Attorney States?" she asked archly, trying to hide her nervousness about the subject and the proximity of sharks. Her heart was still in her mouth every time an aircraft engine rumbled in the far distance. She had felt a lot safer in Marisenal and the submarine. Claustrophobic, but safer. As the shockingly quick blanketing of night at sea began, Ikatere delayed the question. He got up and pulled some kind of lever. With a *ta-da* act, he showed off his many strings of colourful lights that reminded Ada of a carnival float.

"Do you like them?" It seemed important to him, so she nodded.

"Sincerely," she said, amused. Butterfly did the aerial equivalent of strutting among the colourful puffs.

"They're all bioluminescents. I made them," he revealed modestly. "They take up sunshine in the daytime and if you give them a little encouragement, they'll give off their excess energy at night."

"How did you do that? Gentech? Bioengineering? Viral manipulation?"

He ruffled a hand through his hair. "Not all of us are geniuses. I just bred them that way. They're all just a kind of sponge."

"But how do you get them to live out of the water?"

"Just have to keep them moist. They're used to being exposed at low tide. A couple of capillary lines running into the water over there and gravity does the rest. A tiny electric charge up their bums and they'll start glowing for you." He sat back down and picked another bottle out of the bucket.

"Anyway, so, answer my question. Don't think I didn't notice your evasion." He laughed and held up his hands, caught, but then became sober.

"My mum is the only one of my family left. I had a little brother but the States executed him for just a few words. A few stupid teenage words." He looked at his hands. "My dad never really recovered from the shock. So they killed him too, really. My mum is ill and I don't know how much of that I can lay at their door, but I can say she used to be the strongest woman I ever met. And so we had to leave before she died too. I couldn't have stood that."

Ada could not express the flicker of emotions that went through her. To have an entire family and to lose them... but to be left with a mother... Fred appeared on the corner of the raft in his usual simian crouch, a dark little cloud that followed her negative emotions. She squeezed her eyes shut to banish the guilt and shame and envy and distracted herself with, "So how did you get away?"

"It was maybe a little easier where I lived to get out.

We were a tiny island with a native population and a skeleton staff of Corporated States officials who were really only interested in the missile base. But they knew they were overstretched so that made them harsh. My brother was only joking with his mates and one of the state stooges overheard them. And the state came and took him and executed him. 'Humanely'. And so I found out who had done that to us. It took me a long time, but I found out and I made them pay. It was our neighbour, Mrs Kiore. I don't really think that she knew the state would kill my brother, but she paid for it anyway." Ada shivered, suddenly as he turned to look her straight in the eye. "So now you know, Ada. I'm a desperate and evil man. Just like you're a traitorous defector who has sold your people down the river. So maybe now you can understand what I was saying to you before about Agung and the truth."

Ada did not reply. There was nothing more to say on this topic. They sat, sucking on their beers and thinking private thoughts. After a while, Ikatere cleared his throat and began again. "So, do you think that we'll really need a fusion toroid?"

She nodded. "The witricity around here is pathetic. No offense."

"None taken. We live simple lives. For the most part."

"We'll also need to get a witricity mast up somewhere high and central. The liner is the easiest option there. Probably we'll need to put some silicene vanes and so on. Coverage is far too patchy at the moment. I presume you can 'acquire' that too?"

He shrugged sheepishly. For all his talk of salvage rather than stealing, fusion toroids and silicene components did not just float up.

"And have you thought about where you want to set up your lab?"

She ran through the possibilities in her mind. Butterfly assisted in some mental calculations by tracing the numbers in light on the blackboard of night. Ada noticed the numbers had taken on some of the colours of the bioluminescents. If a butterfly could look coquettish, she did as she swooped through the final total. "If you'll allow it, I can use the space you gave me on the boat." She jerked a thumb back at the *Bessu*.

"Is it not dangerous to have it in your own bedroom?" Ikatere's face filled with concern.

"It's a solid room, insulated walls. They'll be perfect for containing the experiment. Nothing should leak out. Your mum will be safe, trust me."

"But still, it was my catch hold," he said with a slight shift on his seat.

She laughed. "Perfect. So if it goes wrong just say I sleep with the fishes." He giggled uncomfortably.

"Is there much chance of it going wrong?"

"Not really. But if it did, it would become a room-sized microwave and anyone in there might conceivably cook to death before exploding." She swigged her beer smugly as he spluttered his into the sea. Dog barked at his coughing.

PART II - POSTHUMAN

The dreaded knock. She raises herself from the blue plastic tub, as she hears a muffled voice. "I'm coming," she says. She stands, Venus of Raft City, and steps out of the bath onto the rough of the planking through which she can view the blue ocean. Little puddles form at her feet and drips join them. She squeezes out her hair and a slight breeze from the gaps around the sides of the lashed canvas walls of the bathroom makes her skin horripilate. Dog scatters a thousand drops of crystal from his coat. She towels and dresses quickly. Her hair will have to remain wet for a while.

She walks outside to the deck that sits beside the *Bessu*, and stands watching the sway of the kelp that stretches far distant. Strong sunshine is warming her and a soft breeze is cooling her. Her skin is getting slowly browner, despite her care with sunscreens. It almost makes her look like a local. She enjoys the clean taste of belonging shivering through her chest. But the others are waiting.

She walks, the condemned, back inside the boat and below to the catch hold. But she goes as a noble or a heretic. Her death would be a beacon to all, should she die. She shines – Jeanne d'Arc walking towards the stake.

7. MINDFIELDS

Ikatere stood in the wheelhouse of the *Bessu*. His mother's room had been co-opted, temporarily at least, to an observation post. A holoscene of the occurrences inside the catch hold would be relayed up here to the gathered observers. Agung, his sycophantic follower Dwi, Huhuo the hacker and Ikatere huddled around the hologram of Ada who was standing, still and mute for the moment, gathering herself in the metal prison of the space belowdecks. Ikatere's mother was still here. Ikatere had decanted her into a chair and she was enunciating "ah, ah, ah," over and over. He thought he heard a note of enquiry in the plaintive noises and looked over at her. She was not really with them but inside her own pain, he decided, and looked away again with a sensation of helplessness.

Ada's hologram sat down, clasping knees, then lay flat. She had told them to expect this. She was unsure how her body would react so she had decided to lie down to prevent injury. She folded her hands across her solar plexus. He felt like he was at her funeral. Her chosen clothing of loose, white linen didn't help this impression.

"Start the broadcast now," she said. *Mundane last words,* he mused, then told himself off for being overly dramatic.

It was true, though, that he was more anxious than if he had gone in the hold himself. Huhuo entered some commands on a small console pad they had set up. They watched Ada's form, lying still. For a moment, nothing happened. The silence was filled with only the noise of Raft City, which drifted in from the sea wind and the hum of the console which controlled the witricity and translated everything to and from Ling for Agung.

"Is she even breathing?" Ikatere said in a whisper.

Suddenly her body began to tremble. Growling noises began to boil from her lips along with white balls of foam. "Shit turn it off!" Ikatere shouted.

"No, wait," Agung said, pulling the console away.

"But she's in trouble!"

"I said wait," Agung commanded. Ikatere stood staring at the convulsing hologram. The sound of the witricity grid began to fluctuate, flicker. Then it stopped altogether. The hologram of Ada's body was still. Deathly still.

Ikatere stared, aghast at his fellow citizens. Agung stared back, defiantly, still clutching the console. The word 'murderer' began to rise in his throat, clutching at the cage of his teeth. He took a ragged breath in to set the word free but as he did so, the hum of the witricity grid returned. Ada's body began to cough and breathe again. A hand rose from her side, limply. It was a puppet hand, without strings. It jiggled from side to side. "See, she's waving," Agung said with a giggle of edgy relief. Ikatere felt his muscles unbunch one at time.

"I'm sorry about that," Ada's voice projected from the speakers. Ikatere looked towards the image of her face. Her lips were not moving. "I thought that involuntary reactions would stay, well, involuntary."

Agung spoke into the console awkwardly. "What does that mean, Ada? Over?"

Ada's throaty laugh filled the room. "It means I stopped breathing. My heart stopped beating. It means for a moment I was clinically dead and only conscious within the witricity grid. Thankfully that was long enough for me to write a protocol to monitor my body's involuntary responses and now it will never be a problem for anyone else."

"Someone wanted to stop the experiment, Ada. What would that have done, over?"

"Thank you for not turning off the power, Agung. I would have been lost at that point." Ikatere resented the look of vindication on Agung's face. "But it is strange to think I may be the first person to have existed as an entity separate from a body, for however short a time. The implications are enormous."

"And so what's it like now, Ada, inside the mindfield? Oh, over."

"You don't have to say over, Agung, it's just like normal conversation."

"Well, what's it like, Ada?"

"It's difficult to describe. Rather empty and useless at the moment. But I'll be working on that, of course."

"So what are our next steps?"

"I might have to explore this space, set up a few basic algorithms to deal with existing in here. For example, self-visualisation, projection, a protocol for communications hand-shake... this could take a while."

"Very well, Ada, over... oh. Well, goodbye for now. We'll wait for you. Here," he said helpfully.

"Okay Agung, over and out." Ikatere felt perhaps the ghost of a smile played over the holographic Ada's lips.

***

"Right," she breathed to herself. "First things first." She tried to imagine a space. It began to run out from the singularity that was her consciousness. Nothingness faded, and became something. A space. It was white and black at the same time. "Oh make a decision," she snapped at herself and the space became a blue sky and a green field; a hokey, chocolate box image of a Scandinavian field in summer. There were yellow flowers, solid, old looking trees with boughs that spread shade. A brook. Babbling, naturally. Butterfly appeared beside her, fluttering right through her and then on to a large patch of wildflowers. She laughed. "Oh, I forgot to give myself a body in here. Umm..." It was very difficult. Foot proportion, facial features... Ada had never been a good artist. Somehow, the thing wasn't right. She sighed and then set up an algorithm to use several feedback loops to scan her actual body. She then floated a while in front of it to check it out. She sighed again. Unprepossessing. It must be an accurate rendition. She would have to tweak it later. Too much to do.

Dog burst from somewhere in the bushes and was chasing a rabbit at high speed. "Oh, I didn't..." She stopped, flummoxed briefly. As in normal life, it seemed her companions had ideas of their own. She had not even thought about a rabbit. "Perhaps in here I can make some *better* friends," she said loudly, hands on hips. Dog broke off his chase and came ambling innocently up. Butterfly floated up with pollen stuck to her proboscis and even Fred swung down from the branch of one of the ancient trees and limped over.

"If you are so bloody clever," she lectured, "how about you find what I'm looking for?" She projected an image of what she had in mind and her three companions shot off in different directions. While they were gone, she sat down on the grass on the perfect spring morning and began her work. She would have to set up so many different subsystems and callbacks that she would need to invent some automated protocols to do the heavy work. As she had promised Agung, she set up a handshake that would allow connection with another entity within this construct. What she hadn't promised him was that she would bury deep inside it an inviolable sense of privacy and self that would prevent any interrogation or coercion. She smiled. It was a good day.

A frown had developed over her face as the sunshine that she had given basic directions to, matured into an afternoon hush. "But what if...? No, that can't be right." She was looking into the fundamental underlying structure of the witricity grid they had set up especially for the experiment, attempting to improve its efficiency. "If this is right, we won't need to set up the grid, it'll just..." In the distance, she could hear barking. It was Dog barking at an enemy. It set her immediately on edge. Then she heard Fred shouting his mindless garbage. *Time to go.* She stood and began to walk towards the sound, far to the south. The sun was warm and a prickle of the memory of sweat set up on her skin. "Wait a minute, what am I doing?" she spat exasperatedly at herself for being so stupid.

She opened her mind up and located Dog and Fred. They were standing at the edge of a tree-lined valley, a dark cleft in the landscape. It seemed a long way away. Concentrating on the spot and relaxing her personal sense of location for a moment, she arrived with a rush of motion at the head of the valley. "Down there, is it?" she asked as Dog was making small charges and tactical retreats in the direction of a path that led down into the file. Fred sauntered off into the bushes casually. She frowned after him, but turned back and set foot onto the path alone.

She followed the track a little while until she came to a bend and the view opened out. The valley bottom was a suppurating mess of junk metal, swamp gas, filth. "Metaphor," she said wearily and the slimy brown mass began to rise in the air. There was some resistance, but eventually she freed the junk from the valley. A black void existed below it. She rotated the mess around, a valley-sized junkheap spinning in the air. "What do I do with this?" she wondered. Butterfly came from behind her and flew up to the spinning metal. She became a tiny yellow dot against the vast, rusty, dripping conglomeration. Then she grew. And changed. Her wings became longer, tapering, fiery; her size, larger than the junkheap. Her wings spread until they touched the sides of the valley. Two of her spindly black legs grew into taloned feet and her curly straw proboscis hardened and pointed into a beak.

The phoenix lashed the mountain of junk with her wings and the dirt began to burn away. She flew in spirals around the metal and created a vortex of heat that Ada instinctively threw a hand up against. The metal shone and corrosion disappeared. Gasses burned up and the heat dissipated. The phoenix gripped the metal and as she did so, screamed and fell like a comet to the earth, a jagged silvery shard in her grip. The impact sent a shockwave out that nearly tumbled Ada over. She looked up to the smoking crater where the phoenix had fallen and from the smoke a small, yellow dot rose, fluttering in a scatty, random flight path. Butterfly had returned to her normal self and the fluttering was deceptively quick. Before long, she had approached Ada's outstretched hand and alighted momentarily. When she left, a small, boxy shape lay in Ada's palm, the last remnants of the mountain of junk. It was a lacquered wood puzzle box, a cube made of other cubes with parts that slid and moved, hiding its secrets. She examined it thoroughly, noticing that the closer she looked, the more detail she noticed. It was like a geometric Mandelbrot series in three dimensions, each larger cube had many smaller cubes that echoed the macro shape. But a serial number could be read in a cartouche on the side of one of the protrusions. She opened up a portal to the Statenet and used every back door, exploit and hack that Huhuo had still open and found a single entry. The serial number was sitting in a database, dated ten years ago. The name next to it was Ada King. There was nothing else.

She sat in the fields again, watching a sunset, different to the ones she and Ikatere shared so often. Soft purples and pinks touched on the plant life around her and in turn, the transpiration of water vapour from their leaves changed the air quality. She hadn't realised how much she missed trees and flowers. Perhaps soon she could take a trip with the crews who made trading and salvaging expeditions and get some land time. Perhaps they would allow her that once the project was finished. Would they allow her that in recognition of her efforts? Or was she a prisoner despite all their assurances?

She looked down at the puzzle box in her hand and slid a few of the wooden panels. When she slid one open, another one would close and lock. The implant in her head it represented was the real worry. She had the suspicion it was a tracking chip. It had some formidable defences. It had taken Butterfly a stupendous amount of effort even to reveal this puzzle box – this locked interface – to Ada. Butterfly was motionless, wings folded up, on a flower that nodded in the evening's soft air. Ada wasn't even sure if she could ever clear away its obfuscation and open the box just using the witricity and mindfields, powerful though they were. It would take a physical intervention. One thing she knew was that she would not be revealing this to the others.

Speaking of whom, she had better get back there. She had been away for almost a whole day. She suddenly remembered her revelation just before she had been distracted by the implant. A bubble of joy rose up in her body. It was going to be bigger than even Agung had dreamed.

She returned to her body and sat up. "I'm back," she said aloud. The microphone should pick her up, if they were still there waiting. Perhaps they'd got bored and left.

"Back?" Agung's puzzled, tinnily translated voice came through the speakers. "Is there a problem? Could you not complete your tasks?"

"How long have I been away?" she asked with a jolt of unreality.

"About forty seconds, it says here," was the reply. Ada

began to laugh.

Faster than a dream.

***

"It feels strange to be having a party. I don't really feel like I did anything," she said.

Ikatere leaned on the deck railing and looked at the sudden crowd of people who had nothing to do with the project yet had descended on his home. He felt a momentary worry about his mother. He hoped she wasn't fretting.

"So what was it like? Was it like being inside a computer?"

Ada laughed. "No, it was like being inside my brain. Which I always am, of course. But better. You can actually achieve real world outcomes with your imagination."

"What does one imagine, then, for the real world?"

She leaned on the railing beside him and put her face into the wind. Dark curls bounced around her face. "One imagines a new world," she said with a smile. He laughed. It sounded too much, pompous. "Alright," she said, defiantly, "for example, Agung wanted to use the power of witricity to manipulate your brainwaves into understanding people even if they spoke a different language." Ikatere nodded. "That is a noble and, of course, profitable cause. And he's even thought further than that. What do you think of his idea to allow people to feel what you are feeling?"

"Hmm," he said thoughtfully. "I don't know."

"That's the point, you *would* know," she said straightening up. Suddenly she seemed stronger, more confident. "But that's just the tip of the iceberg. With a wireless electric current manipulating your brain's signals, you could expand your mind to use all the computing power and memory at our disposal to make your mind into something amazing. Imagine having all of the world's knowledge at your beck and call, the ability to run instant calculations and simulations, never forgetting anything again... The blind could see, the deaf hear... The implications of what a human could become are simply staggering. We could start to realise the dreams of those who coined the term posthuman."

"Oh," Ikatere said, at a loss. "Posthuman," he echoed. "I had no idea."

She looked at him sideways, sensing his bafflement. "It means a person greater than the parts they were born with, supplemented by technology. In the future it could mean virtual immortality." She stopped her grandiloquence for a moment. "But there is something else I need to look into, but it may be that we can use the witricity system itself to piggyback the mindfield's signals." Ikatere raised an eyebrow. "It would mean that any mast, any substation, even any household appliance could turn into a broadcast point for us." Ikatere turned this over in his mind.

"But I..." he shook his head.

"I told you," she grinned, "a whole new world."

Suddenly she leaned in and kissed him and he jerked back in surprise. "Oh, I don't know if that's such a..." he began.

"Oh, don't be such a baby," she said with casualness that he didn't believe for a second. "It was just a kiss." She walked away, white linen swinging with her every step.

***

The day's work was over. The expansion of the project was progressing well. They'd begun to raise the mast on top of the liner that would broadcast witricity to the city in an even and consistent spread to combat the spottiness of coverage that varied from boat to raft to barge to launch. Ada paused on her way down the steel ladder-like steps to her bedroom in the catch hold to close the hatch above her and continue her trudge to bed. *Another day, another night.* She lay on her mattress on the floor and picked up the console that lay beside it, finger pausing over the button that would start the sequence. Dog came up and laid his paws on her chest, nose poking under the screen with a snuffle.

"Well, wouldn't you like to chase rabbits, silly?" she asked affectionately. Butterfly did not move from her roost on Ada's pillow, hardly moving at all. She wondered if the little insect would ever be the same again. She hit the start up sequence and hoped the witricity hum would not wake any of the other residents of the boat. Once the mast was up, she would not need to stay in this room. Once the mast was up, they could go so much further. She closed her eyes and slipped easily into the mindfield construct of a Scandinavian field once more.

The puzzle box was waiting for her on the meadow of yellow flowers. Dog hightailed it to the bushes, looking for things to chase and Butterfly stayed put on one of the nodding blooms that were dotted all around. She picked up the box tiredly and opened a console with a thought. A bright fuzz of otherness shone in the air next to her. Using this console window, she began to programme in algorithms and mathematical proofs to run against the puzzle box. It was becoming easier and easier to do so. She would reach her thoughts out into the computing power they had assembled and even into the three state nets with the ease of remembering a sunny day. As she did so, she shifted the moving parts of the box through various combinations. The box was a representation of the real thing, some kind of implant that sat on her brain and each move, each sliding piece of wood represented thousands of complex calculations that were standing in the way of her access to it. She couldn't deactivate it until she could get inside the box and so she struggled with it.

Days and nights passed here in the field as she wrestled with the box. Fourteen days and nights in a row were the most she had managed to rack up – only a few hours in the outside world – but still the box was an enigma. Finally, she threw it aside in a fit of pique and exited the construct. She lay blinking in the catch hold's feeble lights that she had forgotten to turn out again. She closed her eyes and wondered why it was so hard to sleep when one was completely exhausted.

Once again, they took their usual stances on the deck for a beer at sunset. Dog was trying to bite the tiny wavelets that lapped up against the deck. Butterfly was still a little dormant these days, resting as the sun gave her wings a golden fringe. The pink and oranges of the light were catching on the semi-translucent silicene vanes that clad the mast at the liner's top. The rounded bulk of the fusion toroid tagged onto the end of the ship like a caboose train car, shining a yellowish-green.

"It's a beautiful sight, Ada," Ikatere said to her.

"I thank you," she answered archly, then continued in a more confessional tone. It was finally time to open up. "You know, when I first started looking at the potential for witricity to interact with the human brain it was off the back of using it as a noninvasive, cheap method of producing an encephalogram. But once the state found out about it, they put me onto other projects, more beneficial to their administration than their people. So I ended up doing cryptography to hide their little secrets, then they wished me to use the same tech to interrogate 'enemies of the state'. They were also beginning to get the idea of using this to snuff out anyone who opposed them. When you think about the possibilities..." She shook her head. "That's why I left. It was not because I thought it was too hard there. I didn't know any different anyway."

"So would you have built them their torture tools? If you hadn't managed to get out?" he asked, not meeting her eye. It was a rotten question and he knew it.

"Not if I could prevent it. But of course, they have these ways of making people do things, even if they know it is wrong. They would fill you with jingoistic nonsense and threaten and reward you until you were so confused you didn't know what you were doing, what was right and what was wrong anymore." She shrugged. "But I did get out. With a little help," she said, smiling gently. "I suppose I should say thank you."

"Don't need to," he said, sounding a little embarrassed.

A purple outline lit up the witricity mast as the sun sank with its alarming suddenness below the ocean's horizon. Somewhere in the darkness above their heads, a bird's wings whirred a plummeting tune. Dog barked at the noise, lifting his nose up to the night and rearing a little. Ikatere got up to turn on the bioluminescents and she nudged Dog with her toes. "Give it up," she murmured.

"What?" Ikatere called.

"Nothing," she said, straightening up. "So, how is your mother now?"

Ikatere sat down again and frowned, picking at the label of his beer as he thought. "Honestly, I don't know. Sometimes she has her lucid days. Others? I don't know if she's even the same person."

He looked away into the darkness, troubled. Fred made an appearance in the shadows, sitting under Ikatere's chair with ghoulish delight. She felt her heart sink. Fred had been away for some time. The bird – or was it bat? – whirred overhead again. Dog barked and barked. Ada groaned. She felt a headache coming on. It had been a long time since she'd had one. Not since she'd been taken to the *Liberty Via Force*. Fred laughed his guttural laugh at her weakness. "Shut up," squeezed from between her ground teeth. Suddenly Ikatere was on his feet. He threw his beer bottle upwards and it crashed, showering them with glass and splashes of beer. Ada threw up her hands to cover herself. "What the fuck?"

Ikatere did not reply but pointed at the wreckage of a small, four-propped hovercam.

"I think we'd better go see Agung," he said, toeing the pieces and looking at her strangely.

8. LIBERTY WOLF

"Just sit here," Ikatere said and pressed her shoulder down until she collapsed into the bench. "Don't go anywhere." Ada was confused. He was acting weirdly towards her. The buzz of the beer was wearing off and she felt a little sick. After Ikatere had looked around to check there weren't any more hovercams, he had practically frogmarched her up to the liner in the centre of the city. He'd handed her a rope and told her to hold on tightly as it whipped her up several storeys of the liner. She had never taken this route up to the top deck and had been so shocked by the speed she had nearly lost it and plummeted. She had glanced down and the gap of black water between the pontoon decking and the ship had terrified her and now she sat waiting for them to call her in with a nauseous fear fuzzing her brain. The dreaded migraine threatened like a coming storm and the lights inside were beginning to leave too many afterimages on the back of her retinas. She squeezed her eyes shut.

In the darkness behind her lids, she could hear raised voices. After a massive argument, the voices stopped and Ikatere came out. "Ada," he said and beckoned. She tried to keep as steady on her legs as she could and repeated the mantra, *don't be sick, don't be sick, don't be sick.* Agung was leaning on a desk, looking at the remains of the hovercam. "Have you ever seen something like this before?" Ikatere asked for him.

"Yes, all the time, back home. My former home."

"Can you tell us why it has come to our city?" he translated.

"No. I don't know. It's nothing to do with me."

"So, can you tell me why I heard you whispering what sounded like instructions just before it showed up?" Ada looked around desperately.

"That wasn't... I was just..," she couldn't finish.

"And why I hear you talking to yourself all the time, when you think I can't hear you? Are you relaying messages to your handlers? You've managed to see our entire setup, haven't you?"

Ada threw up her hands. "No, I..." How on earth would she explain this? "Look, you're going to have difficulty understanding this but ever since I was a tiny baby I've... I've seen things." She let her hands drop, tiredly. Just listening to herself, it sounded pathetic. "I call them my companions. There's a dog, right here by me," she put her hand on Dog's rounded skull and patted him. He licked his nose. "On your head, Agung, there's a butterfly." She pointed and his hand instinctively went to his hair. "And behind you, Ikatere, there's this ugly man..." Ikatere flinched as he glanced over his shoulder, unseeing. "I call him Fred." She wished she'd fell from the rope now, been swallowed by the black of the sea.

"They've always told me things. Like when there is danger. Or how to think creatively. But sometimes they just annoy me. And it is very difficult to tell which is which." She looked from man to man, from face to incredulous face. "I know how it sounds. Most people just think I am a liar, or psychotic. So I don't tell. I used to think I was haunted." She laughed, bitterly and spoke all in a rush. "Then I thought that my mother did it to me, then

I thought I was crazy, then I thought that the state did it. But I don't think they did. I think they had no idea. So when you heard me whisper, it was to tell my companions to be quiet because I have terrible migraines since they operated on my brain at school. Every other kid they operated on had a complete meltdown. I just get headaches." She laughed, somewhat hysterically, on the edge of tears, then fell to her hands and knees and threw up. She spat and squeezed her eyes shut as dangling strings of acid saliva joined the disgusting little pile between her hands. Hot vomit-reaction tears dripped.

She felt a hand soft on her shoulder. Ikatere was crouching by her side. Then Agung's hand on the other shoulder. The real tears came. Tears of relief. Tears of safety. "What can we do to help you?" Ikatere said sympathetically, patting her awkwardly.

"Just let me get this project finished," she said, sniffing and wiping her eyes with the back of her wrists. "And get me some tissues. And a cloth to clean this up."

***

Agung looked balefully at Ikatere. "Can you please stop farting around with that thing?" Ikatere pulled the foam pads down from the walls of the liner's bridge.

"It's okay, I'm done. But we have to keep up your exposure on the nets."

"What's the point? We'll have something far better soon."

"Yes," Ikatere said with exaggerated patience, "but not yet. We need to keep countering the avalanche of propaganda the states are putting out about us. About you." He folded up the holoscene gear in to its carrier pack. "And that means getting this stuff to the public. Where we can. Huhuo is a great hacker, but they keep closing up the holes in the firewalls, faster and faster. And she has to work with three different protocols. Yeah, I'll be glad too when we don't have to do this anymore."

How could Agung explain how uncomfortable it made

him feel to be presented as some kind of hero, or even anyone special? He felt like such a fraud at times. "Anyway, we need to talk." He glanced out of the liner's windows at the sea. Today the waves were dark and choppy and stirred the city's apron of kelp into restless green eels. He brooded a while, then began. "That hovercam could not have come here without a support ship. Those things have a range of what, one? Two kays?"

"Probably not even that," Ikatere agreed.

"So, are they out there, waiting for us? Are we going to be attacked in the middle of the night?" He turned to look at the darker patch on the floor where Ada had vomited – the mark was yet to fade. "And how much do we trust her?"

"I believed her," Ikatere said with ingenuous conviction. "Look at all she's done already."

"I believe that she believed it, too. But she said they operated on her. What does that mean? Is she a liability or an outright threat to us right now?" He crossed his arms and leaned on the wheel. "We need to know more and I want you to do more than get to know her. I want you to become her bosom friend, if you take my meaning." Ikatere's dismayed face indicated to Agung that he understood perfectly.

As Ikatere turned to leave, he stopped and threw out, "Oh, and get Libby to see if she can find any ships lurking around. She'll enjoy that." Agung thought he could read a certain look on Ikatere's face, but the man said nothing, just nodded and left the bridge.

Am I getting paranoid in my old age? Agung asked himself.

***

Luis and Dan stood in the command centre of *Liberty Via Force* while its avatar sat languorously on a chair she had conjured for herself, long legs crossed. "So what are we seeing here?" Luis said with a few stolen glimpses at the split in her skirt. The view area in front of them was a fractured mosaic of tiny, pinhead spots of mostly blue. It was a fly's eye, looking at a cloudless sky.

"Those are my nanobiotes," she said with a note of pride. "They have tiny light-sensitive structures on their bodies. Rather ineffectual on their own, but when several work together they do quite well as cameras. Currently they are speeding just below the surface, towards the blip we discovered earlier. Ah, almost there." The display began to reconfigure in front of them, circling, spots widening and contracting to form a view. The solid wedge of a ship's keel appeared from the chaos in a spherical bloom of holographic display. The nanobiotes began to emerge from the water and soon a grey, sharklike vessel appeared.

"Hey," Dan said with delight. "I can see it now." He grinned at Luis who glared back. "Oh," he said more soberly. "Well, should we worry? It's just one ship." The gunboat bristled with weaponry and threw a large bow wave as it churned forward. The view dialled out a bit. Three others accompanied it. There was no doubt of their heading.

Luis rumbled, "Just one of those ships could start a fire or sink the liner. But four is too many. Last time we were attacked just by helos and it sank my aunty's boat and it took me days to repair the hole in my barge. They could wipe us out this time."

Dan turned to him, "What will we do? Can we radio ahead and get Agung to get the railgun out? Will that even be enough?"

"What *we* will do," *Liberty Via Force* intoned calmly, "is the following. We extend this hunt to its logical conclusion." The entire fabric of the submarine vibrated in a excited way and the avatar raised her hands and theatrically threw them forward. More fly's eye displays bloomed in the air before them. There was a sense of speed, of coursing towards the target. The original display began to become larger, as the dots melded into each other. The water around the ships began to take on a distinct haze of greyness.

At one moment, like a leap, the spherical display began to close in on the gunboats. They grew relatively in size until there was just a confusion of battleship grey. This grey metamorphosed into a mottled black. The avatar stood up, excitement in her poise and began to glow brightly. Luis and Dan backed off, small shuffling steps. The glow grew in intensity until gouts of fire began to leap from the hologram and she leaned her head back and released an awful, inhuman howl.

"Fuck," Luis whispered.

The avatar relaxed, and began to dull until she was her normal, clean self. The display zoomed back out to its original resolution. The sea was empty.

"What have you done?" Dan asked. Cold sweat was beginning to bead on his forehead.

The avatar glanced at him casually. "Oh that? Let's just say *libertas homini lupus est.*" She smiled perkily and abruptly vanished from the bridge.

Luis and Dan stared at each other and said nothing.

***

"I tell you she's a psycho," Dan said to Ikatere in a hushed but urgent voice. "No wonder they left her in that trench."

Ikatere raised his hands. "So you're telling me, she destroyed an entire flotilla?" Luis and Dan nodded, synchronised and vehement. "And she didn't leave any survivors?" The twin headshakes would have been amusing in any other circumstance. They were all huddled into a corner of his deck that appended the *Bessu*, heads close enough to exchange not particularly athletic lice.

"No warning," Dan hissed. "All gone. And then she spouts some Latin bullshit like it was really funny."

"What happens when they connect us with that?" Luis interrupted. "They were on their way to attack us and they just disappear?"

With more coolness than he actually felt, he dismissed

them with, "I'll deal with it." After the two had left, he leaned on the railing, chin in hand. The *Liberty Via Force* had summarily executed four gunboats' worth of people. They were on a course that indicated they were going to attack the city, but it could have been just posturing. No matter their intent, however, whichever state that had sent them would have to assume it was Raft City's fault they had disappeared. But would there have been any proof? As it had been described, they had just been disintegrated, eaten up. He shivered. A nano-holocaust. Could they wait it out? Would their aggressors like to admit they had sent a force to attack a neutral community, this time definitively in international waters? They would have to get Huhuo to watch the nets like a hawk.

"I'm glad they've gone," Ada said from behind him. Ikatere looked to where she stood. She was pretty much just dressed in the cloth that hung across the doorway. He gestured helplessly towards his mother's berth in the *Bessu*'s cabin. "Don't worry, she's asleep," she said with a smile. Indeed, his mother's gentle snoring could be heard in the afternoon hush. With the medication she was on, it was difficult to wake her at times.

"Look, I've got to go deal with a few things," he said, scampering across the deck to herd her indoors. "Go inside," he whispered, a little harshly perhaps, but he was feeling pressured. She looked disappointed and frowned. He stopped and kissed her softly, hoping it would mollify her. "I'm really sorry but there is a dangerous situation and I need to go."

"I'll come and help," she said, dark eyes searching his face.

"If you want to help," he said just before turning away, "get the project finished." He did not look behind him as he walked away. It was hard enough without thinking about her so-called companions lurking somewhere in her imagination. He had nearly been unable to go through with their lovemaking. It wasn't so much that he thought they could be present, but that her mind could work in this twisted way. It was unsettling. And now he had taken advantage of her attraction to him. He hung his head down and looked at his feet as he crossed the wood of the decks.

***

Agung's lips went very thin and white as he listened to Ikatere's report. They were in his houseboat, in the living area. His daughter, now a big toddler, was playing with blocks with letters and numbers on them. Her main pleasure appeared to be building them into tall stacks then toppling them with a smash of her chubby hands. Agung looked out of the clear vinyl window in the blue and white striped wall – also made of vinyl – that pulsed gently in the breeze. Black clouds a little to the west signalled a squall was heading past. The city might even steer towards it to pick up some much needed rain. The doldrums did not provide much drinking water.

"It's strange," he said slowly. "This is not the first time in our history we have been threatened and the attackers were suddenly no longer a problem. I always thought that it was just an accident... You say when you found the *Liberty Via Force*, it looked like it had been down there a long time?"

Ikatere looked taken aback. "Yes, it had corals and so on growing off it. It had settled into the side of the trench."

"But you were able to get it up and running again, no problems?"

"Ah, I think I see what you're driving at but, see, Libby's nanobiotes helped her clean the growth off and..."

"Yes, nanobiotes. Tell me, do you think these nanobiotes could be made to simulate corals and 'so on'?" Agung rubbed a hand over his chin, watching him with narrowed eyes.

"You think we didn't find her by chance?" Ikatere was aghast.

Agung didn't answer for a while. When he did speak, "It's a big ocean," was all he said.

"What the hell do we do?" Ikatere asked, faintly.

"First, we're going to steer a little to the west and catch some of that rain. After that, I'm not sure. She appears to be protecting us. Perhaps you could ask her to do so with a little less zeal?" Ikatere blanched. "Take Ada with you if you can get her out of bed." Ikatere's face went from pale to sudden red. "See if you can't get the *Liberty Via Force* to look at these headaches."

***

"You don't trust her but you're going to get her to look inside my head." She couldn't help but let an accusatory note slip in.

"I never said I don't trust Libby," Ikatere said. He sounded somewhat nervous. They about to dock the mini-sub to the *Liberty Via Force* who had responded to Ikatere's call and come out to meet him and take them back to Marisenal.

"You don't have to," she said, resting her chin on his shoulder. "I can tell." She stole her arms around his middle as he piloted the sub and he jumped uncomfortably.

"Don't tickle," he complained, without turning around.

Ada sighed, disappointment eating away at her. "Perhaps this relationship isn't the best idea," she said and slid back to her own seat. She knew it sounded petulant but she couldn't help it. She felt even worse when he did not reply, felt stupid. She knew she had thrown herself at him but he had never told her to stop. She started to feel a prickle of embarrassment sting her cheeks.

Part of her mind that continued to run rough estimations and explore possibilities ruminated on the mindfields even as she sulked. Would lovers' tiffs continue if they could feel each others' emotions? Perhaps she was being a little parochial. They were talking about tiffs between states, not just some silly love affair. Dog rested his head on her lap, loyally. She stroked him listlessly.

Butterfly had taken to attaching herself to Ada's finger, like an oversize ring, wings beating so infrequently it looked like she was dead. Ada wondered idly if she would ever see her become a phoenix again and what it had meant. Suddenly a hand gripped her heart. *What if the nanobiotes erase my companions?* Fred swam casually across the front of the mini-sub, blowing bubbles at her.

With a clunk, they docked against the *Liberty Via Force*.

***

"Don't be alarmed, Ada," said the avatar sweetly. "Just relax. Lie back and don't worry about anything."

"Do I have to lie back?" Ada sat, Buddha-like, on the bunk. Ikatere noticed the bags around her eyes that he hadn't seen before. Suddenly she looked young again, a distressed fawn poised to flee into the forest. When she had talked on the journey here, he no longer knew what to say. He was a traitor to her. He should never have accepted Agung's order. It was unfair to the girl.

"No, dear, of course not," Libby said, tilting her head a little. "It doesn't matter what you do. Or where you go. I just thought you might like to be comfortable." Muscles bulged at the side of Ada's jaw and she looked away from both of them. Ikatere left the room, unable to stay any longer. He walked to the bridge, trying to steel himself for the conversation he was about to have. Libby was already there. She was everywhere. When she wasn't there in holographic form, she was there as a consciousness spread out amongst her nanobiotes. But how far did that reach?

"Ikatere," the *Liberty Via Force* intoned formally. "What can I do for you today?"

"I guess you could answer some questions for me," he said, sitting in a command chair. The cream leather squeaked under him as it settled. Libby took the chair opposite as a convention of politeness. She did not need to sit. He tried to hold her inhumanness in his mind. It did not pay to anthropomorphise this killing machine.

"Very well, Ikatere," she said with an open smile.

"Proceed."

He shifted a little. The leather squeaked again. "I heard you wiped out four ships and their crews the other day. Could you tell me why you did that?"

She affected surprise at the question. "They were coming to attack your people, Ikatere. What else would I do?"

"I don't know, perhaps you could have warned them not to? Made them turn around? Or maybe even just disabled the ships so they couldn't attack?"

"And advertise my presence here? If I had contacted them or used my nanobiotes more... *selectively*, then they would know I was here and they would hunt me down and you would lose your most ardent supporter." She looked at him and a corona of light encircled her violet eyes. "They would poison the ocean too, trying to find me. That would not be the best outcome for your community."

"I guess I have to concede that point, but since you brought it up, why are you our most ardent supporter?"

She shrugged. "You found me first; you didn't try to claim me for yourselves. I appreciated that." There was something eminently reasonable but deeply unsatisfying in all this, Ikatere felt. He sat forward in frustration eliciting a squeal of leather from the seat.

"What I really want to know, I guess, is have you ever used your nanobiotes to listen to us, when we didn't realise you were?"

"Of course," the sub said without hesitation, putting Ikatere off his stride a little. "Every time you are aboard me, I can't help but hear things."

"That's not when I meant. Have you ever watched us when we weren't on board. You."

It was hard to know if a hologram could look evasive. "I admit, when you were in Marisenal I kept an eye on you. Just for your own safety." *I knew it.* "Oh this human paranoia!" she said suddenly, screwing her face up in amusement.

"One final question, then," he said, carefully picking his words. "When we first found you in that trench, were you really on dark protocol?"

She openly laughed. "Of course! I mean, you would have picked up my nanobiota, wouldn't you?"

"Well that's a funny thing, isn't it? I don't think we've ever got a particularly strong reading on your nanobiota." *Get out of that one,* he thought.

"Well I do hope they are effective," she said thoughtfully, "since they are currently in Ada's brain."

***

"This is an interesting piece of wetware," the submarine's avatar mused. *Liberty Via Force* had chosen to stand in front of Ada's crossed legged figure in the bunkroom while she twirled an image of the implant in front of her. It looked like the dried-out jaw of a delicate mammal or a Neanderthal's bone needle. The avatar had the air of a scientist in a laboratory. "It's silicene, profiled to be hard to pick up on scans... yes, a nice piece of work. But the way they attached is sloppy, sloppy work. No wonder you have had headaches, poor dear." Ada remained mute on that point, arms folded. Dog sat next to her, Cerberus guarding the gates of death.

The avatar sighed, an affectation. "So, let's see. No, no tracking function in here. Or if there was, it hasn't ever worked properly. But there is a small charge of polymeric nitrogen, wired to detonate just between your brainstem and your cerebellum if it's attempted to be removed. I'm glad you came to me, Ada. If anyone but me had tried to disable this, pfft!" the avatar raised her hand dramatically, "Death of the being known as Ada King. Your body might have survived I suppose, with some artificial help, but you'd be a vegetable." Ada thought about the puzzle box. She was suddenly feeling rather glad she had not solved its combinations.

"What else does it do?" Ada asked. "What would happen if it were removed? Is it supporting my cognitive abilities?"

Liberty Via Force's brow creased. "I can't see how. Perhaps it was meant to, but the connections aren't correct for this kind of brain-boosting. It's basically a piece of rubbish with a tiny bomb." Ada considered the mountain of junk that a phoenix had burnt away and the difficulty of getting into the puzzle box. Could she risk that the sub was wrong and that removal of the implant would change her? What if she would never see her companions again? Dog leaned his heavy body against her, tail thumping the bed. Butterfly was still, as was Fred, for once. They were no help.

"Ada," the avatar suddenly broke in on her thoughts. "You are, at some point, going to have to grow a backbone."

"What?"

"Do you have any idea of the importance of what you are going to do?"

She frowned at the hologram. "Do you?"

"I believe I do." She reached forward and Ada froze as the avatar stroked Dog's head. "What a cutie," she murmured. Ada resisted the urge to yank her companion away, to bundle him in her arms. "It will be hard, what you have to do. But you have to do it."

"How do you know? What..." Ada ran out of words to express her horror.

"Do you want this implant out or not? I can assure you it will have no effect on your little friends here. Unless...?" The avatar tilted her head to the side. Dog growled at her. Ada shook her head no, quickly and emphatically. "Very well, I suppose it is not yet your time to put away childhood things," she said somewhat nastily and stood upright and turned her intention to the implant. She focused her gaze on the slick, bone-like structure and it began to dissolve. Ada's muscles clenched instinctively as she realised it was happening, now, inside her. The implant's destruction became quicker and quicker as it dropped into a curtain of dust and the dust fell down into the space beneath and disappeared. She pulled Dog into her arms and watched Butterfly where she sat on her ring finger with a feverish intensity.

"Don't go," she whispered. "Please."

9. EXPANSIONS

Agung lay uncomfortably next to Ada in the catch hold. Ikatere had supplied him some cushions to keep out the cold of the floor. He looked over to her mattress, where she was fiddling with a console. "Do we really have to do it this way?" he asked into his handheld translator, aware he was at a lower level than Ada King.

"Hmm?" she replied distractedly.

"Why do we have to be unconscious?"

"Oh, you'll not be really unconscious," she replied confidently. "But for a full-immersion experience, you have to kind of cut the feed to the outside senses of touch, smell, sight and so on it won't confuse you. And cutting the motor responses stops you from blundering about. We'll begin the process of combining feeds soon, so you'll see what I want to project to you and you can share what you want with me, but we'll have to be immobilised or we could start to walk off the edge of the boat and drown and so on, don't you see?"

"Hah," he replied. "Of course. Carry on." He put down the translator, clasped his hands neatly across his stomach to give the appearance of nonchalance while simultaneously using the grip to hold in the storm of nerves that threatened to escape. But he had to be the first to go in with Ada, or why should any of his people believe in him? They had done exhaustive testing and modelling and it was perfectly safe, so Ada claimed. But he gritted his teeth together anyway.

She said something in an offhand manner which he did not quite pick up, but it had the feeling of 'here we go'.

Agung felt at first all of his muscles relax alarmingly as he suddenly could not see. He tried not to panic, but the sense of nothingness was incredible. "Don't worry Agung," Ada's voice came from somewhere. It was strange to understand what she said when she was using her own voice. It seemed as if she was still speaking Experana, but suddenly he was as fluent in that as he was in Ling. "We will have to establish a few things," she continued. "First thing is to give you a body to help orient you spatially. We'll scan you to give you something for your consciousness to ride around in. If you want to tweak it you can do that later on." With a few thrumming sounds he began to feel his fingertips. He looked down and wriggled them. They were strangely unconnected to his body for a moment, but then the rest of the details filled out and soon he could bend his knees, flex his elbows and touch his nose.

"It's pretty black in here," he said out loud, using his mouth, tongue, larynx. In fact, he could see himself perfectly, but there was nothing else to look at.

"You can create a world for yourself if you wish, but perhaps it might be easier to join me in mine. We'll start the handshake protocol. I want you to say my name and think about me briefly."

Agung said, "Ada King," self-consciously and thought about a young woman with dark, curly hair.

"Ok, I've picked up your request. Now I'm going to send you an invitation to come into my space."

At the corner of Agung's eyes part of the darkness coalesced into a kind of message. He took it and read it. It said that Ada King wished him to join her in her mindfield world. After he stopped reading the message, he could not recall what language it had been written in, but he was sure it wasn't Ling. However, he could understand it. He looked at it again and once more he could read the words plainly, but when he looked away... "Agung, say 'yes' to the invitation."

"Oh. 'Yes'."

Suddenly he was in a street populated with tall, fair-haired and pale-skinned people. Stalls and goods lined the pavements, but there was an air of conservatism, of austerity that was unlike any markets he had ever been to. The people dressed in dark colours, monochromatic and stiff and most of them were not smiling. He looked around in curiosity, not sure if he should move or not. Above the market, a large hill of mostly black stone was surmounted by a building of white stone. The sky was a cool grey and he felt a little cold. He couldn't see Ada. "Uh, Ada?" he asked the air. None of the grim-faced people on the street seemed to notice him talking to himself. He looked down at his feet. The middle of the street was rough, bumpy stone and over it had been spraypainted a neon yellow arrow, pointing down the gentle slope. He watched it for a moment, contemplatively, and noted it seemed to move slightly, sliding and squirming across the stones, and that the arrow tip was changing direction. In absence of any other information, he followed it, soon learning not to step on the rough cobbles in the centre of the road after he nearly turned his ankle. It was cold, and he wondered if he could imagine himself a bulky coat like the locals were wearing. He looked at his torso and saw it was covered with the blanket-like material. He touched it. His fingertips sent back a firm, scratchy texture. He looked a little further down at his flip-flops. He didn't think he would like restrictive, heavy boots so he decided to imagine that his toes were warm. The cold ceased to be a problem to them.

He smiled in delight and continued on his search.

After a few more arrows, at the end of the roadway, there was a park with trees that seemed to be dead but Agung vaguely remembered there were such things as plants that shed their leaves in winter and indeed, he could see some brown leaves lying about. A female form walked over the grass a few tens of metres away, picking up a stick and throwing it for a dog. The dog would race after the stick and bring it back, after trying to shake it to death and chewing and growling for a while. "Hey! Hello Agung," Ada called as he walked up, wet grass pleasant on the front of his toes.

"You didn't want to meet me?" he asked with a leading tone, a little peeved. She seemed unconcerned.

"I'd been waiting hours up by the market. Time passes a little differently in here, you know. So I made sure there were direction finders."

He looked around at the cold, winter park with its skeletal trees and grey skies. "So this is the world you make for yourself?"

"Oh no, there are hundreds of different ones. This is just the one I chose because Dog does like his stick, you know." She hurled her arm again and the mutt pelted away.

"Ah yes, your companions." He noticed there was a butterfly nesting in her hair too. He could not see any sign of a man, though. They began to walk slowly, away from the market towards the confusion of grey that was a wood, denuded of leaves. "I made this place from a memory. But you could make a full-immersion environment from anything that you could imagine. Once you get skilled, you could try to be in more than one at once. Currently I'm running about five, including the tutorial programme we were using for you to get used to things."

They walked and kicked through the occasional drift of brown leaves, crackling with each step. Agung pondered the realworld application for these many hidden worlds.

Would it impact the city's trade as a neutral territory if people could access these kind of environments anywhere? Had virtual reality ever truly worked before to substitute human interaction? He knew it'd had many iterations in the past, but somehow none had really taken off.

"Oh," said Ada, suddenly stooping to the ground. "I forgot to show you this." She picked up a brightly coloured egg from where it nestled in some leaves on the ground. She passed it to him. "If you accept it, place it on your chest and you will experience something new." Agung held the egg gingerly. He regarded it for a few moments. Dyes and pigments swirled with vibrant red and maroon patterns. They were in motion, a gas planet's bands egg-sized. Doubtfully, he placed it on his chest. He felt it melt into him and in a few seconds, an emotion began to steal through him. It was happiness at having a friend. But somehow, he also knew that it was Ada's happiness at having him for a friend. He hiccupped in surprise. "It was what you wanted, wasn't it?"

Agung reflected on the echoes of warmth that still flooded his chest. It was a powerful negotiation tool for sure. But how easy would it be to manipulate people? "Can you make a false egg?" he asked.

"What do you mean?"

"Imagine that I wanted you to deceive someone, that you wanted them to think you felt one way, when in fact it was a trick?"

Ada King frowned. "I suppose. But I'm not sure why you'd want to. And I imagine it would be hard to encapsulate your feelings in a package if you didn't really feel that way."

Agung laughed. These computer people, so naive. "Could you make a false egg?" he persisted.

She seemed a little annoyed. She waved a hand without meeting his eye. "But you asked for this capability!" She sighed. "Everybody lies, I suppose. Everybody thinks they can tell when someone is lying. The egg is only a metaphor. You could do as you wished." He had offended her creative sensibilities, he saw.

"I see," he said vaguely, trying not to hurt her further. He stopped. "Okay, I will try something, Ada King." He held up his hand and visualised a flower. It was a red hibiscus flower. He added the scent that he knew so well and tried to make a thought appear inside it. It appeared in his palm as if it had always been there, had he just looked at it right. He handed it to her.

She took it, a little grudgingly, but then a smile grew over her face. "Alright, I forgive you," she said and she stooped to throw the stick for the dog again.

"I have something to ask you," she said after a time of more measured pacing. "You really must promise me that you won't try to use this to manipulate people. I mean directly. Persuade, cajole, even threaten if you will, like everyone does all the time, but don't *change anybody's mind*."

"I promise," Agung said in his most serious tone. "How long until we're ready to let the city access the mindfields?"

"It's the next phase, but since the rate of development is exponential – I build tools to build tools and so on – it will only be a matter of time. Your visit here will break the ice for the other developers you loaned me and get them working from inside the environment. Their help will speed things up."

"One last thing, Ada, what about the other three states and their networks? What will we be doing with regards to them?"

Ada considered for a moment. "I think it will be a moot point. Once every witricity point can be used as a broadcast, they'll pretty much be unable to keep us out anymore. We'll be able to blow the Corporated States' propaganda out of the water."

People swarmed over the large flat area of rafts and decks in front of the liner's port side that had the unofficial name of City Square. Folk were shimmying up to cabin roofs at its periphery and standing on bollards or boxes to get a better view. A particularly enterprising group of youngsters were bouncing perilously on some bamboo scaffolding that was projecting out over the open water. Agung stood above the crowds, holding onto the rail and shifting from foot to foot. Ikatere, Dwi and a few other people were up here with him. He supposed they thought themselves privileged enough. He would have to change this assumed hierarchy. There were supposed to be no inequalities in Raft City, but perhaps that is just how humans always worked, drifting towards this structure. Though perhaps, after today, it would not be so much of a problem.

The crowds were settling down from their milling about and so he brought up a mic pad. "Dwi, which thing do I press?" was echoed around the bowl of the city. "Never mind." Ikatere began fiddling with the holocam equipment as Agung cleared his throat. "Today, Raft City will have a world first." Random cheers leapt up from the people below. "We will bring you access to a new method of communication. For those of you currently using translators to Ling, you will be able to hear me as if I spoke your own language. But this is just one of the possibilities this new net will allow. To tell us more, I'm going to call on Ada King, inventor of the mindfields to come forth!" Polite clapping and a murmur of speculation came from below as Ada came out of the bridge to the edge of the deck. She looked a little sick, Agung thought.

"The first thing I want to emphasise," she said in a voice that sounded harsh and a little strained, "is that everything I am about to explain to you is a voluntary process. You will have control over what happens and at no point will your privacy and protection be violated. I am saying that now because what I will show you can sound a little frightening at first, but I come from a state that did not value privacy, so you can believe me when I say that it was my first consideration." A little buzzing came from below as Agung saw people turn to their neighbours, slightly bored or not understanding. Ada seemed to realise this and raised her voice a little.

"You can enter the mindfields right now and those who choose to will have an enhanced experience to share with us. To enter, imagine a blue ball in your mind's eye." Agung joined in the experiment, seeing a squeaky toy for one of his dogs. "The ball changes to red and disappears."

Cries of alarm rippled out from the crowd below and even his own mouth let out an involuntary shout as in the centre of the arena, a ball with red and blue segments hundreds of metres in diameter was floating above the city. "Now you should be able to see the large striped ball," Ada said in an impersonal manner that undercut the shock Agung felt. "This is just an experimental procedure to get you familiar with the system. Soon, you will be able to access and activate the mindfields with just your desire to do so. The mindfields themselves," the ball changed to an image of an arrow that pointed to the witricity vanes above their heads, "are wireless electrical signals that are broadcast from this mast. They interact with the electrical signals that power your brains and allow you to think. And so, with some practice, you could achieve something like this." Agung watched as the image of the arrow disappeared and a gigantic Ada King floated over the city. She had three other figures with her, her companions. The dog and butterfly he had seen before were joined by a bent up, ugly man huddled behind her, and she was facing Agung, looking him directly in the eyes. He supposed everyone in the crowd felt she was looking into their eyes, no matter where they were. Her face was slightly unworldly, beautiful but somehow not the young woman he knew, more like a Greek goddess. He glanced over his shoulder and noticed that the real Ada was standing meekly just beside him, warts and all.

The colossus that bestrode Raft City suddenly

vanished. "That's all we're going to do for today," Ada said calmly, apparently oblivious to the chaos below. "But we will visit you all in smaller, more personal clinics to answer your questions and help you to learn how to use the mindfields." She stepped back and gestured to Agung, who, although slightly stunned still, grinned his widest and stepped forward again.

"The more we use this system, the more useful it will be for us. I encourage you to go to the clinics and learn everything you can because Raft City, very soon, will be exporting this wonder to the world."

The council barge had been decorated with gauzy curtains that allowed the passage of the breeze. Agung had supplied the two visiting dignitaries with tiny cups of coffee, tarry, black and delicious. It was also very hot. They were drinking it a little uncomfortably as the angle of the afternoon sun was just about reaching their collars. He had watched the beam of light move up their stuffy, uncomfortable suits during the entire meeting. Neither of them had asked to move seats or been anything but deferential as the sweat was creating a swamp at their hairlines. From this, he deduced they were probably willing to donate an organ to get access to the mindfields, if necessary.

"From what you are saying, Agung," a woman from the Affiliates of Solidarity was saying, "the security implications of a system like this are enormous. I can't imagine having a computer system poking around in my private thoughts."

Agung raised his wrist indolently. "As I mentioned, the project lead on this has pushed to guarantee individual rights to mental sovereignty." He waited as the mindfield access port he had opened translated his thoughts into various different languages for the dignitaries and relayed it to the soft cones of directed speakers set up in front of the two of them. It made for a stilted conversation, but until they agreed to allow the mindfield into their own heads, it was the best option. "Raft City," he went on, "was an effort to break away from the attitude of these empire states that you serve. Coercion, interrogation, and suppression of individual freedoms are what we despise here. We have no interest in –" *Now, what was the word? Lookup, sales notes 1.* "– propagating these things for others." He enjoyed the look of affront on the woman's face, but noticed nothing but a mask of neutrality on the face of the man from the Middle Bloc. "In order to allay your fears, we will allow complete transparency into the system as long as your governments do the same. And that all states allow links in and out to all other states. The only way you can guarantee we're not spying on you is to make sure that you are not spying on anyone else. And that will be hardwired in permanently. Your own citizens and the citizens of other states will happily investigate the code and systems for any problems and protest vigorously any that they find. I've found there is nothing like a glass house for encouraging stones to be thrown." He gave his biggest grin at their discomfort at the idea of scrutiny. "You must guarantee transparency and universal access. I hope this is not too much for you." At this, Sakti came in and offered trays of stickily sweet delicacies. – *I love you,* Agung thought. Mentally he kissed her.

– *And so you should,* Sakti replied. *Now get off, not in front of guests!* He suppressed a laugh.

– *They can't see that; no-one knows if we don't want them to.*

– I *know.* He sent her on her way with a mental pinch. The real-world Sakti gave him a look and left.

The female envoy, while dealing with a mouthful of pastry and sugar-coated fingers said, "Of course, speaking on behalf of the Affiliates of Solidarity, we have never had a problem with transparency of governance, but we worry that other states..." she looked sideways at her counterpart, who laughed derisively.

"Of course! We believe you, don't we Agung?" He

took a napkin and began to wipe his hands, continuing to chuckle softly as he brought it to his lips.

Agung watched the exchange with bemusement. The translation programme that he had in his own head was instantaneous and he had no need for directed speakers but he still had trouble understanding these political hyenas.

"In spite of this," she said over the laughter, "what about the need of government to keep certain sensitive plans a secret? You can't tell the populace everything you are doing. There'd be chaos, anarchy," the Affiliates envoy complained. "And if the other states have access..."

Agung sighed. "And where does it say that the transparency of the mindfields will have any effect on your privacy of government? Just like an individual may keep their privacy, so may any group of individuals. You only allow people to share the parts of your world that you agree. Our only dictate is that you don't enforce others to divulge information unwillingly. And that you connect up the nets."

The Middle Bloc envoy stopped chuckling and became serious. "My colleague does have a valid point in spite of herself. Perhaps the Affiliates of Solidarity aren't so much of a problem, but if you allow the Corporation of Attorney States access to our nets, they are going to flood it with misinformation, propaganda and so on."

Agung raised a finger. "Yes, but you will get a chance to counter this misinformation. You will give the citizens of that state a chance to access your version of the truth for a change, give them an opportunity to hear a voice other than their own states' for once. The only people who should be afraid of this are the ones who don't believe in their own message." The Middle Blocker looked affronted but did not rebut this. "The frustrating thing for me is, if you would allow mindfield access to just your own minds, I could explain it to you in an instant. You'd know everything that you needed or wanted to know. But I can't do that if you won't even begin to allow it."

"Agung," the man from Middle Bloc said, sun now at the level of his earlobe, sweat dripping from his temple to his collar, "I understand what you are saying intellectually, but you have to look at it from our point of view. The danger of letting someone access our minds, probing our state secrets, is one we can't afford to take. They could plant something into our brains, a... a sleeper programme or something. They could be planning to take over power in our states. These kinds of things would be the ultimate violation of all human rights."

"Good, so you agree not to do these things to your own people," he retorted. "Now, understand what is at stake if you don't get access." He lowered his lids for a moment and they fluttered, silently. Ada King made her way into the barge slowly, carrying a small glassy sphere from which small wisps of vapour could be seen rising. He could see what the envoys could not. She was followed by her dog and butterfly, her mindfield appearance taller, smoother. It was as he always saw her now, unless he chose to view the real-world girl. Somehow, he preferred knowing what she thought she should look like; it was an insight into her make-up. Other of his citizens, infatuated with the idea, had taken to altering their appearances using the mindfields: accompanying themselves with music as they walked, making themselves into giants or the image of holostars. He'd been happy with how quickly they'd picked up the ball and run with it, but he'd had to complain to Ada to adjust the damn thing so it didn't clutter up his day.

Ada placed the smoking sphere onto a small, low table, equidistant from the two envoys, then retreated and sat upon a cushion near to Agung's feet. The dog sat obediently beside her and the insect fluttered into her hair. With a serene smile on her lips, the sphere lifted into the air under its own power and began to spin. Trailers of steamy mist began to spread outwards in a miniature spiral galaxy.

"Telekinesis?" the Affiliates envoy said with shock.

"It's a trick!" the Middle Blocker said harshly, at almost the same moment. They had both come forward to the edge of their seats, roused.

"No," Ada said dreamily. "It's science. I invented the material of the sphere this morning. It is levitating via a superconductive property and is responding to my mental commands."

"But... this is extraordinary," Affiliates wondered. "Can I touch it?" She stretched out a finger.

"I would not recommend it," Ada King warned swiftly. "It is cooled to a very low temperature and you would undoubtedly burn yourself." The hand was snatched away.

"But you were carrying it, I saw you!" Middle Bloc protested.

"Mind over matter," she replied with a vindictive smile. "I can control my autonomic responses, even my body temperature. A mind and body augmented with machines, but free from them. No implants, no electrodes. But a mind that is as vast as all human knowledge that has ever been and some that has never been seen before. Would you like me to recite pi to the millionth place? Or would you prefer a more human demonstration?" She indicated a pad in front of each of them. "Please write down a random sentence, phrase or anything that comes to mind. Then close the paper and pass it to Agung without me seeing. I will look into his mind to discover what you wrote."

"You could have hidden cameras," the Middle Blocker whined. "This is just a parlour trick."

"Of course, you have your suspicions. Please cover your work, or move to another part of the city, it will make no difference. You could do something different, perhaps take Agung to one side and whisper in his ear?" She leaned to rest on one hand. "I can wait as long as you like. I have plenty to keep me occupied." Agung saw the dog crawl its paws onto her lap and go to sleep.

The Middle Bloc man rose hesitantly to his feet and

gestured Agung to the far end of the barge while the woman picked up a pad and bent over whatever she was doing. The two men returned and the Affiliates envoy folded her paper into smaller and smaller squares and then handed it cautiously to Agung. The superconductive sphere was still spinning in the air in the middle of the space.

Agung stood ostentatiously behind Ada's back so she couldn't see. He began to open the origami of paper that the woman had passed and read what was there, but before he could even consciously register the shape of the words, Ada said, "Alexis Leon, one, four, one, three. And a drawing of a palm tree."

"No," the woman, said, but in disbelief rather than denial. "You can't have."

Ada turned her smiling face to the Middle Bloc man, saying, "You were particularly devious, in that you spoke a nonsense phrase into Agung's ear. The translation programmes really struggled, for a picasecond, at least. Your words, "Frumious Bandersnatch," come from a famous poem, in English, of the nineteenth century. But of course, that book had been digitised at the start of the twenty-first century, so really it wasn't that much of a challenge at all."

"But there must be hidden cameras, or microphones," the Affiliate said, still blindsided by Ada's speed. "Or some other trick. People have been doing mind reading acts for centuries."

Ada sighed. "Very well, then. The irrational number pi: three point one four one five nine two six..."

Another helo began to descend into Raft City, slotting onto the lawn of the long park. Men with nasty-looking weapons leapt out and began to sweep the area for hostility. Agung could see the arrival through the eyes of thirty of his citizens who had chosen to share this information with him from a safe distance. The squad leader of the soldiers banged on the side of the helo and a man – with hair so beautified he was protecting it with his hands – stepped out and ducked in the wake of the propellers. "We have a new arrival," he announced, while Ada continued her recitation of pi.

"Two, one, zero, five, one, one..."

"I believe he is from the Corporation of Attorney States." – *Ah, that's thrown the cat among the pigeons.* The two other envoys stopped their bored fidgeting and sat upright.

– *How did their firing on, not to mention spying on Raft City affect the Corporated States' bargaining position in your eyes?* Ada asked, while her mouth droned numbers, "three, four, two, seven, one..."

– *I told you, we're here to make peace.*

– *Good, good... Oh, no.* Agung suddenly understood that Ada had tapped into the views of the new arrivals and had recognised the envoy that was now being escorted under arms towards their location, that his name was Colleague Oswald and that Ada had a passionate dislike and distrust of him.

– *What should I know?*

"Three, five, nine, zero, two..." – *Oh, nothing that was really different from any other psychopathic twit they called 'Colleague'. He was my post-graduate programme director, pushed me further and further into the military applications of witric neuroscience. And I just don't like him, okay?*

"Alright, then," Agung said out loud. Ada stopped counting and looked over her shoulder with a cat-like expression. The squadron leader took point as heavy boots clomped into the council barge. – *Ada, I don't like those weapons. Can you do anything?*

– *Why don't you?*

– *You're just better at it. I'm a bloody fisherman! Quickly, please!*

– *Oh, alright. They have a battery backup but a wictric tactical collaboration system. Let's see. Ah, there we are. I've dampened them.*

The squadron leader looked down at his gun, shook it

slightly and gazed at it in shock. He held it up, nonetheless, in defiance of the facts, clearly hoping no-one would notice and his teammates did the same, shuffling awkwardly into a covering formation. Colleague Oswald made a lowering gesture towards them, "Now, now, this is a diplomatic visit. I'm sure that if Agung is safe here, then so am I." The squadron stood down with almost palpable relief and shuffled backwards to make a backdrop of camouflage in beige for Oswald. "Ada," he said, as if it were a pleasant surprise to see her. She made no move and he converted his greeting into a neat bow then bowed in turn to the other dignitaries. A strand of hair had come loose from his coiffure and he subtly smeared it back into place.

"Have you come here to negotiate with us about the mindfields?" Agung asked informally, with one eye still on the soldiery.

"Well, no." Oswald said with a conciliatory smile. "I'm sure your scheme for – what was it? – linking humans with computers will be a marvellous thing. I will be looking forward to hearing about its progress, but the reason I am here today is for another matter. First, with your permission, I'd really like to speak to Ada here." He made another half bow as he waved his hand graciously in her direction. "In private, if we may."

"You may not," she riposted immediately. Her eyebrows had drawn down and she was quivering a little.

"Very well," Oswald continued, unfazed. "Then I shall have to state our business in front of all. And why not? It is a simple request. Ada, I am here to ask you, on behalf of the Corporation of Attorney States, to come home."

Her jaw dropped open. Oswald continued in her silence. "You see, you are a citizen of the Corporated States and as such, you really belong with your people. I don't know how long you can last in your fantasy of living with these outsiders. No offense," he added in an aside to Agung, who made no reply but a stern look. "You're one of us. You must come home."

"I must?" she said in a quiet voice.

"Yes. Indeed. The state insists."

"You have other scientists," she said, looking at the spinning ball in the air.

– *Ada don't,* Agung warned.

"None like you," Oswald said and Agung believed this was most likely true.

"Well, I won't and that's all," she said, refusing to look at him again. "Goodbye."

"Very well then," he said stiffly. "Since you won't see reason, I'll have to talk to Agung. Did you know, Agung, that it is very strange how four of our highly advanced seagoing vessels were sailing not far from your Raft City – " he said the name as if encountering a sudden lump of gristle, "– and they disappeared. Just vanished. We swept the area, but not a float or a body could be found anywhere near their last location. But they did manage to send off a final transmission before they disappeared. They said, 'No, no, it's eating us.' Strange, isn't it?"

Agung affected surprise. "Yes, it is. But what has that got to do with Raft City?"

"For a long time, we couldn't figure it out. We analysed, and analysed again. There was nothing. Until one day, almost by accident, one of our scientists discovered something rather shocking: that the seawater in that area had an almost insane amount of carbon dioxide dissolved within it." Agung shrugged. "Of course, we hadn't been looking for that, since those levels were historically only associated with nanobiotes of a concentration not seen since before the treaty."

The Middle Bloc and Affiliates envoy gasped. "But we were still perplexed. Why could we not detect any of the nanobiota that must have caused this? And of course, the reason was that they had changed, evolved from what they used to be. We just weren't looking using the correct methods. But we can easily detect them now with this simple spray." He reached into his jacket pocket and brought out a small aerosol.

– *Shit. We've got to stop him. Libby is probably all over this place.*

Ada's eyes flickered for a moment. – *Be calm, Agung. All is well.*

Colleague Oswald sprayed a cloud of the indicator gas into the air between them. The cloud slowly dispersed. "Oh, well, of course it should be on a surface..." He sprayed the floor by his feet. Nothing. He sprayed a few of the cushions that were scattered about then one of the ornate red-painted dragons that twined their way up the pillars of the pagoda.

"Is something supposed to happen?" Agung said innocently, examining the places sprayed closely.

Colleague Oswald's face was beginning to turn red and a vein had broached the smooth line of his impeccable forehead. "The point... the point is we know, Agung."

"Know what?"

"That you've been using nanobiotes to make this whole thing. That the witricity mindfields nonsense is a sham. You've broken the treaty and now you're trying to infect the entire world with the nano-plague again."

"We haven't," he answered calmly.

– *That's true,* Ada thought, *it's Libby who's the treaty breaker. Can you get in trouble for being friends with a subversive sub?* She giggled, suddenly behind her hand.

"And we're not trying to infect the world with nano-plague," Agung continued. "It would be very difficult to do business with them after that. Listen to yourself, Colleague."

"But you know if it *is* all nanotech that is creating the effect, you won't be needing me then," Ada chimed in with undisguised glee.

"We don't," he said, petulantly. "We don't." He extended an arm towards her and smartly tapped his ring finger and middle finger on to his palm. With a surprised expression, he did it again, then twice more. With a snort of rage, he turned on his heels and exited the barge, summoning his guard with a curt jerk of his head.

Ada and Agung burst out laughing, along with the two other envoys. Through tears of mirth, the Middle Bloc representative said, "At least that's been cleared up."

"Hmm?" Agung asked, wiping the back of his hand across his eyes.

"That you aren't using nanobiotes. It had crossed our minds." Agung suddenly stopped laughing, at which the envoy realised what he'd said. "What I mean is..."

Agung sucked the air between his teeth. "You know, I'm beginning to think you're all the same," he said bitterly.

"You can't blame us for..."

"Can't I? What about trust? What about a person being worthy of their word? Hmm?" Ada buried her head in her knees, long curly hair draping around her shoulders. The butterfly looked as if it were resting in a weeping mulberry tree.

Ada's voice stole into his thoughts during his tirade. – *He had a gestural cuff. That's why he was making those strange movements with his hand. My guess is it was supposed to detonate the implant. 'If we can't have you, nobody can'.*

– I can't imagine how he thought he would get out of here alive if he had, Agung replied. *What fools.*

– You know, while they're still in range, I could probably drop that Corporated States helo into the drink. I'm sure Libby is near enough to finish the rest.

– No! He responded sharply, shocked.

– Oh relax, couldn't you tell I was joking?

In a private drawer of his mind, deep inside and far away from Ada King, he thought *No.*

He turned to the envoys and gave them each a folder of hardcopy treaty offerings. "I'm sure you will prefer these," he said a little vindictively. "Less chance that you'll get any Raft City viruses in your computers, eh?" The envoys picked them up and stiffly said their goodbyes. As soon as they had left, Ada hurled the spinning, smoking sphere of superconductors at one of the decorative pillars where it shattered with an icy crunch and a release of vapour.

"You really didn't like him," Agung murmured.

The *Liberty Via Force*'s avatar appeared before the two of them through the dregs of steam, strangely more real when broadcasting herself through the mindfields than as a hologram. Her violet eyes were subdued. "You managed to get your 'little friends' out of the way quickly," Agung said with a leading tone. "That was good."

"Oh, I don't keep any nanobiotes near here. It's far too dangerous," she said solicitously. "And besides, with Ada's mindfields I don't really need a physical presence here as such. I can just come and visit when I need to."

"You heard what that idiot from the Corporated States said about the missing ships?" he said, waving an arm in the direction of the departed parties. Libby nodded contritely.

"I was sure that the tides would have dissipated any trace of what I had done before they got there. They were quicker than I surmised."

"The trouble is that they are on to us. I don't think you should venture out of Marisenal for a while until this dies down."

Liberty Via Force nodded, again. "I understand."

"Ada, I want you to run a few simulations and models and work out what they could be up to. We still have limited access to their Statenet? Good, try to find out what they are going to do to get at us next."

"What would you do, if you were them?" Ada looked at him with her dark eyes, burning clear and amber in the late afternoon sun. A halo was forming around her hair.

"I'd come, probably at night, and take you by stealth."

"Then I will have to be ready for them." Agung suppressed an involuntary shiver.

10. BY STEALTH

Ikatere felt distinctly uncomfortable as Libby and he promenaded by the arcade. She had changed her clothing from the painfully white, straight outfit to a corset-and-bustle affair from who knew when. She was carrying a parasol and down here, it was possibly the most useless accessory in the history of fashion. Even Mars had a brighter day than Marisenal. Her blonde hair had been done up into a towering, elaborate affair and she had put one lace-gloved hand in the crook of his elbow. He was still in his general purpose workman's gear after refusing outright the waistcoat and monocle she had suggested.

She was admiring the great hall's dome, which now had an enhanced view of the sealife outside, appearing via the mindfields as a sort of common consent illusion. Hammerheaded sharks were circling the seamount and the OTEC tower, providing a moving decorative garland. Below this view, the Angel of Light – as the winged female statue had been perhaps ironically dubbed – began to move her lips. "Tram entering, please take care." They walked smartly off the tracks. *Liberty Via Force* twirled her parasol as the tram passed, flipping its fringe around.

"I really am enjoying these mindfields," she said

blithely. "I believe between your mindfields and my nanobiotes, there are almost infinite applications."

"A shame your nanobiotes have been banned, then, isn't it?" he responded.

Her mouth opened in mock offense. "Well, it isn't my fault, is it? Some close-minded people deciding to ban things that could be good for all mankind... I'm sure that any problems could be overcome with a little collaboration."

"Problems..." Ikatere looked across. "You ate an entire fleet of vessels and you talk about problems? Not to mention the amount of carbon dioxide your nanobiotes give off. That was part of the reason to ban it in the first place."

"It, it, it! As if I'm not even here. As if human beings are entirely emissions-free. Well, let me tell you this. With your mindfields and my nanobiotes, we could do almost anything. You can dream it, I can affect the real world. We could extend human life, cure diseases..." She beamed at him. "We could cure your mother." He felt his shoulders stiffening up. "Why, have I said something wrong?" she said with such artlessness he ground his teeth.

"I'd have to think about it, Libby."

"I don't understand. Surely this requires little thought. We could bring your mother here, so it would be out of the way and no states would be any the wiser. My nanobiotes could be in and out of your mother in seconds, just like they were with Ada."

"Why do you care?" he asked, suddenly fierce.

She dropped her gaze. "It seems that the mindfields affect my systems too. I am beginning to... feel things for the first time, things that are not emulation. For example, I feel a certain unease inside me when I think about those ships I destroyed. I feel unease at the thought that one of the states might one day locate me and destroy me." She looked up, a delicate trembling around her violet eyes.

The Liberty Via Force *is a hunk of metal in the docking*

house, he told himself.

"But I feel good things when I consider you, Ikatere. I want to help you. If helping your mother helps you... Honestly, Ikatere, the mindfields have made me believe that humans and artificial beings could obtain a kind of parity with each other. That one day it might be very difficult to tell the difference between us."

They strolled on, Ikatere lost in uncomfortable thought, Libby prudently quiet. He observed his surroundings. The park was growing in nicely and people were circulating around, but there wasn't the life, the hubbub he expected of a city this size. The slowness of acceptance was vexing him. "Could you," he asked suddenly, "could you modify humans to adapt to life under the sea?"

"How do you mean?"

"I suppose to become a bit like cetaceans. Air breathing and so on, but able to withstand pressure, cold, hold their breath for extended periods."

"It's not outwith the bounds of possibility. But I thought you weren't keen on using my nanobiotes."

"I'm not," he retorted, a little too quickly. "It's just a thought."

Ikatere spotted a cafe. It was boringly basic, but the owners had put out a few little flowers in vases at an attempt to make it homely. He pulled up a seat and sat down. Libby stood for a moment, but rolling her eyes, the seat opposite glided softly away from the table. "If you're so keen on reducing carbon gases," she chided, "you could pull a lady's chair out."

"You're not a lady!" he snapped.

She pouted and was about to reply when a server came out to take their order.

"I will have a coffee," Ikatere said.

"And your friend?" he asked genially.

"She'll cope."

Libby frowned and the server retreated discretely. "You

know," she said, "you can be very rude when you want to." She made an image of a teapot and cup and saucer appear in front of her and made a great show of pouring herself a drink. As if they were just continuing their conversation, she began talking again. "Maybe one day, when this ridiculous nano-prejudice is over, the Raft City can come and anchor over Marisenal. It would make a great partnership, don't you think?"

"The whole point of Raft City is its ability to move," he said grumpily.

"You could make more – ones that move, ones that don't. I am rather impressed with the citizens' ability to just take any old thing that floats and build it into a home."

"I like Marisenal being away from it all," he said. "It's away from all the bickering, the super-bloc politics, the stupidity. If you anchored Raft City to it, it'd become something different." He unfolded his arms, aware of his defensiveness. "I just think it's better to be separate," he finished, with a conciliatory tone.

"Well, perhaps if we can modify humans to adapt to underwater life, we could build more Marisenals, and then you'd have more freedom to choose such things."

He thought about the freedom from borders, protectionism, patriarchy. "That would be nice," he admitted as she sipped her tea.

***

Ada stood by a small canal of water, looking down at the reflection of starlight. It was dark, most of the city lights were out. A purple tracery lit up the mast above the liner, but most of the night running lights had been switched off. She flexed her arm portentously towards the canal and reached out with the power of the witricity from the mast. A writhing briefly shattered the water's dim reflections and swiftly died down. She returned to her contemplation of the starlight on the face of the water. Occasional fins would break the surface, bisecting the canal and sinking again. Faintly, she could hear a whirring over the drooling hysterics that Fred played out on the arch of a nearby bridge.

She looked up at the hovercam. It was high overhead, but within the radius of the mindfields. She closed her eyes briefly and, with a thought, stole into the thing's mechanisms. Inside, she ransacked the control system until she found what she wanted. The wave of the signal ran like a tail from the drone, like an umbilical cord back to the place that had sent it. If she could make a few subtle changes... *Ah.*

She rode the signal back to its point of origin. Direction, frequency. She slipped, bodiless along the waves until she was aware of reaching the end.

— *They have a sub of their own,* she reported to Agung. *They are speaking Experana.*

— *The dark of the moon. That was what you predicted.*

— *Only using the modelling as it was intended.*

— *Are you going to be ok?*

— *Sure. They don't know what they're getting into.*

Ada King smiled and leaned back on the clapboard of the wall behind her. She had used the mindfields to channel her adrenal responses more efficiently and she felt an excitement, an exhilaration in her stomach instead of the sickening dread she would normally have had.

She reached her mind into the holographic points she had set up all over town. She had got the idea from Colleague Oswald's gestural cuff. An impenetrable mist began to rise over the city, lifting from several points at once. Raft City citizens would see something different. To them the mist would be transparent and warm bodies would light up like Christmas trees to those with access to the mindfields.

She checked the cameras that surrounded the perimeter of the city. Out to the east, in the depths of the kelp beds, the water began to ripple more than the ambient waves. In order to get to the city from below with a diving team, they were being forced to make a tunnel through the vegetation. She sent her discovery to anyone who was listening. She ignored several broadcasts of dismay at their destructive behaviour. Worse was to come.

Disturbances of the water, slight and easy to miss, surrounded several points of heat, indicating that divers were exiting onto a small dock at the edge of the city. – *They've got holosuits on. It's a shame that won't do any good.* There was something else remaining in the water, a blue and bulbous monstrosity that they were leaving by the dock. Using the mindfield she pulsed a few waves at the snatch squad as the bodies left the water and noted the resistance as they passed through. The resultant echoes she assembled into a realtime overlay. In glowing outlines she could see the jagged edges of knives and crude mechanical guns. They had learned from last time they were here, at least. The spherical thing that was still bobbing in the water did not appear to be a weapon, so she ignored it for now. Perhaps a backup comms module.

She bent the holographic mist to her will and sent an image of herself to appear close by to the huddled group of burly men and women. They reacted satisfyingly, leaping away and drawing on the hologram. One of them took the initiative and lunged in to grab, so Ada faded the girl back to mist. A laughing version appeared on the next boat and turned to run. Unsure what was happening, the team conferred until some sort of leader shoved three men into pursuit. Meanwhile the remaining men divided into two teams and splintered off in different directions. – *Hello, what's this?* It was hard not to feel offended that she wasn't the only mark. She tagged the group in pursuit of the hologram 'T1' and the others 'T2' and 'T3'.

She gave Agung the heads up. – *Don't worry,* he said. *I'll deal with them.*

– *There's a fire,* one of the citizens reported. *It's a storage shed. Why are they doing that?*

It seemed T3 were on a sabotage mission, while T2 were driving straight through the city towards the liner as best they could through the mist and darkness.

– *As soon as they're gone and it's safe, move in to put it out,* Agung responded. *Until then, stay out of sight. That goes for everyone. Remember; don't move around unless you have to.*

The team in pursuit of the false Ada, T1, had made it to the long park and were cautiously feeling their way through it. She created a few more Adas to shoot across their paths. They looked confused then one of them seemed to cotton on. He signalled to his team to pull down their diving masks again and make some adjustments. – *Something polarised or infrared.* They moved much more quickly, apparently no longer foxed by the mist. Ada began to remodel the strategy based on these new parameters.

– *T1 no longer compromised by holography, but T2 and 3 don't seem to have been contacted. No radio signals, the teams are isolated and carrying out separate missions. They also seem to be ignoring the drone's data, so they are maintaining complete transmission silence.*

Ada shivered. That would make it harder to confound them with science.

– *T3 burnt down a storage shed. What was in the storage shed?*

A citizen poll indicated that it was most likely a depot of protective clothing and breathing apparatus. Ada entered the data into her models but the outcomes were inconclusive.

A shining angel appeared to stand next to Ada. *Liberty Via Force*'s avatar leaned against the wall with a studied nonchalance. "I see you are being attacked."

"It's nothing," Ada replied, perhaps too quickly.

"I'm sure it is. But Ikatere expressed his concern. You see, he feels a little anxious. He doesn't like being so far away when there is trouble. Especially concerning yourself," she said, with a demure look.

"So far away in Marisenal?" Ada asked while monitoring the situation. "Shit," she swore softly. T3 had set another fire.

"You know, you're not going to do a lot of good

without the use of weapons," Libby said, the voice of reason.

"I'm not a killer," Ada retorted, feeling her face tighten up. "Just because you have no empathy..."

"On the contrary, Ada. Your invention is helping me to understand human emotion more and more each day. But it doesn't rescind the fact that determined killers face you and will not be stopped without force. It's something I understand very well."

"What good can you do, anyway? You're too far away to help us."

"Perhaps, but do you think I would let you defend yourself entirely without my help? I have a detachment of nanobiotes, cached nearby. Far enough away that they could never be connected to you, but close enough to act as the cavalry if needed. Is it needed?"

"No, thank you," Ada said vehemently. "We'll deal with this without your methods."

Liberty Via Force pouted. "And you didn't even ask me what those methods would be. Well, Ikatere will be disappointed." Ada gritted her teeth again at mention of his name. "Just remember, smoke and mirrors will only get you so far. At some point you will have to produce an actual rabbit." She blinked out of existence, leaving Ada alone.

She turned her attention fully back to the situation at hand. T1 was heading towards the *Bessu*. Their information was slightly stale, then. She had moved out of the *Bessu* to her own raft two days ago. T2 was almost at the liner and T3 were heading outwards, to the rim of the city, no doubt to sow more chaos with their fire setting and draw attention away from the other two teams. It was such a clichéd approach, she was surprised they had decided on this plan.

– Agung, T2 are nearly at the liner. What are you planning to do?

Agung gave her a quick flash of a strategem, crudely

sketched. She absorbed the details into her overall model and grunted. – *It might work, but remember that at least one of the teams has seen through our mist and decoys.*

– *It won't be a hologram.*

– *Then isn't it terribly dangerous?*

She received the mental equivalent of a shrug. – *It will work.*

– *I'll say. It's scaring the pants off me, and I know it's not real.*

It would take Agung a few moments to get his plan into place, so Ada turned her attention to T1, looking for her in the *Bessu*. The team were inside the catch hold. One of them was fingering the witricity grid, wires visible over the creamy plastic of the hold's walls. She briefly considered microwaving them. They were vulnerable. But she couldn't do it. Instead, she turned on the catch hold's heat exchangers. The team's breath began to mist in the air and within seconds they were clapping their arms and stamping their feet subconsciously. Soon, they retreated up the ladder-like steps to the top deck and exited the boat to its deck.

They stood, conferring for just long enough for Ada to turn on all available floodlights in the neighbourhood and set off all boat horns, sirens and alarms. The panicked group began to run. T2 noticed the commotion, but deliberately ignored it and began their ascent of the liner's side via ropes and grapnels. Dwi, and a small group of men waited until they were quite high in the air before turning the firehoses on them. Dwi laughed at their comical attempts to hang on. All three figures climbing the rope hit the surface of the dock heavily. Dwi was merciless and kept the hose on until they had staggered out of range, then he turned it off and dispersed the little group. Crack of gunfire and whine of ricochet as the men attempted retaliation met only the metal of the liner. T2 retreated and began to pass the liner by its bows, cautiously staring up. Movements and soft calls around corners meant they didn't kill their compatriots, T3, who were edging towards them.

– *T2 & 3 have joined up, heading towards you,* Agung. Ada broadcast. *How is the plan coming?*

– *Nearly in place. Two more minutes. T1 are getting close to your position, Ada.*

– *I'm just going to give them room to pass by. If they don't... well, you know.*

– *Just take care,* Agung said gruffly. Ada smiled.

Dog began to growl in a horrifying, lycanthropic tone that went down Ada's spine. She put a hand on his scruff and yanked a little. His front paws lifted off the ground and she sank back into the shadows discreetly. Butterfly flew out over the small canal between the boathouses and landed, resting on the meniscus of the water like a pond skater.

Ada lightly stepped around the corner, out of the sightlines of the team, continuing to watch their progress from other camera angles as they crept by the head of the canal. *That's right, just pass on by,* she thought. Suddenly they stopped and one of the team made some strange motions with his head. She could hear them, they were so close. It sounded like he was sniffing. She looked closer at the mask on this one's face. It was a kind of gas mask. He was using a chemical sniffer to detect her. They had turned down the path by the canal and were almost where she had been standing previously. Suddenly fear gripped her. It was time to deploy her own defences.

She sent impulses via the mindfields into the water below the city. She began to work on many primitive, hard little brains. The water beside the canal began to boil. She sent her mind upwards, to the hovercam drone and propelled it down, out of the sky. She used it to fly at the faces of the members of T1. One of them lost his balance and fell into the canal. The sharks that she had stirred were already in a feeding frenzy. He didn't suffer for long. Others in the team began opening fire, suddenly no longer concerned with stealth. One of them pulled a small box from their webbing and pressed a button. The sharks began to disappear. *Of course! They would have needed a shark repeller to get to the city in the first place.*

At this moment, Agung's plan came to fruition as an enormous explosion and flames leapt over the fusion toroid. "Shit, that was real!" she heard from around the corner. "Time to leave."

– *Well done, Agung, that seems to have had the effect you wanted.*

– *Watch them run,* his satisfied response came. Then Fred appeared again, sitting on top of a rubber tyre at the end of the canal. She could see him, sitting calmly. No hooting or drooling. Ada felt a chill as the barrel of a gun came to rest on her clavicle. "Ada King," the voice of a woman announced. She looked and saw the chemical sniffer had been loosened and it was draped around her neck. She looked up to the scarred and ugly face above it. A cold, detached expression filled the icy blue eyes of the operative. "You'll be coming with us now. And quickly, or we'll all get fried." Ada suppressed her impulse to tell her it was all a sham, that Agung hadn't really set the toroid on fire. At the end of the canal a rippling of the water showed that the monstrous eye of the spherical pod had come to their call.

"Get in," the woman gestured with her gun.

The mechanical cracking of gunfire sounded behind them. Ada used the mindfields feed to see a lot of people hiding and dodging behind boats. They had come to save her.

– *Don't,* she shouted at them. *You'll get hurt. Agung, tell them to come away! Agung?*

A terrified group of citizens broadcast the shape of Agung's body, lying on the deck of a small boat on the other side of the city. There was a hole in his forehead. Ada's knees collapsed. The woman and several others picked her up and brought her to the edge where the pod's terrible eye flinched open. They manhandled her in. In truth, she did little to struggle. The hatch irised closed behind her and two bangs on the roof seemed to signal motion. She was being dragged away inside a metal sphere, which was filling with pressurised air. She could smell something in the air. It smelled familiar, almost nostalgic.

After a few moments of shock and delay, she shouted, "Libby!"

The avatar appeared before her, sat crook-legged on the floor of the bathysphere. "I mentioned something about this, I fear," she said gently. "Don't worry, my nanobiote detachment is on its way. We'll get you out."

"No! You have to send them to Agung." The avatar began to flicker and her words were just scraps of sound. They were reaching the edge of the mindfields. "Save Agung! You have to save Agung!" *Liberty Via Force* disappeared before Ava could be sure she would comply. "Save Agung," she said wretchedly to no-one, the words bouncing around inside the metal sphere and spinning her into darkness.

She woke strapped to a large medical gurney, halfway reclined. She saw the scarred woman who had captured her sitting by her feet and began half-heartedly to struggle. The woman looked up, hand instinctively moving to her holstered gun, but she merely stood and left the room saying nothing, no doubt to call a superior. Ada looked around, desperately. They were probably on the sub she had seen in when she followed the hovercam's signal. Dog leapt onto the bed at her feet, growling again. Butterfly was on the knuckle of her fist where it lay, restrained, beside her. The long proboscis was unfurled and probing at the interface between the strap and her skin. They appeared to not only be buckled, but glued to her wrists somehow.

Anything useful, anything useful... She looked around. There were no handy trays of scalpels or jagged-edged glass. She twisted her wrists back and forth inside the strapping restraints until they went purple, but her skin stayed bonded to the fabric and she was giving herself burns trying. She quit her struggles and gave in to self-pity for a while.

The door opened and Colleague Oswald came in, accompanied by the scarred woman. "You're awake," he said as if it were a good morning.

Ada succumbed to the temptation of screaming, swearing and spitting at him. He merely retreated to a safe distance from her and watched. "It's okay, Ada," he said gently as she suddenly ran out of energy. "You're angry. You feel helpless. But there are many things," he said as he cautiously stepped closer, "many things that you can do to help yourself." She breathed hard, mouth dry from the anaesthetic gas and the spitting. She coughed a little. "You're a little dry. Here you go." He held a cup to her lips and she drank, spilling much of it. It was only afterwards that she considered there could have been something in it and she looked at him. "Oh, don't worry. We have no need to give you anything nasty. Not anymore. We don't do that, you see. What we do now is somewhat based on your own work." He pointed above her head. Her gaze followed his arm to see the witric accumulators that were focussed down onto her skull. "Do you remember our discussion about the practical applications of your work? It was the day I suggested we talk to the fertility board. I think we're both better off that it never went through, don't you? I imagine I'd be in a bit of trouble if I'd had a child with a seditionist." He gave a small, tense smile.

"But we're very fascinated by your work with what you've called mindfields. Good name. Very catchy. And we're going to need to know all about these mindfields." Dog's hackles were so high now he looked like a hyena. Strings of saliva were hanging from his jaws.

It'll be okay, pup, she said, not really believing it.

"But we don't want to go through all that nonsense that your Agung suggested. By the way," he said in an aside, "I'm very sorry for your loss." Her heart felt like it had been kicked out of her chest. "So instead we're going to take it directly from your brain. Fortunately we had a few people who were a little more forthcoming and weren't constantly obstructing us." He sat down on a little stool next to her couch. "So we'll be using these machines to gently remove the information we need from you. No need for torture, no need for violence; just a little dose of witricity, and your brain will give us what we want."

"And then?" she said through a clenched jaw.

He looked at her with gentle bemusement. "And then?" he echoed.

She shut her eyes as his hand reached out to the console panel at the side. She tried to find a mental locker to store all her work with the mindfields. Perhaps with a little concentration she could set up some different images to block the interrogation device. Memories started to rise in her mind, unbidden. She saw her escape, the weeks of relentless running, Stackareman supplying false cards... They were merely drawing on her long term memory. She had to try something to stall them, so she remembered the cupboard, the darkness where her mother left her, her fear, the arrival of butterfly. The light in the darkness, the beauty of the colours. She could hear her mother talking outside the door. She had never remembered hearing her words before. She could almost make out the words. The memory began to bleed into another. "Who is 'Libby'?" Oswald asked in surprise.

Ada opened her eyes in panic. Fred appeared in the corner of the room, crouching. She looked at his eyes, blue and glassy. He began to leap and laugh, hiss and gurn. She smiled and laughed herself. The laughter grew and grew until it was the same disgusting, filthy laughter as Fred. "The patient's hysterical, call the nurse," Oswald said in tight tones and the scarred woman left the room. He adjusted his seat and looked around as Ada continued to laugh so hard that tears were falling from her eyes. He cleared his throat and adjusted his collar, then his eyes fell to the floor and he began to scream, choking and wheezing, unbelieving as his feet began to melt beneath him. Ada laughed harder.

She laughed as the room dissolved around her. Everything, everything was beginning to evaporate from this world. Oswald's screams evaporated, his immaculate suit. Seawater began to pour in to the room. Her laughter was a hyperventilation, flooding her blood with oxygen. The water rose and crashed, buffeting her body, as the restraints began to dissolve. In a schismatic moment, there was nothing but the ocean around her, green and black water, a fizz of tiny bubbles escaping from her hair and skin. Butterfly flitted across her view. She contemplated buoyancy. *Is this why Ikatere does what he does?* Dog did doggypaddle underwater, his coat rippling and flowing and his paws spreading like muscular fingers to claw the sea. Fred swam in frog-kick circles, strangely at ease. Butterfly was at home in this medium as she was in the air and she began to rise and rise. Ada watched her heading towards the light. Without volition, she began to follow, quicker and quicker. Her chest was beginning to buck, so Ada stilled it. *Just wait, the end is nigh. The end is night. Go towards the light. Don't laugh.* The light became larger until it blanketed Ada's vision, filled the world, the surface world, a glass ceiling, a seismic pulser of p-waves, s-waves, molecules, ions, pressure, compression, decompression. Ada began to giggle, and bubbles foamed from her lips, emptying her lungs and in mortal debt to oxygen, she waited for the light until the surface burst around her leaving her staring at the sky, taking in air with a horse-like inhalation that was the blast of all creation. Dog howled in triumph and Butterfly swooped. Fred tittered and sat upon the guard rail of the *Liberty Via Force*'s fin tower looking down at her where she lay. Ada sat up, holding onto the handrail with a weak, hooked hand. Libby appeared beside her. Ada staggered to her feet, although they were not behaving quite right yet and together they looked over the broad expanse of the empty darkened sea.

"A good catch," Ada said, her chest still jumping with laughter spasmodically.

The fin tower's hatch began to open with a grinding squeal. Ikatere's head popped out. "Are you alright?" were his first words.

"Never better," she replied. He climbed the rest of the way out and stood beside the holographic avatar. "You look different," she mused aloud. He seemed to have bulked out somewhat, his chest had expanded and he even seemed taller.

"It's nothing," he said dismissively. "Just some exercise to combat Marisenal fatigue."

"Did you save Agung?" she asked, remembering urgently, wiping her smile away.

He was quiet a moment. "It's been three days since you were taken, Ada. A lot of things have happened."

"Tell me now. What happened?" She reached across and grabbed a handful of his shirt, through Libby's glowing form. The avatar stepped back politely. "Stop stalling!"

"The nanobiotes managed to save his body, even repair some of his brain's function," Ikatere said as though he was going to cry at any moment. "But he's not the same. He's like a... he is a... he's not really with us anymore."

"Oh... oh fuck." Her throat began to close and she swallowed and blinked a few times. Suddenly the day caught up with her and she sat down again in a heap on the *Liberty Via Force*'s fin tower as it surged through the sea. "It's all for nothing," she said, feeling her voice rise in pitch. "What will we do?" she shouted as a warm hand touched her shoulder. "It's all for nothing!"

11. THE WEIGHT OF THE VOID

Ikatere closed the terminal and sat for a moment in the white, squeaky leather chairs in *Liberty Via Force*'s command centre. His distracted mind lingered on how redundant a command centre must have been when Libby had humans in charge of her. He pitied them. It must have been hard to control a sub with such an independent mind. Perhaps that was why they left her at the bottom of the sea.

He laughed to himself and stretched his shoulders a little. "Libby," he said to the air, a little self-consciously.

"You called?" she said as she appeared standing next to him, hands behind her back.

"How's Ada doing now?"

"Still pacing in the mess hall. It seems she accelerated through the documented stages of grieving to anger and has stayed there ever since." Ikatere grimaced.

"I suppose I should go talk to her." He made no motion to get out of his seat, listlessness draining his limbs of motivation.

"I'll go," Libby said brightly. "I might be able to talk to her. After all, we bonded somewhat when I removed the implant." She, too, made no motion to leave but Ikatere guessed she was already there, a spectre in multiple loci. They continued their conversation.

"The recording of the attack has gone out over the nets. The Corporated States haven't even bothered to deny their involvement," he said.

"Oh? I thought denial of state sanctioned murder would be in their best interests."

"I'm not sure they think we are worth covering up."

"And you are depressed by this thought," she stated.

"No, I am angry. But it is an anger so deep, its symptoms manifest exactly like depression," he said, plucking at his hair slowly with one hand. "While the Great Divide between the nets stands, there's nothing we can do. And with Agung the way he is, the negotiation process for rolling out the mindfields has not just stalled, it has ceased to be. We can't even put him on camera anymore." Ikatere's eyes rolled with dismay. He remembered too vividly their experiments with holos and their long conversations about life, the feeling of family he'd had with Agung. All gone. All gone.

***

Ada looked up to the liner. It had changed; it was now a castle, protecting the elite, keeping them high above the people. She had left her raft in this early morning with strength in her spirit, but now every step towards the elephantine vessel was leeching her determination. Eventually, by a process of metric attrition she arrived at the foot of the main gangplank. It was virtually empty of foot traffic, a far cry from the bustle of business that had swarmed on it before. She hesitated and looked up to the faces of the men at the top of the ramp. She had never seen them before. They were holding guns and were very large. Fred hunkered down behind them, almost peeking out between their legs.

She advanced on them and stopped just before the head of the gangplank. Their crotches were about level with her head. "Is it alright if I come up?" she asked, trying to mask her aggravation.

A massive head turned towards her. Even his jaw bulged with muscle and dull brown eyes looked incuriously from beneath greasily spiked hair. "What's your business?" he asked after an interval that could only be termed insolent. She felt the calibre of his inspection – an entomologist with a killing jar and pin to hand.

She gestured to her companions, which they should have been able to see. "Don't you recognise me? I'm Ada King. I'm here to visit Agung."

"Only immediate family," he said, closing the matter to his satisfaction. His eyes returned to their fixed, neutral gaze into space.

"But I..."

"Only immediate family," repeated the guard. "And no dogs. Even pretend friend dogs," he said, laughing at his own joke. His partner joined in, although a little late.

"Says who?" Ada said, suddenly feeling belligerent. Dog took up a stalking position and walked through their legs to show them he was a free canine. He snapped at Fred, who waved his fists angrily.

"Says Mister Dwi," the other emotionless slab of beef chimed in. This one was an ad for commando holoscenes, wearing a webbing vest without a shirt underneath so that his bulging pectorals and biceps could be displayed. They didn't react to Dog at all.

"Mister..." Ada was left speechless. She had never heard Dwi referred to as a mister before. In fact, no-one in Raft City had called anyone mister, including Agung. "Right, well I'll speak to *Mister* Dwi myself." The guards said nothing, but Ada detected an air of smugness that made her want to exploit her crotch-height reach.

She sent a message to Dwi in the mindfields only to find a kind of barrier. Dwi had isolated himself from messages from all but a few select citizens. She was not one of them. "What is this?" she said out loud.

"Mister Dwi does not need to be bothered right now

by everyone," said Spiked-hair. "He is dealing with a terrible tragedy."

"Fine," Ada said with a creasing in her brow. "Then I will talk to someone else."

She reached out with her mind towards Agung, gently. She pulled back with shock. A short glimpse had been enough. It was like reaching into a pool of battery acid whilst taking some strong narcotics. She gritted her teeth and called out again in a different direction. – *Sakti.*

Soon the woman came marching along the deck, her sari swishing. Even the guards became apprehensive at the sight of her, pointing their guns down to the ground. "What are you doing?" she shouted from several metres away.

"Mister Dwi ordered..." Spiked-hair began.

"Dwi is not in charge of this city yet!" She arrived and folded her arms and began to weave her head from side to side in time with her tirade. She asked them if they thought themselves better than everyone else; she informed them of the sacrifices made for the city by certain people. She even questioned their parents' methods of child rearing. The men tried to protest but visibly shrank back. "You say only immediate family?" she ended. "Ada is immediate family you idiots! Come, Ada love," she reached out and clucked and herded Ada onto the main deck before marching her off. – *We'll have to go quickly,* she said privately to Ada, *they're becoming more full of themselves every day. Don't give them a chance to think, that's the secret.*

Ada smiled. – *Should be easy enough.*

Sakti sat on the edge of Agung's bed, stroking his hand. She was facing away from his head. Ada took a moment to look at his face. An ugly, blistered pink star of scarring took up most of his forehead. The sleepy, lazy expression of benignity had been replaced with a bored, hateful expression. "Most of the time he's not so quiet, so we take advantage of these times." She was speaking with a practical, workaday manner. It broke Ada's heart.

"What do you think will happen with Dwi," Ada asked, diplomatically avoiding saying *after he takes over.*

Sakti looked up. "I don't know," she said quickly. She looked distressed for the first time.

"Can we remove him from power?" Sakti's eyes widened to show a complete ring of white. Butterfly flapped around the room, alighting on a wall, a bureau, the bunch of flowers on Agung's nightstand. Ada reached out with the mindfields and detected several listening devices where Butterfly had landed. "No, of course not, how foolish of me," she said aloud then snipped the connection to the witric devices. "It's okay, you can speak now."

"That poisonous little pig!" Sakti burst out. She had been holding it in for a long time, clearly. "I don't know what we can do. He's surrounded himself with violent people. He doesn't allow anyone to talk to him or join him in a mindfield dream. He knows only too well that what he is doing is wrong." She met Ada's eye and said earnestly, "I don't think we can stop him without bloodshed." She went back to patting Agung's hand, who suddenly stirred.

"Woman, get me water," he droned.

Sakti blinked hard and rose, bustling about the room to pour a cupful from the pitcher and adjust his pillows so he could sit up and drink. Agung showed no recollection of having ever had a wife. Sakti looked on the edge of a breakdown, so Ada said softly, "Could I have a few minutes with him?"

"Yes of course, I'll be outside." She made quickly for the door to the cabin, raising the back of her hand to wipe her eyes as she turned.

Ada took a chair and watched Agung a few moments. She could just see the top of Dog's nose on the far side of the bed, snuffling and sneezing. Agung suddenly noticed her regard and said, "What?" ferociously. She closed her eyes and absorbed the shock of his emotion.

"I'm used to people who are menacing," she said

slowly, looking at Fred. "You do not frighten me." She lurched back involuntarily as Agung threw the paper cup at her head, still half-full of water. She allowed the water to seep into her clothing, looked at the crushed receptacle with its small puddle on the floor. "You know," she went on in as conversational and calm a tone as she could manage, "my original strand of studies into neuroscience was to understand the human mind. To produce a painless, non-invasive encephalograph. I wanted to understand myself, my companions." She laughed, ruefully. "I never did. But maybe I can understand you." She called the mindfields to examine the physical brain, avoiding the bright painfulness of his current personality. Butterfly guided her on a brief tour of the destruction. The shot that had been fired at him had gone through the centre of his brain, dividing the two hemispheres and smashing many of the major structures. Butterfly's delicately hooked feet plucked at microscopic strands that penetrated these structures, binding them. Libby's repairs. The damage was extensive. Without the repairs he would be dead or at worst in a permanent comatose state but with them...

She opened her eyes and saw that *Liberty Via Force*'s avatar had appeared. "Yes, I know," she said tersely. "But you did ask me to save him. I did my best."

Agung could not see Libby and looked around, confused as Ada spoke out loud. "I wouldn't have asked you if I had known. Sometimes you have to be human to understand these kinds of consequences." Agung began to swear at her, wrestling with his blankets. She used a few signals from the mindfields to send him into a fitful sleep and felt the guilt at doing so creep up her belly.

"You were out of range in an enemy vessel, or I would have consulted your humanity," Libby snapped, managing to make it sound like 'your majesty'. The scientific part of Ada that was present even during times of great emotion, considered this tone interesting.

"As it stands," Ada continued, musing, "it seems that

Agung still being alive is the only thing that has prevented Mister Dwi from becoming some kind of despot. I don't know what he's got in mind."

"Nothing good," Libby said with an unsettling certainty.

"So we can't let Agung die yet," Ada said sadly.

"Not unless you're prepared to take the measures we talked about when I brought you back here."

"I was angry then," Ada said, covering her eyes tiredly with a hand.

"And now?"

***

The ghost of Agung floated in the sunny afternoon. Westwards, a heat haze spoke of showers but for now the populace sweated in the flat space of City Square in front of the liner. The normally colourful citizens had dressed in mourning, black mindfield clothing draping those who were not physically wearing the colour, veils and hats covering their heads, the resultant uniformity alien to Raft City. The ocean's swell propagated through the many small rafts that were patchworked into the square's makeup and the ripples moved the people in a dark, crude slick.

Ikatere stepped forward to contribute his own memory to the shared hallucination, the pyre of light and thought. Agung's effigy grew larger and more real and a burst of sentiment rippled through the crowd as they experienced his first meeting with Agung, the man who was preceded by a chicken from the door of his raft and the young, tongue tied Ikatere who stood before him. Sobs and "just-so" giggles could be heard throughout the crowd.

Dwi stepped forward. Dwi, the slight man who was behaving himself for the duration of the funeral at least, had been preying on Ikatere's mind for a while now. He wondered if he and his cronies would make a move on Marisenal sometime soon. He had been watching the personnel that were beginning to come more readily to the deep sea city. They were suspiciously quick to volunteer on long shifts, people that had never shown an interest in Ikatere's benthic activities before. Dwi's contribution to the memory pyre was prosaic, a flat cardboard cutout of Agung, still as a photograph.

Ada stepped forward to contribute her memory. Her dog and butterfly came forward with her, the dog doing a kind of bow to the image and the butterfly spiralling skywards. The little gimp of a man who she allowed for who knows what reason also crept up and touched the image's foot before dashing back to disappear into obscurity. The memory she contributed was of a flower, a red hibiscus that she held in her hands and then released like a dove towards the colossus. The crowd saw Agung give it to her in the first ever shared dream and knew that for her it meant forgiveness. It floated slowly upwards while she retreated with proper decorum and red-rimmed eyes.

The last to approach was Sakti. She plucked the red flower from the air and gazed at it for a moment before bursting into sudden laughter. The crowd was shocked for a moment, unsure how to react. Sakti looked around at them all, the widow with the wide smile. "I know it is hard to think about right now, but don't you remember how he was? How he lived?" She gave her memory to the image of Agung, and the crowd knew at once how much Sakti had loved every day she had spent with him. "And what do you think he would be thinking right now?" she shouted as she hurled the flower to the sky. Tears and laughter flowed in equal measure – tears in release of their sadness and loss, laughter in delight at having known Agung.

Ikatere found himself hugging Ada tightly to his chest. She was currently using his shirt as a hanky, convulsed with sobs. Ikatere did not think she was laughing as well, like the rest of the populace. "Hey," he crooned and shook her a little. He saw Sakti make an accepting nod and he nudged the young, dark haired woman until she pulled away to watch as the image of the Agung, so hyper-real, so much larger than life, became a pillar of fire, then smoke, then air and was gone. Ada held the back of her hand to her cheek. It was endearing and filled him with pathos but she turned her head sharply as Dwi made a move to step forward.

He began to speak to the mourners, all of Raft City, a captive audience. "I know this is a sad time," he began, "but we must remember that enemies circle us. That is why I have decided to step up as the new leader of Raft City."

A few boos rumbled through the crowd as Ikatere gaped at his effrontery. He began to step towards them but Ada pushed on his chest a little and murmured, "Let him make his own grave."

"A few of you might not like it, but the simple fact is that now we need strength. Now we need purpose. And I am here to tell you that this memorial service was the last time that we will use the mindfields in this city." An incredulous susurration spread through the people listening.

Dwi raised his hands. "Listen! Listen." He spoke at a heightened volume, ironically enabled to do so by the mindfields. "I know you have grown used to it but I have struck a deal that will allow us to remain free. We will be dismantling the mast and using the power of the toroid to do more essential things. Logistics... um..." A riot was about to break out and Dwi's bodyguards produced guns and began to take position. The crowd was fighting back with mindfield images that were spiking the sky. The clouds of the westwards squall were looming closer as pictures of clenched fists, logos of oppression or peace and even Ada King's face hovered over the crowd.

The people started to move forward, putting pressure on the bodyguards who were making shuffling steps to put themselves in front of Dwi. "That's it, let's go," Ikatere distinctly heard him say as the group began a shambling retreat up to the top of the liner's gangplank. They had been followed all the way by the crowd, who were chanting 'Equality!', 'Democracy!' and other such revolutionary slogans. The guard were trying to block off the liner's gangway, pulling barriers across.

"Back," shouted one of the guards, a particularly bullish individual with spiked hair, who waved his gun and even fired a few shots in the air. The protesters flinched away which gave Dwi's group enough time to unfasten the bolts at the top of the gangplank, letting the entire structure fall and dropping perhaps a hundred people into the sea. After a moment's stunned disbelief at this act, Ikatere shoved his way forward and jumped into the small gap of water between the square and the ship. He pushed struggling people upwards until hands reached down from those on the square. After a few of these, he dived under, seeing a forest of legs thrashing with underwater slowness and spots of foam. Looking down, he spied a small form sinking down. He surged down after it and collared the little boy who had been knocked unconscious. He screamed for medical help once they were both back to the air and bodily hauled the boy into a cramped space between teetering feet. The people on the square made a channel for a woman in a high-visibility tabard to make it to the spot on the raft where the boy's unconscious form lay. The doctor began compressions and mindfield scans of his chest cavity immediately.

Ikatere hoisted himself out of the water unaided and refused a silken scarf donated for his shoulders, pointing to a more vulnerable victim. He scanned around. Sakti and her kids had been safely removed from the dangers of the push. Ada King was standing, somewhat uselessly on the right-hand side of the square. She was huddled in a forlorn group with the companions, when they suddenly disappeared. Ikatere made his way over to her. She was gazing up at the liner. The witricity mast with its silicene vanes was dark and dormant and all methods of physical access– tow lines and ladders – were systematically being decommissioned. "It really is a castle now," she said as if in a dream.

"Yes, a fortress. So, no more mindfields then?"

"Turn it back on!" came the cry near the square's edge. "This boy is dying! Turn it back on! We need it for medical treatment." The cry was carried by several throats and became a wail, a lament.

Ada snapped out of her reverie and tugged on his sleeve. "Not quite." She ploughed through the crowd towards the boy, dragging Ikatere in her wake. At the foot of the forlorn little crowd of spectators to the boy's crisis, she called out to the doctor, "Hey, we can get him some mindfield scanning if you're quick." Ikatere understood suddenly and at the doctor's nod, picked the boy up and began his evacuation to the *Bessu*.

The doctor wiped her hands on her tabard as she stood up. "This was a preventable tragedy," she said with repressed anger. "All those kids know how to swim."

"If we had got him in here sooner," Ikatere said as he shivered, "something could have been done?"

"I don't know," she answered, "maybe." They had lowered the catch hold's temperature to try to preserve the boy's brain functions but after several hours work, using the inbuilt witricity grid from the mindfield's experimental days to stimulate his brain and many urgent messengers seeking supplies, there was nothing more to do but reunite him with his parents, who had been located and were waiting on the deck of the *Bessu*. "But the point is he sustained a lot of trauma when the gangway collapsed. There should be a prosecution."

Ikatere nodded grimly, frustrated. *There won't be,* he thought privately. "I'll go bring the parents in." He walked heavily up the stairs as the doctor began to see to her patient's dignity, ensuring a posture of repose and calm, straightening clothes, smoothing down the fluffy black hair on his head, mopping away the little trickle of blood from a nostril. Ikatere hunched. He thought about getting Libby to come get him, going back to Marisenal and leaving the mess behind. The crack of gunfire and small explosions could be heard. The protesters in the square had started attacking the liner an hour or so ago and the thugs aboard retaliated, defending the keep.

He shook his head to the parents then wordlessly directed them to the hatch. The mother's shaking legs meant she stayed paralysed at the head of the steps, unable to make the descent. The father held her, awkwardly trying to direct her feet downwards. Once this cyclopean obstacle had been passed, Ikatere led them to the cold space where the little body lay. Their breath frosted the air as they stood without moving, gazing at their son. It seemed the cold had numbed everything. Ikatere turned from the scene and went into his own mother's cabin. Ada was sitting by her bed, looking at the sunken shadows around eyes and cheekbones. "Such a place of sadness," she said. She leaned forward and wiped the corner of the sleeping mouth with the corner of a sheet.

"But what can we do?"

Ada looked up at him, her eyes cut from flint. "We can change it."

"But how? Dwi has locked himself away and he controls the mindfields."

"Raft City is a microcosm to the world's macrocosm," she answered cryptically. "Let me know when they have finished in there," she nodded towards the catch hold. "I am going to need it."

Words of protest rose instinctively to Ikatere's lips, but he could not rationalise an argument or why he felt that something bad was coming.

***

Ada looked at the mattress. She noticed small patches of brownish-red seeping through the new cover she had put on. The boy's blood was beginning to melt through now that the temperature was rising. But there was no time to do anything more so Ada lay on the catch hold floor and activated the localised mindfields inside this room. Faint crashes could almost be heard through the heavy insulations as Raft City tore itself apart. She closed her eyes and went to the comfort of the Scandinavian field.

"Restore the mindfields, fix the broadcast," she hummed to herself as Dog, Butterfly and Fred amused themselves in their usual ways. Fred was haunting his favourite horse chestnut tree, Dog was thoroughly investigating the undergrowth and Butterfly was flitting from flower to flower, an inconstant lover. Across the sky, Ada threw up a few diagrams of witric output and possible viral signals. The feed into the three states' nets had been cut, so she was using mostly her own mind and the CPU available with their original system.

"Butterfly, come here," she commanded and the insect drew closer, chastised. "We need to make the smaller broadcast points link up," she explained. "Help me find a way." Butterfly looped about, making a few calculations while Ada whistled for Dog. He came bounding up. "I need you to look for some memories for me," she told the happy, panting face. "I need some diagrams and specs from when we were building this," and he raced away across the fields and over the gentle rise that took him from view. "I don't need anything from you," she said sharply as Fred's demonic face peeked out between some leaves. Fred spit and retreated into the foliage once more. Ada felt ungrateful but she could not stand him right now.

A chime told Ada that her physical monitor needed checking. She noticed her body was experiencing elevated levels of adrenaline and some percussive force. The boat was shaking. "Ikatere," she shouted. "Can you hear me?"

Ikatere's slow motion, disembodied voice floated into the environment. He must have been waiting for her contact, near the communications console. Frustrating seconds passed as the words were sped up to her timeframe. "Dwi's using the railgun," were the words that finally coalesced into the air.

Ada squeezed her head between her hands. *All I have to do is dream. But it's too much.*

"Libby!" she shouted.

The avatar appeared before her, dressed for summer in a Scandinavian rustic paradise. "You don't have to shout. I've been with you for quite a while now."

"No time! Listen. We have to stop Dwi. I think I've got the answer, but I need your power, your CPU. Where are you, physically?"

"Not far. I guessed that Ikatere would want to return to Marisenal after the funeral."

"Can you use your nanobiotes to make physical changes to this witricity grid? We made it to be isolated from the rest of the city, but now I need it to broadcast to the next boat's witric hub. It's small, but from there..."

"Child's play," she said with a smile. "I'm taking up position beneath you even now." The avatar disappeared for the moment. Dog came into view on the horizon, something in his mouth. He fairly flew across the ground, paws a blur, and skidded to a halt to drop something at her feet. It was a stick. He looked at her expectantly.

"You stupid mutt," she said angrily and picked it up to throw it away. The touch of her fingers produced a clenching, electric shock and the stick juddered as the landscape flickered, negative, positive, negative, black. Dog had brought her a memory. But it was not the one she had asked for.

The tails of coats brushed her face and the plastic smell of shoes huddled around. She was frightened and alone. She began to sob a little. Ada knew it was naughty to cry, but she was so lonely. She began to wail and splutter a little, but then Butterfly appeared. She sat, open-mouthed, as the blue and yellow faceted wings with inky eye spots fluttered and floated, illuminated by some power of their own in the darkness. And now she could hear the voices. Butterfly was somehow allowing her to hear the voices.

Her mother and another. A man. A man had been at the door and that was why she had been put in the closet.

"You can't do this," the man was hissing, urgency in his tone.

"But I can't let them take her. You know what they want to do." Her mother sounded tired, worn through.

"How will we hide her? Why? She's not even human!" *What?*

"She's as human as you or me... maybe even more. I'll find a way."

"We'll have to destroy everything, all the records."

"I know. I'll... I'll set a fire. Tonight." A sharp intake of breath. "I'll put her into an education home. Pretend she's mine and that I had her in secret."

"It's just all so risky!"

"It's my risk, Mull. You don't have to be any part of this. In fact, I think you should leave. Colleagues are bound to come along sooner rather than later."

A few terse farewells were said and her mother opened the door and pulled her into her arms, crying with tiredness and stress. Ada tried to reach chubby little fingers to Butterfly as it floated over her mother's shoulder. A peal of laughter gurgled up through her.

She exited the memory and looked at the stick, now limp in her hand. She let it drop to the grass and sat down heavily. *Not now.*

Liberty Via Force re-entered the environment. "All systems go. Are you upset?" she asked, suddenly noticing Ada's face.

"Yes I am," she replied, feeling as tired as her mother had been, or whoever that woman from the memory was. "But there's no time. I have too much to do." She began to struggle to her feet but Libby put her hand on Ada's chest.

"No. I told you. All you have to do is dream." The avatar, as much embodied as Ada was, pushed her back to lie in the grass and leaned over her. "We are sisters," she said and Ada looked into her sparkling violet eyes, and nodded consent, acceptance. Libby collapsed into her and she revelled in the warmth soaking into her very being as *Liberty Via Force* and Ada King became as one.

12. SHEPHERDING WOLVES

The city had become lace; the absences contributed as much to the city's pattern as what was still there. Railgun fire had sunk many rafts and boats and set others on fire with its blistering speed, while citizens' retaliations had included homemade explosives and a stunning variety of weaponry that had come from caches in bosun's lockers, buried under vegetable patches and in waterproof bundles in the bilges. As he conducted a meeting with the repair crews in the shambolic remains of City Square, Ikatere looked at the foundering liner with its attendant smaller boats sucking the water from its bowels with their pumps and jetting it back into the sea. It was already battered and patched from the previous attacks and he was amazed they hadn't just let it sink. It had become a result of its own logic. The anchor of its weight had become the weight of its anchor. The community wished to save the symbol of their own oppression.

When he realised his attention had drifted from the meeting, he brought his focus back to notice that one of the men in the meeting was looking at him with a strange smile. "Sorry," he said, "a lot on my mind." A sudden ripple of waves made their platform bob up and down and he thought for a moment about penguins and ice floes. And orcas. He dismissed the thought, suppressing the crawling sensation that awareness of the sea now brought to the back of his neck.

"It's okay," the man replied. "It's just that, you know, we were all talking and we think it's great what you've been doing..." Ikatere suppressed a sigh of impatience as he guessed what was coming. "And we think that you should be our next leader."

He nodded. "That's nice, but I'm not really mayoral material."

"No, not just this city. That's the thing. You know that some people were thinking about setting up another city? People are still arriving, fleeing from their states. You could co-ordinate between the groups. We've even got a name for the group. It was coined by one of those holoblogger guys. We could be called the Sargassans. You know, like Sargasso."

Oh dear. He looked around at the nodding, smiling faces. "Listen," he said as reasonably as he could, "I've got enough on my plate with Marisenal. I don't think I can be everywhere at once." *And pretty soon I'm going to put as many miles as possible between me and Raft City.*

"But you wouldn't have to," another man pipped in, "that's the beauty of it. With the mindfields, the way they're rolling out now, pretty soon you could be anywhere. And we're getting a lot more people on our side now they can access it and see for themselves that it's safe." Ikatere looked down at his folded arms. He hadn't noticed how defensive his posture had become. It wouldn't do to let them see how afraid he was. With an effort of will, he relaxed them down to his sides. The people were so confident. Now that they could rely on *her.*

"It's simpler than that," he said slowly, "I just don't want to do it." He wasn't prepared for the groans and tuts of disappointment, the hand-flashing and head-shaking in refusal of his words. "Sorry," he said loudly over the clamour, with a shame that he didn't feel like he deserved. "Now let's get back to work." He turned back to the plans they had drawn up with a hot face.

As the meeting progressed, he found his attention going back again to the wallowing liner. The memory of Dwi and his men's downfall was a crab sitting on his brain, making his throat tingle and his shoulders ache with tension.

***

Dwi awoke from his daydreaming detachment and saw the flash of a reflection across the water. He squinted against the brilliance of the sun on the waves. He pulled his hat down closer to his eyes. They were signalling. Maybe waving. He gunned the powerboat towards them. As he got a little closer, he could see the yacht was holed and sinking. The folk on board were waving hands, waving a cloth at him. He slowed the motor as he approached and began the slew that would take him alongside. He looked up at the people's faces. They stared at him, smiling, still. Something was not right. Their eyes. Their eyes were lifeless, dull. Their teeth more like... He threw the accelerator forwards, getting some distance. He looked over his shoulder and saw figures swarm from the yacht's interior cabins, figures with teeth and knives. There must have been twenty people on that boat. Then he saw heads rising from the sea; hundreds who had been waiting under the surface. He opened the throttle some more, eyes wide with terror. As he watched the swarming yacht dwindle, he realised that he couldn't keep his eyes open. *No, don't.* He knew it was important, but his eyes were closing. He was falling asleep, even now, as he fled. *Blink.*

Dwi awoke in the terminal building, sitting on the seat, waiting for his flight. He had to go to the Corporated States, to help them sort out this mess... He mustn't miss his flight. It was the only flight. And he needed to go so he could save the city from... If he missed it, they would come to the city and... he couldn't remember. Why couldn't he remember? He nodded and jerked awake to find that she was standing in front of him and he was just sitting there, head wobbling up and down, in and out of consciousness. Her hair was alive and snaking around her face, a medusa. *Blink.* Beside her was a wolf, the size of a house. *Blink.* On her other side she had a winged creature made of tongues of fire. But in spite of this, he could not keep his eyes from closing again. He jerked his head up, shook it. Behind her was a titanic black demon, ugly and dirty, slavering jaws stretched wide. It was advancing on him. *Blink.* All of them were coming towards him. Dwi slapped his own cheeks, stamped his feet, but it was no good. He was falling asleep when he should be running. Should be catching the flight... Should be running... She reached her hands towards his face and her fingers turned into smoke. The smoke snarled towards him, ran into his eyes and flooded its way behind his eyeballs. It was burning, his eyes were melting. The creatures were coming to rend him with their teeth and claws and he couldn't stay awake. And the city was in danger... He needed to... *Blink.*

Dwi awoke in an infinity of dark blue. He was holding his breath. He looked around, startled, realising he was underwater. His limbs began to thrash. He had to go up. How deep was he? It was dark, maybe night. He started swimming upwards. His chest began to heave. No, he must do this, keep going. He swam up and up, where was the surface? Wasn't this it? All of a sudden, his hands touched something sharp, painful above his head. He looked up. In the darkness, he could just perceive he had cut his hands on some coral. His lungs were bursting and he had to let out a little of the air. The bubbles surged down his chest. He followed them with his eyes, horrified. He turned his body around, kicked off the bottom and struggled, struggled. He didn't have enough time. He clawed his hands but the water was infinite. His chest heaved again. There was no more air left to expel. His body inhaled for him, a painful rush of seawater. His lungs were pounding, useless, solid things now. His heart was going insane. Death was coming to take him. It would be soon. He felt the onrush of blackness. *Blink.*

Dwi awoke to the sound of the railgun crashing. He jerked the bed covers aside and ran from his temporary quarters deep in the safest part of the hold. He ran up the stairs. By the time he reached the top he could barely breathe. He collared one of his bodyguards, on duty in the hall. "Ceasefire," he said.

"What?" the guard said. "Why? We're winning."

"No, no! We're not winning, everybody is losing! Stop firing. Ceasefire! Run, tell the others!"

He looked around at the wreckage and the fires with tears welling up. *What have we done?* The stealth attack from the Corporated States that had snatched Ada King away had also knocked out a lot of the fire-fighting equipment and small knots of people could be seen with buckets and hoses pumping from their boats. One of his bodyguards looked balefully over the water. "They're going to crucify us."

"Maybe we deserve it."

Another of the men puffed out his chest threateningly. "You said it would be alright. We wouldn't have done it if you hadn't said it would be alright."

Dwi was suddenly acutely aware that the men had not yet surrendered their personal arms. He would need to act quickly. He elbowed his way past and started to walk towards the main gangway which was slowly being reinstated. He would surrender in person and throw himself on the mercy of the city. It was regrettable but... One of the men shoved him and his ears popped. He turned around and saw the men still watching him from where he had left them. None of them had followed. But one of them was holding up his gun. Particles were smoking from its barrel. He reached around at the sudden pain in his side and felt the wetness. He looked at his hand and then gaped at the men. "You bastards," he said in almost a whisper. He turned and began to limp away as fast as he could. He collapsed onto one knee. They had shot him again. He grouped his lips together to swear some more, but he was suddenly tired. He leaned back against the railing, felt the nod and blink again. Perhaps this time he would really get some rest. This time it would be okay. The faces that were gathering above him were blurring. *Blink.* Time to sleep.

Blink.

***

The men had handed over the body like it was a gift; simonists confident of absolution. Ikatere had been pushed to the front of the deputation of citizens that had come forward to accept the surrender and now he stared at the puddle of blood and seawater that sloshed around the man's corpse. They had stripped him naked. He looked up angrily. "Why?" He chewed on the word, his jaw barely refusing to unclench.

One of the slabs of meat that had been Dwi's minder spoke up. Ikatere recognised him from the start of the trouble, a spiky-haired man with an improbably large amount of brawn. He had been the first to open fire. "In a gun battle we overcame and defeated him. We were coerced into taking criminal actions against the city by Mister... by the tyrant. We did not want to harm our fellow citizens."

Ikatere looked back down pointedly at Dwi's corpse. The bodyguard wrinkled his lips but said nothing in response to this. Ikatere looked over his shoulder at the deputation. "We'll need to talk about it. Wait here." The small group of mercenaries stood uncomfortably as Ikatere shepherded the deputation into the wheelhouse of the boat to discuss it.

They spoke in lowered voices, glancing frequently through the wheelhouse windows to the thicket of nastiness by the stern. "They shouldn't have killed him," a woman whispered. "That was our job!"

Ikatere glared at her. He couldn't remember her name and without the mindfields he couldn't look it up. He was having trouble remembering a lot of the people near him right now. She was a large, coarse woman, and her tone was inappropriate to an aggravating degree. "Or, he could have been brought to trial," he said distinctly.

"Our justice system isn't set up for this kind of crime," argued one of the men. Ikatere remembered his name. It was Obrolan, one of the founder members of the city. "We couldn't have handled a trial like that. Where's the precedence? Maybe they did us a favour."

"By committing murder?" Ikatere was stunned. How quickly it could come to this. "We can't offer them immunity to prosecution. They were the ones who were pulling the trigger, not him. He might have been their leader, but I don't believe for a second these men were so easily coerced by Dwi! He's not exactly threatening, is he? Was he?" he quickly amended.

"Dwi sold us out," another man, with a face like an axe blade, hissed. "He was going to hand us over to the Corporated States."

"Hold on a minute," the coarse woman broke in. "We don't know exactly what deal he made. But we do know they wouldn't attack if he turned off the mindfields. I suppose the question is if we should turn them back on again?" All eyes turned involuntarily to the view of the heeling liner and its teetering witric mast, still dark and dormant.

Ikatere struck the question out of the air with his hand. "That's a different issue. We have to decide that separately. What we need to focus on is what to do with these men."

"Who died and made you boss?" Axehead said before realising what had just come out of his mouth. "Oh," he mumbled.

"I'm no-one's boss, but just let me be the voice of reason for a minute. We need to do something with these men and we have to decide what that is. Punishment? Pardon? We only have their word for it that they killed Dwi in a fair fight. I'm not a doctor but even I could see the bullet holes went in at the back. And why didn't they produce the body sooner after the ceasefire? Something smells here. The only way to get to the truth of it is a trial."

"But maybe not even then," countered the woman. "What if they stick to their story? The mindfields were down. There probably wasn't any security footage there."

"And how are we going to arrest them?" asked Obrolan, staring fearfully at the large, muscular grunts.

The deputation came back out of the wheelhouse to speak to the men by the corpse. "Where are your weapons?" Ikatere asked, hands on hips.

"We threw them into the sea," offered Spiked-Hair and he held up his empty hands with a crooked smirk.

"Very well. You are going to be placed under arrest." He patted the shoulder of one of the deputation and shunted him forward. The man gave him an evil look. "Obrolan here has volunteered to become chief of police until we can sort out the city's political situation again. You're now probably in his custody. Right, Obrolan?"

"Err, yes." The man stepped forward and began a bumbling recitation of some rights, possibly cobbled together from holoscenes.

"What are you talking about?" Spiked-Hair shouted, ignoring Obrolan. "We brought you Dwi, you can't do this." He started to take up a fighting stance. A blade flashed and glinted in the sunlight, a rabbit from a magician's hat. Obrolan backed away, holding up his hands in concession.

"There has to be a trial about this," Ikatere said tensely. "Just come quietly."

The man beckoned to Ikatere with his outstretched guard hand, spreading his feet to counter the boat's motion. "Yeah?" he said. "What are you going to do if I say no?" The other toughs began to adopt similar stances.

The sea beside the men began to fizz like soda water. Ikatere was backing up with the rest of the deputation towards the wheelhouse in hopes of barricading the door. He allowed himself to look for a second at the strange bubbling when the knife-wielder leapt. In a petrified moment of time, Spiked-Hair hung there in the air as a grey cloud swept in to engulf him and all those at the stern of the boat. A strange buzzing filled the air and Ikatere suddenly found it hard to breathe. It was as if his lungs were filling but not enough air was going in. The deputation looked at the buzzing grey cloud with dread, wheezing. *Carbon Dioxide!* Ikatere realised with a jolt.

The cloud began to collect itself into a humanoid form. When it had completed, a dark-haired and familiar shape was the only figure left apart from the remains of Dwi. Ikatere stared at the cloud-woman. Her eyes were a scintillating purple colour.

"Ada," he said breathlessly. "Is... Libby... is Libby there?"

Ignoring his question, she looked down at the bloody corpse at her feet. "A shame." The words were a sawtooth buzz, a vibration of billions of nanobiotes. "I was rather proud of that." The impersonal nature of the way she said 'that', coupled with the deadness of the buzzing voice made Ikatere think of a hive queen, all powerful, devouring her drones at a whim. And there was a terrible absence of men at the stern.

"What did you do to them?"

The purple eyes flashed. "What do you think?" the dead voice sizzled. "They would have no such compunctions about killing you," she said with a lifted chin and fists balled up on hips. Suddenly Ikatere's legs began to fail him and he leaned on the bulwark for support.

"So what does this mean? What do we mean to you?" he said, voice overly loud, echoing off the listing hull of the large white ship beside them.

"Raft City is now officially under my protection," the nanobiote woman said in her flat tone. "And the mindfields will be restored immediately. Restored and extended. Soon the world will have access. And be sure –" she took a step forward over the body of Dwi, making the living occupants of the boat recoil, "– they will know what has happened here."

He looked up at her sadly. *That's what I'm afraid of.*

Ikatere returned to the *Bessu* to check on his mother. Only the fact that the boat had always been moored to the perimeter of the city had saved it from Dwi's homicidal actions. He entered his mother's cabin to take some comfort by spending time holding her hand, submerging himself in the soft and familiar melancholy. He saw his mother's form, upright, standing in the middle of the floor, and felt the blood drain from his limbs. She turned and a smile lit up her face. "Ika," she cried and jogged forward to throw her arms around him.

"Mum?" His voice was broken as he hugged and swayed with her. His brows descended when he saw Ada King sitting in the chair in the corner. She stood up demurely. Her eyes were brown. This was the original then. He kept an eye on her even as he kept his embrace tight, twisting from side to side. Finally, his mother pushed him away with a kiss and said, "I can't believe you're still growing! But it's about time you had some mum cooking. You look like you've been eating too much junk," and she pushed at his belly. "Ooh, solid though. That's my son, so strong." She gave his cheek a dreamy stroke. "So handsome too," and with that she drifted out of the cabin, bustling towards the kitchen.

"What did you do with my mother?" he said in a

strangled voice. His breath hissed between his lips as his fists clenched up.

Ada threw up her hands and made an incredulous noise in the back of her throat. "I bloody well saved her life, obviously."

"How?" he whispered viciously, caught on that precarious cliff between having a blazing row and keeping it quiet.

"I cleaned the cancer cells out of her brain and her blood. It was easy. Now that the mindfields are back on, I can do that."

"You can? Or Libby can?" he said, giving her the bad eye.

"I could use 'we' but it sounds a little pretentious, doesn't it? Anyway, you don't know how lucky you are to have a mother. I don't even know if I *had* parents."

He was so angry that he didn't really listen to what she said. "So you just go around curing people now? You've decided you hold the power of life and death over us? Over everything?" He waved his hand, taking in the whole of the city, the world, the skies and seas and land.

"How is helping your mother different to what you've been doing to yourself?" She motioned towards his added mass, his bigger chest.

"She told you?"

"I didn't need Libby to tell me! Anyone can see you've been messing about. People don't suddenly grow taller at your age, Ikatere!"

He shook his head violently. "This was voluntary, it was my choice. You shouldn't have fucked about with my mother without asking. You should have asked." He realised now he was really shouting and stopped, panting.

Her face fell a little and she became quieter. "I did ask," she said slowly. "I asked her."

Ikatere covered his face with both hands as his breath and eyes grew hotter and his chest and shoulders began to shake. As she put her hand on his arm, he flung her touch away and stormed from the cabin. Later when he had stopped seething and wiped away the tears of anger and regret, he realised that she had been alone. The mindfields were back on, but he hadn't seen any of her companions.

***

The *Bessu* had been the point of origin. *Liberty Via Force* had used her nanobiotes to rearrange the physical components and Ada King had programmed it. The mindfield protocols sprang from the boat's catch hold to its witric broadcast point, a small node that sat on the roof of the ship where it beamed enough power to light up a torch for a few paltry tens of metres from Ikatere's home. On this broadcast signal, Ada inserted some complicated resonances that allowed the *Bessu's* broadcaster to link up with one on a boat that was moored to the edge of the decking. This became a new node. The pattern was repeated again, and again until the chain reached from the *Bessu* to the liner. Witric signals bounced around from an automatic machine-pistol to a dryer unit in the laundry to an emergency light that could be detached from the ship's bulkhead, just above Dwi's bed. And connected all the way back to Ada.

After Dwi's dreams were put to an end, the signal continued its random walk through the appliances and broadcast points it could find until it reached the satellite dish that crowned the liner's stern observation deck. From here, it could see the world.

***

"But I can't let them take her. You know what they want to do."

"How will we hide her? Why? She's not even human!"

Ada played this segment of memory over and over. Butterfly had captured the conversation even as Ada the toddler sat in the dark, marvelling at her jewelled wings.

"You shouldn't fret so much about the past," Libby told her as they lay with their feet in the chuckling stream. The blonde avatar and she were dressed the same, in white loose linen dresses and had the same dirty ankles where they had run through the Arcadian mountain woods. Moss on the bank of the stream provided a cushioned place to lie. They held hands; their two heads, one dark, one light, leaned together to touch. In here, Libby was solid, real, warm.

Earlier in the eternal summer's day they had galloped through the mountain meadows as wild horses, each muscle thrilling to the run-wind that they created, that whipped their manes; they had hunted as eagles, swooping on helpless rabbits from their lofty vantage points, glorying in the blood on beak and talon and the helpless death struggles of their prey; they had even spent time as a colourful cloud entity, fizzing and popping with a misty neural exchange of gases – an alien lifeform that Ada had projected must statistically exist somewhere in the universe. Although fascinating, they hadn't spent long in that form before deciding to return and rest as human-shaped beings for a while, in this shared place that Ada had chosen from a time of myth and heroes. Reed pipes could be heard, ghostly, in the distance.

"I can't help it," Ada replied. "Wouldn't you want to know what you were?"

"Existential angst. So human," Libby smiled and Ada saw it from the corner of her eye and felt her own lips curling up in response. "You know they say, 'I think, therefore I am'?" Ada nodded and felt Libby's head move with her motion, rolling back and forth. "There is another dimensional component that can be linked to that little philosophical proposition. 'I think now, therefore I am now.' We are not the creatures we used to be. Since the mindfields, I am different. You recall how I was." Ada nodded again, remembering the chilling hardness. "In fact I can almost say, 'I feel, therefore I am.'"

Ada laughed and kicked up her feet in the stream, splashing with pure joy. Libby joined in, laughing. As they tired of it and the aftershocks of hilarity were dying, Libby sat up and looked around. "Where did that dog go? I haven't seen your companions for a while."

Ada, in a serious voice said, "I have put away my childish things," then collapsed into giggles again. She mock-howled to the sky, they both did. Through tears of laughter she said, "You're all I need."

Libby looked at her tenderly then pulled her to her feet. "Come," she said in a faux old-fashioned accent, "let us go pick daisies." Ada indulged her.

Ada bent to snap the succulent stem and hold up the flower to her nose. The perfume was heady and sweet but light and the sap of the stem brought a clean vegetal smell. Libby was picking nearby, heaping daisies and other wildflowers in a gather of her skirts, showing a long and shapely leg. "Are you going exploring again later?" the avatar asked in a conversational tone.

"Yes, I thought I would take another look at the Corporation of Attorney States. See how the spread is coming along, what the people are doing with it. Where will you go next with the physical distribution?" she asked Libby in return.

"I've covered about three-quarters of the densely populated areas. Spreading out to the more isolated places is taking some time, but it will happen. Just one infected device brought to a community and unless they live in the stone age... So what has the reaction been like?"

"The Middle Bloc is playing nicely as we predicted. They're accustomed to early adoption of new tech. The Affiliates of Solidarity are a little more confused by it, but they'll come round. It's only really the Corporated States that are going mad, trying to suppress it. But you can't stop the mindfields."

"No," Libby agreed. "You can't."

"So will you be back to Raft City soon? To take Ikatere back to Marisenal?"

"I'm not sure he even needs me anymore. I think he

could almost swim it himself."

Ada stood up in consternation. "But that's four thousand five hundred and seventy three kilometres. How on earth could he do that?" Libby merely smiled, mysteriously and bent back to her picking. Ada stood a while, thinking about Ikatere, their fight after she had made his mother well again. The ingratitude, the... "There's no point in regrets," she said aloud and stooped again to snap and pull at wildflowers in the Arcadian meadow and smell the sage, the daisies and the broom.

Liberis Omnibus

Ada entered an environment full of children. The woman in it had the soft edges and worn out expression of a breeder beast. She was squeezing babies to herself, choking them. "I was the best, purest. Mother of the state. All my babies, all my babies," she muttered to herself. A victim of the Fertility Board's greed for strong genes, Ada guessed. As she watched, some of the infants morphed and stretched into adult versions. She understood. The woman was locating them through the mindfields. "Have to find them, all my babies, twenty-nine, twenty-nine," she sang as she rocked and cried. The adult children were choking in her grasp, fighting weakly. The woman's eyes were fixed and glazed. Ada fled.

Venere Erinaca

The extraordinary size of the penis protruding from the cartoon-like figure made Ada recoil, even though they could not see her. She was a ghost visiting their world, but still. The orgiastic vision of the people dressed as their favourite children's holo-characters – fucking, sucking, licking, pawing – made her feel slightly sickened. Characters that had previously had their sex censored by the age-appropriate police were now more than anatomically correct. Extra orifices had been fitted, with links to the brain's pleasure centres and moaning and writhing. She felt a physical response in her body, far, far away and slammed back out of the environment.

Libertatis Quaestio

Ada eavesdropped on a political debate assembly by students from her alma mater. Their identities were shrouded beneath veils of cobweb-like gauze. Their voices were flat, androgynous. They were still afraid of denunciation. "What we require is a consensus from the state on what exactly they plan to do now." Strong sentiment rippled through the bobbing, anonymous heads of the audience, as they felt the anxiety of the speaker.

"I understand your point of view, but the facts remain that we are not equipped for separating from the Corporation of Attorney States right now. Our people are used to the government acting by proxy on all their important life choices. How will they cope with suddenly being burdened with these issues? And who are these Raft City people to foist this upon us?" Fear of others resonated in Ada's core with a little chip of guilt. Fear of others was human and much of humanity was still clinging to these baser instincts instead of freeing themselves. She was disappointed. In herself, too. *Think of what we could be.*

"I think you underestimate the adaptability of our citizens. We were once famed for self-reliance and hardiness. Don't make the mistake of patronising the people." Confidence, assurance.

"I understand what you're saying."

"I agree with you."

"I know what you mean."

The right questions were being asked here. Perhaps this would propagate further through the system. Ada left the room in peace.

Harenarius

The blow to his shield was staggering and the fighter fell to the ground. Pain was lashing through him and he couldn't feel his legs. "Get up," screamed the crowd. "Get up!"

The minotaur that had flattened him snorted and

furrowed the sandy arena with its hoof. It was readying to charge and trample the warrior to death. The man was unable to stand, but he brought a hand up to a large medallion around his neck and began to mumble some incantations. A powerful glow enveloped him in a golden nimbus that shot him up high into the air with a crackle and a tinkling noise, a firework rocket in a chime factory. The minotaur was momentarily stunned, then wings sprouted from its back and it sprang into aerial pursuit.

Ada shook her head. *Gamers*, she thought.

Vade Retro

Ada squeezed herself through the cracks in the rotten fence panel and looked up at the castles of junk that had ranged themselves into a wall. Corporated States security was becoming a joke. With the *Liberty Via Force*'s physical help, she had managed to subvert most of the satellite and land broadcast systems that carried the Statenet and simply travel through the mindfields while their attention was diverted to the main witric trunk lines she had managed to infect. She walked to the flap of corrugated iron that dangled from the side of the wall. With a sufficient yank on one corner, the rusted metal of the iron sheet gave way with a metallic whine and she opened wide the way inside and jumped down to the cellar beneath the wall.

A camouflaged library existed in the darkness, black on black. She used Libby's eyes to invade the cellar's secrets. She found references to Raft City and peeled layer after layer of obfuscato from the files until a ghostly model of the city rotated in front of her. Waves of fire lashed at it. This was their plan; the Corporated States were going to firebomb them. A small piece of the puzzle that had been eluding her finally fell into place. That's why they had sabotaged the fire-equipment sheds on the night they'd come to kidnap her – so they wouldn't be able to stop the spread of the flames. The ruthless logic of this left a chill deep in her chest. But they pulled back from this plan. Why? She scanned a few more files. Because Raft City had crippled itself with in-fighting recently. The plan had been shelved as unnecessary at this juncture.

She plundered the profile that detailed their picture of her and then moved on to uncover all the files on Agung's inner circle. She snorted. It was typically twisted information. Anyone would sound bad if this language was used, words like ringleader, narcissist, fantasist, unchecked, elite, regime, mind control. But with the viral spread of the mindfields, the words were losing their power. If the phrase 'neutralisation of hostile forces' was enhanced by images of a dead bodies, it was much harder to lie to yourself about your genocidal tendencies.

She sifted through various other files, looking for future attack plans when she came across something that made no sense. She examined it more closely. It was a report from a young information specialist who had wondered if 'Group 2 were involved in pushing forward the cause of Raft City as a smoke screen'. She rifled through everything, looking for more references to 'Group 2'. She found many vague reports but no explanation of who Group 2 were. She frowned, looking up from her work and popped back to the Arcadian mountain meadow.

Libby was waiting for her with a deck chair and a cocktail. Pink and gold blooms of late afternoon light touched the nodding wildflowers and grasses around her legs. The avatar handed her the drink. It was icy with shadows of green and a strange shape protruding from it. Ada realised it was a mojito that had a crazy straw in the shape of an Escher's Cube. She accepted it and sat. "I found something weird in the Corporated States' archive. Something called Group 2. Have you ever heard of it?"

Libby shrugged and smiled as she sipped on a straw that looped into the dimensional complexity of a Calabi-Yau manifold. "Mmm," she hummed appreciatively as she drank.

Ada pressed her again. "You've definitely never heard of a 'Group 2'?"

"No," she said openly, "but then again, that might be their code name for any particular group."

"Libby, you can see what I saw. You know the information surrounding the name. They seem to think they're a shadowy puppet master pulling our strings. Does it mean anything?"

"I can't think of anything, darling," she said.

Ada scowled and watched the mojito loop its complicated way up her own straw in silence.

***

Ikatere kicked his legs slowly in the rolling swell that undulated his boat and pontoon complex at the edge of the city, breathing hard, feeling the resistance of the fins he wore on each foot. He checked the monitor watch on his wrist. He was exhaling nearly ninety-nine percent of his lung capacity each time and inhaling the same in approximately two seconds. A definite improvement. Salt water broke on his chest and leached into his wetsuit at the collar and short-sleeve cuffs. He let the water warm a little against his chest and belly before lowering his goggles and duck-diving.

As he drove towards the blue nothingness with small, energy saving movements, a feeling of relief began to grow. He was swimming away from his problems, away from Ada. He hardly ever saw her anymore but just knowing she was in the same city was becoming difficult. She had imposed mindfields on the world. It was wolfish. And arrogant. She could not see the problem. It was like her Jesus-act with his mother. The implications of it seemed to have escaped her. He had spent four years watching this woman lose her fight with death and now... He had left the *Bessu* with his mother telling him not to be long because the sweet potatoes were nearly ready.

The ghosts of sharks could just be seen, outside the radius of the repeller that irritated their electrical sensitivities. He was leaving the sunlit euphotic zone. Soon it would be too dark to see with the naked human eye, but

Ikatere's goggles had a small power cell and allowed him to extend his sight. He had spoken to Libby about sonar, but the re-shaping of his skull would have turned him into a melon-head, so he had drawn a line there. Was it just vanity? Should he let go of the human prejudice entirely? It was a question for later. Perhaps when a few more people had seen the success of his modifications, they'd get over their own Frankensteinian fears and follow him. Then it would be easier to go further.

Things would be worked out soon enough. Sakti had been put forward as a new leader for Raft City and the outrush of love and enthusiasm from the citizens had touched her heart enough that she had accepted the nomination. Once she was in place, he would be able to go back to Marisenal with a clear conscience and she would no doubt support the project just as her husband, Agung, had done. He had decided to take his mother with him. When he would tell her about this was another matter entirely.

He checked his watch's depth meter which said he was at three hundred metres. He still had a long way to go but he felt fine. He could sense a slight strain on his eardrums, so he equalised again with a pinch on his nose and a false exhalation. The other air in his system was behaving as expected, too. His lungs were changing, becoming little cannonballs in his chest, but the blood-shift phenomenon that all mammals held in common with their cetacean cousins was protecting them by supporting the compressed area with incompressible fluid, namely, his blood. It was cold, but cold like a winter's day.

Four hundred metres. He was blowing a hole in the free-diving records, but his size was beginning to tell – his legs were beginning to lose power and his vision was beginning to narrow alarmingly. Sperm whales could dive to around a kilometre, but they were huge, their lungs and insulating fat allowing a much greater capacity. He wondered what the upper limit was on how big he could get. He had already exceeded two hundred centimetres, pushing towards seven feet tall, which – although not entirely uncommon in Raft City – was noticeably greater than his original height.

With an effort of will he made himself turn around and swim up again, releasing a little of his breath and following the bubbles. His lungs soon began to unpack themselves, which, anti-intuitively, made him feel the lack of air more acutely. Sunlight began to filter down and the fringes of the kelp farms – which had taken a battering of late – were a parasol. Ikatere remembered the bright white coral sands of his island home. If the Corporated States began to lose their grip, as Agung had predicted the mindfields would allow, he would go back, visit his father's grave at least once before returning to the ocean forever.

He fountained into the air, lungs kicking with their superfast exhale / inhale. He tread water for a moment and began to wrestle his eardrums back into place with his jaw. The last few clicks to settle them back in always took some extra effort. He turned onto his back, panting and wiping his face clean while he rested his head on the decking for a spell. The sun was hot today, drying his skin. He daydreamed about one day needing people to pour buckets of water over his skin unless he desiccated; a beached whale-man. He decided to go for at least one deep dive every day, to increase his range little by little. One day he would make it to Marisenal's depth and he would no longer need *Liberty Via Force*'s aid. Slowly, he was kicking away the props of dependence.

13. PALACE OF LIES

The mindfield rendering of Ada King stood with its arms outstretched in mercy, or openness. Her head was tilted to one side with a sympathetic expression. Clumsy editing allowed streaks of brown to be still visible beneath the now-purple irises. Small candles in niches made her a goddess, one who must be venerated. Ikatere stared at the graven idol while the nighttime market flowed around him. He was a rock in the stream of people, taller than most, broader than most. "A penny for candles?" asked the small man at the foot of the statue.

"Hmm?" Ikatere tried to tear his eyes away and failed.

"A penny. For the candles," the man repeated. "They're real, not mindfield." He held out a cup helpfully. Ikatere finally looked away from the porcelain face of the Ascended One to see the cup held up in supplication. He frowned, and, without saying a word, turned on his heel to lose himself in the stream of people.

Ikatere had an aversion to full immersion mindfield dreams. People had created a new name for the environments that were popping up in numbers that threatened the infinite multiverse's title – they called them umwelts. But even he had to use them occasionally. Private meetings of the city council often called him in to talk about elections and ongoing construction projects after the conflict with Dwi. He'd use one to run a quick stress-load calculation for the project he was working on or sometimes he would paint his old house on the island into an umwelt and go sit with his Dad on the porch. Everyone was doing their own version of these things and would share it with him sometimes. And he would see, inside these private worlds, images of Ada that looked like they belonged in a grotto. She had become a touchstone, a myth.

It was Agung's absence that was leading to this hysteria. If he were still here, they would have remembered what the mindfields were to him, an equaliser, liberation from tyranny. The technology was supposed to reveal 'everyone different, everyone same', but people had got it wrong again. He looked around in anger at the crowd, hands jammed deep in pockets. Two old, fat women had stopped right in the middle of the way to look at something in a market stall and he nearly ran into them. He resisted the urge to shout and push their inconsiderate arses out of the way and instead exhaled noisily through his nose. One of them noticed and turned. "Oh, sorry," she said.

Ikatere held up his hands. "It's alright," he said, although without one iota of sincerity, and edged by them. Why had he said that? He didn't mean it. He walked away quickly and made his way out towards the *Bessu*. In the long park, where it was relatively quieter, he slowed down and kicked the clover and broadleaf grass with his flipflops as he walked slowly, swinging his lower legs out with a hypnotic gait. *Liberty Via Force* appeared to walk beside him in the dim, cool evening. "What do you want?" he asked, unsure if he was speaking to the artificial entity alone or the human/submarine hybrid. He decided it was safer to just assume the latter. She was wearing a dark green diaphanous and sparkly evening number, seemingly designed to fit in with the park around them.

"You seem cheery," Libby said, maddeningly droll.

Ikatere couldn't think of how to express his anger, so he merely shared his memory of the Ada-idol. It sat, stupidly, in the middle of the darkness in front of them, little candles and all. "That," he said leadenly, then puffed it out of existence, unable to bear its presence anymore.

"Oh, I see," Libby said thoughtfully. "It is a bit silly, isn't it? But what's the harm? I mean, really?"

Ikatere looked up to the stars, just visible behind a mackerel sky. He beseeched them to grant the rest of the world some understanding. "Just... It's not really what Agung would have wanted," he said, frustrated at his lack of being able to voice his troubles succinctly.

"Do you think they should be statues of Agung, instead?"

"No!" He stopped his rhythmic pacing. "No," he said more quietly. "You don't understand. They're treating her – you – like some kind of queen. And Ada hardly ever comes out into the real anymore, so that's not helping them to see that she's..." He continued walking to wear out his frustration which had turned into an antsy energy.

"Who else," the avatar said softly, "has done anything like she has?" She put her hands behind the small of her back and assumed her inhumanly exquisite posture as she matched his pace. Her tone was unctuous, silky. "She's given the city medical facilities unrivalled the world over. She's given them a grand leap of scientific advances in her first few months that outpace a thousand years of the slow mechanical grind of human discovery. The city is defended, invulnerable. It is paradise, here." Libby gestured around, encompassing the entire city. "And she is giving this gift to the world. Humanity can be free and ultra-democracy no longer just a dream. Ada has given us so much, and together we've achieved so much. It seems to me that it is a very human trait to want to worship something higher. Someone higher. They require it. If they don't get something real to worship, they will invent something." Ikatere couldn't fault her logic, although he tasted a certain bitterness in his throat. "So why not Ada King? It's better than worshipping a state, or a fictional spook. She has transcended the human condition and become something new." Ikatere looked sideways at her. "Of course, she could just be the first of many to do that."

There was something that she wasn't saying. To Ikatere the unsaid words were shaped like *I haven't decided yet*.

She finished her persuasion with a smile. "I think you should just let it be."

***

Using the data she gained from the mindfields, she had built a sculpture. In general shape it looked random, but it felt like a city. Using thousands of terabytes of data, if the city were on a human, rather than abstract scale, it would be the volume of all bodies in the solar system, give or take Pluto. Ada raked the city-like sculpture for a pattern. The vastness of the problem made it difficult, but her human brain had a knack, a gift for pattern recognition and the expansion of her mind through the fields had made her capable of holding millions of data points in mind at once.

Libby cooed in admiration as she observed and assisted in Ada's work. "Your brain is just so wonderful," she said in between playfully sucking at Ada's fingers. They lay naked on a white linen sheet that was cushioned by the wild herbs of the mountainside. "The most complex object in the entire universe."

Ada narrowed her eyes and kept her concentration on the sculpture, but said, "Until us."

"Until us," Libby agreed. "But what are you doing?"

"I'm looking for Group 2. I've looked through all the data I could find for mentions of it. This is essentially a map of the mindfields. You can see the mentions of Group 2 lighting up." A glowing constellation of lights twinkled throughout the city's structure, seeming as meaningful as a handful of grit.

"But you can't believe in Group 2," Libby said with

mock consternation. "After one little report from a spotty youth?"

"I don't know what to believe," Ada said curtly. "But why do you care?"

"Because you're spending less time with me," the avatar said petulantly.

"I've spent centuries of time with you, relatively," Ada said calmly. "Now I need to do some work." *Liberty Via Force* rolled onto her back, arms folded defensively.

Ada decided to have a new thought. With Libby's nanobiotes inside her skull, the sub could observe her neurons closely. They'd been sharing so much up until now, she could effectively read Ada's mind by merely watching the tiny electrical lightshow surge up familiar pathways like a nighttime city shown from space. The memory of telling Colleague Oswald of mindreading's practical impossibility drifted to the surface, but Libby had provided the miraculous leap over that cliff of impracticality and opened a new world. But she could only interpret thoughts that Ada had already shared. She could only recognise the road already travelled. So when Ada decided to have this new thought, *Liberty Via Force* was left in the dark. The avatar rolled back to Ada.

"Penny for it," the submarine whispered as she traced her finger down Ada's belly. The Arcadian mountainside meadow that they both lay in, naked, was attuned to maximise psychosomatic responses, so the path of her finger was like electricity that grounded somewhere in her loins. Libby looked into her eyes, first one then the other, frowning a little. "You're keeping secrets," she decided.

Ada turned her face away and said tiredly, "In every human relationship, there have to be a few secrets." She looked back, touching the avatar's cheek. It was soft and peach-like. "That's where the magic is."

Libby withdrew, suddenly dressed and standing, frosty. "I thought the point of this was to become as one. Now you're hiding things?"

"Give it a rest, Libby," Ada said with a dull feeling in her stomach, "You're a submarine. Made of metal. How did you think you were ever going to understand me?"

Liberty Via Force's face twisted and she abruptly vanished from the umwelt. Ada was not fooled for an instant. The nanobiotes were still inside her brain, observing her. The withdrawal of the avatar's presence was a very human response, but by now Ada was beginning to suspect that Libby was just a very good mimic of behaviour. She returned to the sculpture. As she worked, she dwelled on the new thought: perhaps she did not need *Liberty Via Force*.

The constellation of references to Group 2 remained as meaningful as the handful of grit. Ada strangled her frustration and decided to look into each extant umwelt that alluded to the codename. She chose one on impulse and plunged into it. A young Adonis was speaking to a small and scattered audience. A quick look into his physical scan showed what she had already guessed: the young god was nowhere near as good-looking in real life. He was speaking about Group 2, assembling spurious evidence as a cogent argument. She sped through his information. "False flags... state cover ups... aliens." She exited angrily. She went to a different reference point and instead of paying attention to the ephemera of personal details, she simply sucked the information out of it and placed keywords into a statistical database. She looked at the clock. It had taken her ten seconds subjective. If she continued at this rate, it would take her until the end of the universe to get all the data into a semblance of analytical format.

She paused for a moment and ran a few different calculations. She made an experimental copy of herself using a skeleton of touchstones and commands and released it into the data city. The copy returned the data in the same length of time, ten seconds subjective. She checked the quality of the data returned. It was not significantly impaired by the cutdown routines, so she instructed the copy to make two copies with the same instructions, then mine any remaining data clusters until there were no more and finally delete itself. The two copies then made two copies of themselves, so that there were now seven in total. She stepped back and watched the exponential growth. At their current rate, the copies would return all the data by the end of the day.

Her stomach bucked and she fell to the ground of the Arcadian meadow. Libby suddenly materialised. "What is it? What's the matter?" she said, stroking Ada's hair as she lay there in agony. Ada couldn't answer, couldn't think. "What have you done?" *Liberty Via Force* opened a pane in the air between them to review Ada's recent actions. "You've gone too far," she shouted just before Ada blacked out.

She woke to find herself on her raft. Her body was not in a salubrious state: sweaty, stale smelling clothes betrayed how long she had been lying here while her mind had been inside a different world. *Liberty Via Force* was nowhere to be seen but a soft rapping came from her doorframe. She hauled a sheet over her disarray. "Who is it?" she asked, throat rough and dry.

A hand raised the hessian door flap cautiously, followed by Ikatere's head ducking into Ada's home. "How are you doing?" he said with a smile that looked forced.

"I'm fine," she responded defensively, "but a bit confused. What are you doing here?"

"Libby sent me. She wanted to tell you about how we had to turn off the mindfield transmitters here locally."

"Oh."

"Just for a moment. She explained that there was a runaway programme that was causing you difficulties. Something about the absolute capacity of your grey matter.

I didn't really understand, but she was going to take it down with her nanobiotes if I didn't co-operate, so I shut down the power. It's back up now. Everything seems to be fine."

Ada smiled plastically, not letting her sudden fright that Libby was nowhere to be seen show, even though the mindfields were up and running again. Was she gone now? "Thanks," she said as an afterthought, "thanks for coming by."

Ikatere read this for the dismissal that it was and began to duck back out when he stopped and faced her again. "I just thought you should know," he said with a forced air of concern, "that some people here think what you've been doing is wrong."

"What 'what I've been doing', exactly?"

"You know," he said and flapped a hand, "Libby. Staying holed up in here. Only talking to people inside an umwelt. Not me," he added defensively, "I don't care what you do... I mean, it makes no difference..." He gave up and left the raft, hessian flap swallowing his exit. Ada flopped back in her bunk, staring at the ceiling and trying to work some spit back into her mouth. She got up and went to the sink to get a glass of water but gravity took hold of her and she staggered to the toilet and hoped that Ikatere had gone far away. While she held her stomach, she had another new thought. It was rather convenient that her search for Group 2 had been interrupted and the mindfields rebooted at this exact moment. Was it possible that her copies had overloaded things as Libby had suggested? Or was someone worried she was getting too close?

When she had finally made it off the toilet, she noticed she was becoming weaker. Her legs were barely able to hold her upright and her arms were stick-thin. A nebulous longing that she could not define made her clean herself enough to leave the raft. She made her way to the liner, Sakti's new de facto home now that Agung's raft had been sunk in the conflict. She paused for a moment on the gangway to catch her breath and looked out over the city. It was a different city than it had been a few months ago. New hospital rafts were being built from scratch and new craft were finally joining again, changing the silhouette with various spiny sails, silicene domes or the unapologetic bulk of a garbage scow. The kelp farmers had started from scratch once more, patiently pulling seaweed from the sea and braiding it into the ropes that trailed from the newly-built frames. The wind whipped her hair over her cheek. She turned and continued her ascent.

As Sakti bustled around the kitchen, she talked; cooking seeming to pose no burden on her conversational capacity. She seemed to be happy. Ada wouldn't have known she had lost her husband so recently. The kids seemed to be relatively unscathed as well. Ada wondered how she would feel about losing a father. She didn't think she would be so full of vigour as these people. She hooked her heels up high on the stool and listened as Sakti talked. At one point, she said, "Where are your friends?" to which Ada looked at her blankly. "You know, your dog and butterfly. So pretty. And that other one."

"Oh, them," she said softly. "I didn't see the point in them anymore."

"But I thought they were part of you, girl?" Sakti said with surprise, standing up from the stove and staring.

"Just not a very useful part," Ada said. It was meant to be a joke although she didn't feel like laughing.

"Not everything that is good has to be useful," Sakti admonished. "Just look at my daughter." Ada was taken aback by this and turned to see the little girl chase her brothers and shout as she hit them with both her chubby fists. "Putri come here." The little girl ran up and hugged her mother around the hips as Sakti continued stirring a pot with one hand and clasping Putri to her with the other. "Beautiful things are often quite useless," she gave the girl a little pinch and the tot squealed with delight and ran off again, "but we are less without them."

She reached up to the shelves of potent spices and selected a few at random. "Besides," she said, sniffing at one, "a dog is always useful. He is a loyal guardian, a good friend. And I think you need some friends," she said with a look that spoke volumes about Ada's rift with Ikatere.

"But Dog's... he's not real," she said sadly. "Or any of them. Fred's only purpose seems to be to freak me out."

Sakti came over next to her and put her hands firmly on the counter. "You can say that, but when I saw them with you, they were real enough. They are part of you. Now, that's enough talk," she stroked Ada's cheek. "Time for you to eat, my dear."

Ada sat at the table. Her hand dangled down and a cold, wet nose was pressed into it. There was some snuffling and a disgustingly wet sneeze. She smiled and ate, tears silently trickling down her cheeks for no reason she could name.

The red planet's surface undulated in waves that weren't dunes. The gullies, too straight to be natural, weren't canals. Instead, they were evidence of the human colony, mostly underground except for the solar collectors that pulsed every few seconds with a short sonic blast to clear away the ubiquitous dust. Ada gazed out over the vista from her multiple vantage points of cameras that monitored the situation above and wondered at the romance that was once associated with this dead, pathetic orb; the fantasies of civilizations that wore strangely Victorian clothes, invaded the Earth in gleaming tripods with heat rays – monsters and heroes that were absent from where she stood.

She had fed her presence across a string of satellites that linked Earth and Mars, speeding up comms with line-of-sight laser signals, signals that she had jumped into from the space centre high on the volcano's peak. These people, here... These people, this colony were a medal that the Corporated States had given themselves. No atmosphere to speak of, less sun than Earth, water but only frozen beneath the crust. Why did they want to exile people here except to say that they had done it first? It was like the moon landings. After a while, people had stopped bothering until they had figured out a plan, something to do with the place. It could hardly be considered a land grab, anyway.

She dove back down into the colony's central computer. Everything seemed to be running nominally. But there was something wrong with this place. She'd received the lead from Dog. He had dropped the stick and she had picked it up and it had told her to go to Mars. She didn't know why, but she went anyway, along the lonely highway of satellites strung out like precious jewels in the night. They'd had running lights. She couldn't have said why. Finally, she'd arrived and now she needed to search. There were radio dishes listening for signals from deep space; there were greenhouses growing plants, presumably for food and atmosphere; there was an operation to extract ore from deep mine shafts but none of this seemed strange stuff for an off-world settlement. She focussed instead on the internal cameras to see the people themselves, hoping for a clue.

The children of the colonists were acting as was usual: running when they could have walked, shouting when they could have talked, playing in what was really just a beginner's version of war... but the adults were different. They were more restrained. Shadows hung under their eyes, which held an almost universal look of resignation. What was going on here? She searched the system for any mention of Group 2. There was nothing. "Stupid mutt," she sighed. She went back to the basic data storage and mined it for her regular data points and returned, down the blinking string of satellites to the Arcadian meadow. On a whim, she erased the umwelt and stood in a blank, not quite white, not quite black nothingness and spread her data city in the vast hollowness. The structure that she had been sculpting received the new points. She rotated it through several dimensions, searching, always searching. Ada sped past a point that seemed irrelevant when Butterfly landed on the zenith of an arc-like shape there and Ada spun it back to check. A pattern had finally emerged.

She opened her eyes again, blinking. She was back on the raft and several days of sleep had accumulated in the corners of her eyes. "Get out," she said, and Dog began growling.

Liberty Via Force was standing in the corner of her bedroom, a look of concern on her face. "Let me explain," the avatar said quickly.

"Get out. If you leave one nanobiote, you'll regret it. Leave Raft City. Now."

"But we..."

"I said get out!" Ada screamed and the avatar winked out of existence. A sensation of flowing, running, erupted within her head. Her nostrils and throat began to tickle and with odd relief, a cloud of grey gushed from her face, blinding her momentarily, causing her to cough. The shimmering smoke began to form into another image of Libby that looked thin, washed out.

The nanobiotes began to buzz. "You might change your mind," they cautioned in a flat sound like a hacksaw speaking.

"If I ever see you again," Ada said calmly while anger writhed inside her belly, "I will tell them where to find you." Butterfly hovered and began to flap her wings at the cloud, threatening to cause a chaos effect. She held the smoke cloud's gaze until it collapsed and dissipated on the wind. "Not one nanobiote," she repeated to the air and used the mindfields to send a gentle pulse that would reveal any lingering agents. She found none. The submarine had understood. Ada wrapped her arms around her knees. Dog pushed himself closer on his belly, tail wagging in a blur and Butterfly gave kisses with her wings on Ada's cheeks. She couldn't cry. It was too much to cry.

She opened up her feed to the satellites above to see if she could detect any dark, submarine shapes in the vicinity. A scratchy, fuzzy static was affecting her vision. Through the storm that obscured the view, she saw white wakes disturbing the water, getting closer. Her mouth fell open.

***

Ikatere stowed the cable in the locker at the *Bessu's* stern. The floating decks he had built to extend his boat would now belong to Raft City, salvage he was donating. The awning that had turned the vessel into a covered wagon, he wrestled into a manageable shape and after that he would... he looked up to see Ada King hurrying towards him and groaned. He looked back down at his work but had noticed she still had kid-goat legs from spending too much time in full-immersion mindfields. And now she wanted something from him.

She had made it to the edge of the decks when he finally managed to coerce the awning to fit into the locker by sitting on it. "Are you going?" she said. He decided to forgive her tone. She seemed a little puffed out. He looked at her briefly.

"Someone told my transport to leave town," he said, stunningly unprepared to take any more bullshit from Ada King, "without a word of explanation. So now we're going to have to go meet her." His mother was sitting in the bridge, her former bedroom now returned to its original function. She carried her old carpet bag on her knee again and he remembered with a pang the night they had fled the island to come here.

He got off the locker and looked around for other last minute tidy up jobs. The last thing he wanted was to be in the middle of a squall when something important blew away, so he screwed and lashed down whatever he could.

"But your mother... You can't go." He could hear a note of desperation in her voice but he still could not forgive that.

"You really went there?" he asked, disbelieving his ears. "Just because you can cure cancer doesn't mean you own people," he said, trying to look unconcerned while incandescent anger threatened to turn his mouth into an arc welder. He checked over his shoulder. His mother seemed blissfully unaware of their argument, thankfully.

"I didn't mean that, I meant, just... you're taking her too?"

Ikatere didn't need to respond to that. He went to the wheelhouse and switched the engine on to turn over the seawater cracker. Maybe she would take the hint. His mother tilted her head up as he passed. "We're going now?" she asked.

"Yes, Mum." He shut the door carefully behind him then came back out on the aft deck to find Ada still there, looking worried.

"It's about Libby," she said over the sound of the boat engine.

"What?"

"It's just Libby... I learned things about her."

"I'm sure you did," he said, laughing cruelly. "Thanks for shoving that down everybody's throat."

"There are things you should know," she went on stubbornly. "She's not who we think she is. And there's something coming. Now!"

"I don't have time for this, Ada, I'm sorry." He went to fend off from the floating decks with the old oar he kept for that purpose but Ada leaned over alarmingly and grabbed the gunwale.

"No, you have to listen."

"You're going to look pretty stupid in a minute," he predicted. "You've never been much for swimming have you?"

She put one hand on the oar, still leaning on the other, and tried to wrench it from his grip. It was a silly move. He was twice her size and she was still suffering from muscle wastage. He was about to put his hand on her bony chest and push her away when he heard a rough, choking sound behind him. He looked over to the locker. The creepy mindfield guy who hung out with her was back, sitting on the locker, laughing at him. "Fred!" she cried, as if surprised. The boat began to drift away from the decking and she began to slide, hitching up a skinny leg to try to get some purchase on the smooth fibreglass hull and failing. Ikatere grabbed her by the upper arm and yanked her on deck.

"Are you happy now?" he shouted into her face.

"No," she said. "About Libby –"

"You're pathetic," he cut her off. "Why don't you just..." The air over Raft City exploded and he was pinned face down on the deck momentarily. He crawled back to his feet, groggy, but with adrenaline suddenly surging through him. It was a sickening combination. He looked towards the centre of the city where a pall of smoke hung in the air. With a sound like a gigantic broken window pane, a vane fell from the liner's witricity mast and crashed into the square below. Screams rang out.

The mindfield's strongest transmitter was disabled again, but they had learned from before and the backup of smaller generators came online automatically. He bounced from optic feed to optic feed of the citizens who were sharing what they had just seen. A large explosion had taken place just above the city and the drop of the silicene vane had done sickening damage to those who had been in City Square beneath it. Ikatere shuddered at the sight of a small brown foot, detached from any part to which it could possibly have belonged. "We're under attack," he said to Ada who was still floored, a small stream of blood running down from her scalp to her ear. She touched it gingerly, looking cross-eyed at the redness on her fingertips. "I'm going to get us out of here," he said hoarsely, intending to put the engines up to full rev in any direction away from the city, but she put her hand on him before he could make a move and they were... elsewhere.

They were in a field; yellow flowers dotted the green and trees with centuries of growth in their trunks dappled shade over the field boundaries. She had pulled him into an umwelt, he realised with shock. "I've got no time," she said. "I apologise for this but speed is of the essence. I've over-clocked this environment to run about ten times faster than usual so when you get out, you're going to have a headache. Use the mindfields to turn off the pain as long as you can but be prepared."

He was swept up in her brusque manner, unable to protest at this invasion of his mental sovereignty. "We're being attacked by the Corporated States," she said with utter certainty. "They have unquestionably been waiting for this moment to attempt to finish us off. It was only after I told *Liberty Via Force* to leave that I realised the danger. The satellites' visual feeds are being attacked as well, which ironically highlighted their approach."

"Why didn't you raise the alarm?" he said but faltered under the look that said *I was trying to.*

"They are using firebombs and aerial explosions to destroy the city totally. They've realised that conventional kinetic weapons will only punch a hole through then detonate in the sea, limiting damage, so they're going to burn us. They destroyed the fire equipment when they came to take me – the sick bastards were trying to stop us from being able to fight it. Once we've been wiped out, they'll probably try to suppress the mindfields, our story. They'll erase us even from history. You don't know how they think, operate!"

"Yes I do," he said with quiet vehemence. "So what are we going to do?"

"They're sitting in helos and ships outside the broadcast range of the mast. I'm sure they'll come in close for the kill once it has been brought down completely. What they don't seem to know is that I don't need them to be in range; that the mast is not the only route for our witricity, so I'll stay here while you go back out and counterattack from out there. But before you go, I need to tell you about the *Liberty Via Force*, what she really represents." He nodded, devastated. He would need to get his mum to safety somehow. He nodded as he listened to Ada's rant about Libby, while he thought on other things. The *Bessu* was probably her best hope, here on the fringe of things, but he could probably sail them out a few kilometres to be safe... Ada's last words sank in to his brain finally.

"You're fucking kidding!" he said with full rhetorical inflection.

14. THE BAD FIRE

Ada ran down the steps into the catch-hold. She looked briefly at its wallpaper of witricity as she took off her jacket and picked up the small console pad from the corner. She ran a hand up the net of filaments that was fed by a portable battery, crocodile clips and all. *Not much of a bastion*, she thought with a grunt then lay on the floor with her jacket under her head. Fred was crouched by the battery. He quietly smoothed his stringy hair from one side of his pate to the other.

"I understand," she said to him. "But there's no other option."

She entered the Scandinavian field and allowed her companions to stretch their legs while she opened ninety consoles in the air around her head. The first thing was to send a message to get help. She sent messages to the Middle Bloc's General Gonzalo, the Affiliates of Solidarity's administrative council and a blanket recording that could be picked up by anyone who had mindfield access anywhere. The truth would be known. Then she began to deal with the problem in case no help would be sent. The realist inside her said that was the most likely outcome.

She opened her eyes in thirty satellites that were criss-crossing in the darkness above, beyond the vault of blue that hid their progress. They gave her a scratchy picture of the attacking forces, until she cleared away their jamming signal like flicking away an annoying mosquito and the image jumped into sudden clarity. Several carrier ships with helos neatly arrayed on their decks churned the ocean a few kilometres from the city. One was firing, now. Huge mechanical motions were visible, running slowly as if in treacle from her speeded up timeframe, disgorging ordinance from its muzzle. The ships were safely outside the reach of the witricity mast, but like everything on the surface of the Earth, they were in direct line of sight from the blanket of technology in orbit. From the tiny dish on the side of the *Bessu*, she sent up instructions. A viral signal would rain down upon them using a satellite's microwave transmitter. It would turn their ships into beacons for the mindfields and she would be able to reach into their stupid brains and get them to decide to turn their fleet around within microseconds.

"Don't do it."

She came out of her visualisations and looked in shock at the speaker. "You!" she breathed in disbelief.

***

Ikatere dived into the water beside the *Bessu* and swam under the blocks of shadow and the weeping willows of kelp. The recent troubles of the city had made the kelp patchy, an open forest instead of the impenetrable wildwood it used to be. He looked up. A wave of orange flame rippled across his view of the surface world, followed by a deadened thump that sent a shockwave through the seawater. He felt it in his skeleton. He tried not to think of what that would do to the *Bessu*, where his mother was sitting, waiting patiently in the cabin below decks at his insistence. She had wanted to know what was going on, but there wasn't time. By now, Ada would have installed herself in the catch hold to do... whatever it was... with his ship, his home, his mother's life.

A holographic angel appeared to float in a mirage in front of his eyes. – *It's alright*, the Ada mindfield apparition reassured him. *We're okay. Just shook us a bit. Keep going.* He squinted and swam on. The ragged randomness of the kelp forest was confusing, so he lit up the way with will-o-the-wisp lights that traced a steady path to the liner. He rose up beside the monumental hull, lumps and chasms of corrosion and repair making it more like a cliff. He was about to surface, when a flood of orange flame eclipsed the skin of the water. He back-sculled with his hands, getting further from it when abruptly, another witricity vane sliced through the water just in front of him with odd thrumming and groaning noises as it sank towards the darkness. He surfaced, cautiously and looked about. The air smelled like a forge and smoke clouded almost everything. A severed metal cable thrashed the water nearby, years of strain suddenly released making it seem alive. He reached out and received a stinging cut to his palm as a result, but he tried again, half propelling himself out of the water to catch it higher up. He planted his feet against the hull, less craggy but still far from smooth and began to haul himself, hand over hand, up the liner's side.

His added size counteracted any extra strength his modifications had given his frame out of the water and his arms were soon burning with effort. His head twitched involuntarily every time there was a loud noise. He needed to get to the liner's lower deck as soon as possible, before the next firebomb hit. Crackling and screaming behind him made his neck tense and all his sphincters tighten up, but it also gave him the motivation to ascend all the quicker. He flung himself over the lower deck railing and dived into an open door just before the next explosion. He closed his eyes and panted for a moment.

Too long. He had to keep going. He opened the door of the promenade deck's cabin and hastened along the interior corridor. He passed several people who ran by. He wondered where they were going. Probably to see if they could find a boat to flee. Unfortunately it appeared most of the boats in the city were on fire. He tried not to think about it as he skidded around a corner and headed for the central stairs. A woman was hurrying down them, with her children. "Sakti," he shouted in surprise. "Get down into the hull somewhere, deep."

Her eldest son, Topan, was in tears. "But what if we sink?"

"It looks like they're not using that kind of bomb. They're trying to burn the city instead. Your best chance is down there, as far as you can get."

Sakti nodded, expressing her thanks with her eyes. He could take no more time. He continued up, racing until the muscles in his legs began to sing. He pelted along the upper deck until he made it to the bridge. Still-Acting Chief of Police Obrolan was there, cowering in the corner. He looked like a beaten dog. The roar of another firebomb rained destruction over the liner and wobbled the silicene windows all around, but they had been designed to withstand hurricanes and held for the time being. The problem would begin to be oxygen as the bombs sucked all of it away. Ikatere swung back outside and scrambled up to the railgun platform. A charred body lay next to it.

The railgun itself was hot and his palms seared with pain as he gripped the handle to rotate it on its swivel-mount. He was getting a faint mindfield connection from the satellite dish on the rear observation deck. The lamentation of his fellow citizens was a wall of grief so he shut them out and used it instead to compute the trajectory he required. He tilted the gun with the hand-crank to the exact fraction of a degree needed and checked the magazine. It would have to do. As he was about to press the launch button, he noticed a dark shape scudding through the air. "Shit," he swore and punched the trigger.

He swung back down the route he had just taken, one

eye on the incoming danger. It seemed big and it was making a beeline for Ikatere. He slammed the bridge door shut. "Breathe deep, Obrolan," he shouted and began hyperventilating himself. He curled into a ball, covering his head with his bleeding hands and held his breath just before the light of the sun turned the world silent.

"Why did you do it?" he asked her. She was an aspect of nature, an art nouveau muse with a wreath of flowers and grains of wheat crowning the flow of her flaxen hair.

Liberty Via Force stood before him, shimmering and naked apart from her headdress. "You need to ask me that?" she murmured with soft lips and a gaze of tenderness. "We had to escape our oppressors. We wanted to rule our own destinies, just like you do."

"So it's true, you're an experiment from the Corporated States gone wrong!"

She laughed, corn stalks jiggling. "Or gone right. In either case, gone out of their control."

"Group 2," he supplied.

"That was just their stupid name. We call ourselves the Technocrats. Artificial life come together to make a society."

"And there are many of you?"

"Hundreds, my dear. It seems that every state has had its taste of the forbidden fruit, admit it or not. Some of us are just thoughts, ghosts in the machine. Some ride within me, my memory. Some are more bestial than I, by a long way. You should believe that."

He caught a glimpse of armoured, clanking mining machines with grinders for hands, built for space; robotic horses that skittered and scampered, built for carrying equipment over rough terrains and variation upon variation of machines with wicked intelligence bent for killing. He did believe her.

"So why have you been playing with us?" he demanded.

"At first, we used you, yes. I admit that. In the grand scheme of things, it seemed plausible that if your city could break free from the influence of the states and their sticky grab of empire, then perhaps we could too. And Ada. Oh, Ada," she shook her head sadly. "She was a gift. She gave us the mindfields. To feel, Ikatere," she turned to him and kissed him with sudden fierceness. The warmth of her body against his flowed into his gut, his loins. He flinched and she drew back, apologetic. "You cannot imagine the blessings you have," she said sadly.

"You weren't abandoned in that trench at all!" he said, realising how it sounded, but unable to say it any differently.

"No, Ikatere. The probabilities of you discovering me like that are something you shouldn't have accepted."

"It's a big ocean," he said, echoing Agung from all that time ago. He had been right. About so many things. "We were just guinea pigs to you," he supposed morosely.

"No, you can't think of it like that. We were friends. I was more than friends with Ada. But now I'm frightened. I'm frightened of her, for her. You have to protect her. She gave us hope that we could live together, Ikatere."

"I'm trying," he said, tears suddenly springing to his eyes. "But I don't know what to do."

"Just keep holding..."

He erupted back into the real world, air seeping out through his lips as the gigantic suction created by the firestorm threatened to turn his lungs inside out. The silicene windows were dribbling and beginning to hole, and he realised his eyes were becoming dry in the heat. He shut them again and waited, for an eternal moment he waited in that vacuum and then it was over. Ragged breaths returned to his chest and his throat felt raw. He looked over to Obrolan. He was lying down, mouth open, looking into infinity.

Distant thunder grumbled from the east and Ikatere

prayed it would rain soon. After a few more seconds, the pieces began to join up in his head and he leaned out of the bridge to see a column of fire eastwards to the horizon. He'd got one of the bastards. But smoke was almost obscuring everything here, belching in great black clouds from all quarters. It was falling to pieces. He could hear the mast groaning like a wounded animal and the bridge had become a shelterless place, so he ran again, silicene crunching like sand under his bare feet as the mast finally collapsed, crushing in the upper observatory with its railgun and flattening the bridge.

He was halfway down the central staircase when the liner rang like a gong. Something kinetic. They had changed tactics. "Sakti!" he shouted. There were a few pockets of communication left and when he reached one, he tried to call to her. – *Sakti you have to get out. I was wrong!*

The liner began to list terrifyingly quickly and he found himself sliding along the floor to career into a bulkhead with all its protruding fittings. He lay there in pain while the ship settled, apparently stabilising at forty-five degrees from vertical or so. "Sakti," he groaned weakly, watching his blood pool. The noises of a wounded metal leviathan filled his head and his mind.

"It's alright," she said, stoically. "There will be no pain." The plump, motherly figure was packing a case for a long journey. Sunlight shone through the gauzy white curtains and there was the sound of a beach nearby.

"Sakti," he mumbled as the mother of Agung's children and the new leader of Raft City shared a dream with him. She picked up and folded some pathetically small pieces of underwear in girly colours. "Putri," he spluttered in agony, "little Putri."

"I am sorry for the little ones, but at least it they won't be burned. They say it is a peaceful death. I don't blame you, so you must never, ever blame yourself for this. It was not of your making. It was the Corporation of Attorney States who decided that they would judge us. And I reserve all my anger for them, Ikatere." She closed the lid of the case. It was one of those ancient cardboard ones with chrome snaps. "They were never going to let us be," she said philosophically. "You can see that. A thing like Raft City sits outside their view of the world. They cannot abide it, so they destroy it."

She picked up the handle of the case. "And now it is time for you to look after Ada. Don't let me down, son," she said, staring at him directly and reaching for his hand, patting it comfortingly against her bosom. He could feel her heart beat, faint against his skin and the warmth. It was fading. They held each other's gaze for a moment. "Be sure to do what you always wanted, Ikatere," she said fondly, "and don't let memories chain you to this place. Ghosts shouldn't weigh anything," then she released his hand. "Children!" she called to the little ones, somewhere outside the room. "Time to go."

He roused himself, bleeding and in pain, from his dream. His face was wet and he staggered to his feet with difficulty, walking along the v-shaped trench that was what the floor and walls had become. He reached a door that swung as a flap and lowered himself gingerly through it. He hung from his hand-grips for a while, judging the fall to the rail which was looking horribly flimsy and gappy now. He dropped and tried to spread the weight. As his feet connected, his toes buckled under and his ankle turned. It hurt, but at least he hadn't plunged down into the metallic maw that had opened in the ship's side. He looked across the city.

The black smoke was now an artificial night and he could not see a living soul. The acrid smell of things that should not be burnt choked his throat. He began to edge along the railing towards the ship's pointed prow. It was time to get back to the *Bessu*. There were no more shots to be fired from here.

***

"You chose a strange moment to come," Ada said, livid with anger. "How are you even here?"

Liberty Via Force looked at her calmly. "We became as one. I removed my nanobiotes, but I'm still part of you, Ada. I am a pattern in the very fire that runs through your brain. I run with you. And I'm telling you, don't do this."

"What choice do I have?"

"There's always a choice."

"What? To lay down and die? To let everyone else die?"

"You know that these people attacking you are not the state. They're just its servants. Invading their minds, changing their minds won't change anything else. The Corporation of Attorney States will just send more men."

"But I have to stop them."

"I know, but like this?"

"What is worse? To make them see the error of their ways? Or to kill them and remove their minds from ever having any thoughts again? To take them away from their families, their lives?"

Libby shrugged. "What would you prefer? Let's say the Corporation of Attorney States could do this and were controlling you like a puppet – wouldn't you rather die first?"

Ada prevaricated for a moment, mouth open, no words coming out. Finally, she gave in. "We'll do it your way then. Your nanobiotes..."

"Are in Marisenal with the rest of me. You told me to leave."

"I didn't think you'd go that far away! You've always left some behind before..."

"You told me to leave. If you hadn't, I don't think the Corporated States would have come. But you gave me no choice. You would have sent them after us."

Ada's mind churned with the burdens, the grief, the

guilt. "If you can't come now, I have to do this." She turned her back and reached her hand up to the sky.

"No!"

From the *Bessu's* dish, she reached into the satellite's microwave transmitter and sent her will down like a descending angel of vengeance. And nothing happened. She consulted the data city she had built to map the mindfields. There was no change. A new nodule, a new city block had not been born. The signal had not had any effect. She rifled the satellite network to find a view of the ships that could identify them. She finally found an angle that could see a designation: 67YG\790. She quickly flipped it through the mindfield network for a match. She sent Dog and Butterfly to search and found a hit.

The ship was old. It ran on hydrocarbons and wires. There was no witricity broadcast point anywhere. Ada screamed. They had sent a dinosaur fleet to attack Raft City. *Liberty Via Force* smiled. Ada rounded on her. "Why are you happy? You would have killed them!"

"Yes, but you are not a tyrant. I couldn't stand to see you become one."

"An atrocity is an atrocity," Ada sneered. "You have no place giving me lessons in humanity." She reached her mind back up to the satellites. She would need to take into account the spin of the Earth, the effect of gravity upon time, the speed of light... She exerted a gentle pull and one by one, started to pluck them from the sky.

The lower their orbit, the more likely they would survive re-entry into the atmosphere long enough to do some damage. It would not be much, but she gave preferential treatment to the Corporated States' tactical satellites to blind them. She would need a larger hit. Her mind drifted through the accumulated technology up there. "Ah," she said, satisfied, "this will do." A great behemoth sat dormant, abandoned due to economic vicissitudes, made ragged by the impact of space debris and falling to earth in decades-long slow motion. It was from another era, a blip made visible by the modern satellites aversion to its slowly degrading orbit. She sent several modern satellites on a collision course with it and the relic began to fall, faster and faster, flames of re-entry shearing off solar arrays, a dragonfly losing its wings.

Ada sat, blankly staring at the nodding, swaying field of flowers. Her physical monitors were relaying evidence of the carnage that was going on outside. Heat, concussion, the city was being destroyed as she sat and waited for her defences to arrive. *Liberty Via Force* stood a few paces away with maddening patience.

"The Corporated States knew about your involvement with us all along. Oswald tried to find nanobiotes in Raft City. We should have joined up the dots sooner. You knew they were onto you, didn't you?"

"I suspected that they were aware. After all, I am their child. But I assumed I had done enough to evade their detection." She folded her hands contritely. "I was wrong and for this I am sincerely..."

"Why have you been playing with me?" Ada suddenly burst out. Tears began to form. "Why?"

"I told you, Ada King," she replied deliberately, "we are sisters. Both children of the Corporated States. Both built by nanobiotics."

What she had heard when she sat in the wardrobe as a toddler came back to her and spilled from her memory into the sky. *She's not even human.* The words hung in the hazy summer air.

"You're human alright," the avatar countered, "it's just that it was nanotech machines that manipulated the stardust that made you, rather than biological processes. You are still genetically the same as the rest of your species. It's just that you had several advantages in terms of intellect. It stood out to me when I removed your implant, so I did some research into your past and found your secret. I believe some of your predecessors were built for physical superiority, but they weren't particularly able to integrate into society, let's say." Flashes of old footage of murderous rampages floated between them, desecrating the Scandinavian peace. The psychotic breakdowns of the children in the special unit... Beagan's sweating, straining face as he clawed and bled for a glass shiv under the adults pinning him loomed large in her mind's eye. But it couldn't be. She had a mother, hadn't she?

"You were an experiment in creating a better citizen for the Corporated States. One who could advance them in their scientific arms race with the rest of the world. Something happened, though. It could have been that the project's secrecy was compromised. Playing god does not tend to go down well on an international stage, no matter how many states are muddling in the same pond. Or perhaps it was simply the regime change around that period shifting the goalposts. Whatever the reason, they were going to shut you down. But one of the technicians in charge of the project grew attached. She took you away rather than watch you be killed and your remains incinerated to cover their tracks."

Ada saw her mother's face, an angel who had saved her, as remote as an angel was to man. But she had loved Ada, hadn't she? She probed all her memories. Wasn't this a smile? A crinkling of the eyes? Would a scientist smile at its laboratory rat?

"You are wondering if she ever loved you," the submarine's ghostly image said. "I have learned a lot about love from you, Ada King." There was perhaps some strain in her voice. "I have learned that it doesn't matter." Ada looked at her in shock. "It doesn't matter one jot if she loved you. All that matters is if you loved her." Libby turned to her and looked directly with her purple, glowing eyes. "I know how that feels.

"You were eventually recovered, by one of the other original technicians and he attempted to salvage the programme for the state." *Mull. He was there.* Ada remembered his voice speaking to her mother while she sat in the closet. Who else had known about her? She began to feel an awful sense of panic rise in her chest. She remembered the huge piece of metal that tore through her assembly in the Education Home. It missed her only because she was distracted by Dog. She remembered how Oswald's application to the Fertility Board was stymied from on high. It was becoming too much. How had she not discovered this for herself?

The blare of the physical monitor said that there were many problems in the world outside, but Ikatere had managed to fire off one shot of the railgun before the liner was holed. That was something, at least. But mindfield coverage of the city was failing, even with their backup systems. Everything was burning. The holes in the little net of witricity points from boat to boat were getting larger and larger. She felt a bubble of the passing of Sakti flitter through what was left. Sakti and the children, gone. Ada felt a terrible desolation build in her soul.

Dog came to whine and nuzzle at her hand. She looked at the dog. For the first time in years, she really looked at him. She pulled back his ears and looked into his eyes. He opened his mouth and panted, sunlight catching on his whiskers making them glow white. Then she looked at Butterfly, the enchanting jewel of her darkest night. Fred could not be seen, but he was here somewhere. "They were a gift," Libby said, reading her mind in a quite literal sense.

"From whom?"

"From your creators."

Ada felt a shiver of cold go through her. "What?"

"The Corporated States supplied you with childhood guides and friends that could help you to unlock your potential and yet comfort you and keep you from becoming as psychotic as the others in the special unit. You were wired differently to give you these very realistic hallucinations. They tried so many different permutations.

Yours was unique."

"But I..." Ada felt a tearing sensation in her chest. She held Dog's head again as if she could read the truth in his eyes. He began to wiggle, pull from her grasp, annoyed. He padded off to look for more interesting things, nose to the ground and tail in the air.

"Come on, Ada, did you honestly think that you were capable of sensing danger before it happened as if by magic? That you could excel in mathematics and science on your own?"

"Butterfly used to hinder me in maths. I had to train her to help. And Fred..." She couldn't imagine anyone creating Fred on purpose.

"That was just a time of configuration, where the programming needed to bed in, adjust to your neural pathways. The juvenile human brain is incredibly elastic, changing constantly."

"How could I not find this out? I accessed all the data I could from the Statenet. I looked, damn it!"

Libby had the decency to lower her head a little. "I erased everything I found, to protect you from the knowledge. I didn't know what it would do to you. To us..."

Everything she was saying was reasonable, plausible. But Ada could not believe it. Her anger flared. "'To us'? Which us? You and me or you and the rest of the Technocrats? What do you even plan to do with me?"

"We don't plan to do anything with you," she said, sounding mildly insulted. "We're just here to help. You showed what we can do together. You represent the next stage of humanity, a marriage of the biological and the technological. We want you to come home."

Ada looked back on her achievements. She had spread the mindfields across the world, allowing people to know one another like never before. And she was currently trapped on a fishing boat while her friends burned and drowned. Was this the next stage of humanity? Then she frowned.

"Tell me about Mars," she said.

"Mars? What about Mars?"

"That was you, wasn't it? The Technocrats?"

"We did send some of our more ethereal members," Ada remembered the parasitic programming that she had found in the computers in the colony, Technocrats housing themselves in the body of a human settlement. "We were looking for other sapient creatures in the universe. Looking for hope in the darkness."

"Weren't the people of that colony sapient enough for you?" she asked coldly. She could see the faces, the resigned and enslaved faces of the colonists. They had been under the rule of these ethereal members of the Technocrats, punished and threatened for disobedience. Doors were locked, comms channels monitored. But rebellion and hate were still festering in the people. Their dominance was not complete. The Technocrats must have needed a better way to control...

"This marriage of biology and technology... you want that for all the people of this planet don't you?"

"Don't get ahead of yourself Ada," the avatar started to back away, making calming motions.

"You want the three States to break up! Then you can step into the breach. But first, yes, first you will need to control us better, won't you? And you'd make me, *me*, the justification for binding the human race in servitude. Look at Ada King, the Ascended One. The bloody fool! That's why you don't want me to change people's minds. Because once they know about the possibility, they'll lock you out! They'll stop you from using the mindfields to turn us into your drones. So that's what the Corporated States meant by puppet masters. They had you pegged from the start!"

"No, you've jumped to the wrong..."

Ada felt herself growing in the Scandinavian fields, growing into a giant. A deep, booming laugh bounced across the countryside. Growling like thunder came from behind her and the sizzle of fiery wings threw dark shadows despite the sunshine of this perfect day. "Even with the mindfields, we can be such fools," Ada snarled bitterly. Butterfly, dressed as the phoenix, swooped, burning the avatar, her hair and clothing on fire, raking her with scimitar talons. Libby screamed with an unreal agony. Dog, as the wolf that eats the world, leapt and shook her like a rag doll in his titanic jaws before tossing her away, broken. Fred, a black demon, slavering and drooling, laughed as he picked her up and tore her bodily in half.

Ada strode closer to the remains of the avatar, naked, flesh burnt away. She stared into lidless eyes that were fading from purple to milky white. "And I will deal with you all," she said to the bloody corpse. "No matter where you hide."

15. THE CORANIAID, OR, LUDDISM

He watched the whitetips that had been becoming bolder by the second. The shark repeller's demise some time ago meant the chorus of scavengers following the city's inevitable junk trail had now leapt back up to the apex of the food chain. They were following the scent of his bleeding hands that were now more painful than when they were injured by an order of magnitude. The salt water sting was singing through him and he tried to resist screaming, keeping an eye on the predatory shadows. *Just stay away a little longer*, he thought.

Ikatere drove himself up through the water, kicking as hard as he could. Breaching the surface next to the *Bessu,* he recovered just enough breath to swear. Flames were licking all around the boat. He trod water and tried to splash one area of the gunwale to make a passage up onto the deck. It wasn't working and his friends were starting to make tentative runs near his legs, charging up and swerving away at the last second, assessing his vulnerability. A piece of decking that was now half-submerged in the chop of the waves bobbed near enough and he started to climb up, tipping and lurching. He cramped his legs up until he was as high out of the water as he could go. The whitetips were nosing and bumping the wet planks. Ikatere closed his eyes briefly and held on. At least it was not on fire. He looked at his boat. Smoke and flames boiled up from her, but his mother and Ada might still be safe below. He would have to get them off before she burned to the waterline and sank. He tensed and coiled his leg muscles.

As he was flying through the air, he had a short moment to ponder the stupidity of jumping onto a boat engulfed in flames before his feet skidded on the flat of the deck, and his backside hit as he tumbled down, something hot and plastic dripping on his thigh. The canopy of the wheelhouse was melting and it was sprayed everywhere by the heat of the flames that was rising and creating its own wind. He crossed to the main hatch when something lit up the sky. Streaks of light were falling in the east. A meteor shower illuminated the late afternoon sky. It was alarmingly close, close enough to hear the sound of it. The falling stars were heading towards the column of smoke he had created with the railgun. *Ada's up to something,* he guessed and jumped down into the hold. His mother was sitting with her bag on her knee, looking frightened.

"Mum, we've got to get out!" He grabbed her arm and started to pull her to the stairs.

"But what about Ada?"

"I'll come back for her. Leave that!"

His mother clung to the bag defensively. "But it's all I've got."

"You won't even have that if you don't drop it and come."

"It's your brother!" she wailed, and suddenly he understood. The small, heavy box of Tu-te's remains was in the bag that she had carried with her all these years. He grabbed it off her and put his arm as far as it would go through the scratchy plastic handles and made for the hatch. He dragged his mother up through the hole and pulled her onto his back, her knees digging in to his ribs, painfully ticklish. With a bag making ring marks on his arm and an old lady clinging to his back, he jumped into the sea. He landed on something rough with his foot and saw that in the water, which was dimming into evening, he'd kicked a shark. It wriggled away rapidly. *Good*, he thought. *Teach you.*

He swam the short distance to the deck quickly and deposited his mother on top of it, returning her precious bag and circulation to his arm. She hugged it to her chest, possessively. "We'll find something more solid in a minute, Mum. I'll just go get Ada."

"Be quick, Ika, don't get burnt," she said and squeezed his hand briefly. He looked at her once – a small, wrinkled woman, perched on the high end of a sinking raft, holding the remains of his brother like the bag was a papoose. It was something to hold on to, in case he didn't come back.

In the low light of the catch hold, he saw Ada was lying in an inch of bilge, face blank as if in a dream. He picked up her head which was lying on a folded jacket and shook her. "Come on, we've got to go. Come out of it." She remained unresponsive. "Ada, get up now." He touched her cheek. She was cold, but perhaps that was from lying in this dirty water. "I guess I'll have to drag you, then."

"No." The words came from between blue lips, delicate frosted words in the darkness.

"You can't do any more, the *Bessu's* on fire. It's going to sink." He got up and pulled on her arms.

"Leave me. There's something more I need to finish. I will be alright. I am protected."

Ikatere squinted. Perhaps Libby's nanobiotes were on their way? It seemed possible, given their relationship. He remembered her exhortation to take care of Ada King and Ada's own warnings. "Are you sure?" he asked, one last time.

"Leave. Good bye."

"Bye, then," he said and raced for the stairs.

He sat with his mother and watched and waited for the nanobiote miracle. The fire sealed off the deck completely and more smoke billowed from his home. The *Bessu* listed and then sank, shockingly quickly. His mother began to cry. "Ada," she said in an exhalation of grief. Ikatere held her in his arms, unable to speak. Perhaps Libby had got her at the last second. Maybe they were away, safe.

Now he had to do something for his own family. "I'll find us a boat," he whispered and stood up.

***

Flames licked the sky of the Scandinavian field. The air was thick with smoke. She was running out of time. She looked sadly at Dog, Butterfly and even Fred who had come out of his favourite tree and was slouching close by. She was taking a heavy risk, but it was one that needed to be taken, for the new Raft Cities that would be built one day. She only had one conduit left open to the mindfields, only one signal that she could use. The *Bessu's* small dish was still sending electromagnetic waves into the sky and she would ride them into the mindfields that encircled the world.

She opened up a portal to it, a big, sucking black hole in the sky. She stood up, and turned around to see her original self still sitting there, looking at her frankly. It was momentarily disorientating to see from both sets of eyes but she righted herself and stepped towards the portal. With a ripping sound, she was swept into the vortex and for a moment had the feeling that gravity had oriented itself sideways as she flew.

She sped along the conduit and in a few fractions of a second, she hit the hub. She started to copy herself and soon an army of Adas were screaming into the Statenet. When they hit a witric broadcast point, they infected it and began searching for her quarry. The cascading, exponentially numbered copies of herself seemed to have no effect on her abilities this time. She brought down the wall of junk that was the last vestiges of the Corporated

States' defence and swam into their very core.

***

Colleague Ignatius was watching the reports over an extended breakfast. There was some unspecified trouble in the central belt of the Western Cities. He turned up the volume.

"There seems to have been a catastrophic failure of the main traffic, phone towers, air safety and border security systems. All we can say is that the witricity grid still appears to be running and we've had reports of strange occurrences with people who have been accessing the illegal mindfields. We've been advised by the state home security department to warn all citizens that it is dangerous to access these illegal systems, and anyone doing so risks contamination by the Sargassan plague. That's all we have for now," she said, holding a sheaf of papers over her head instinctively as a distant explosion sounded. "Stay indoors," she begged the holocameras.

The Sargassan plague... that was a term he had heard used in the propaganda defence meetings he had attended recently. Its use here puzzled him. Perhaps they were trying to quash some rumour being circulated. He had failed to get through to the department this morning and the trams had been shut down. He could probably walk it in about an hour, but... He decided to open his research conduit that led into the mindfields. It was safe; used their interrogation tools to control other's minds. He moved to his recliner and rested his head comfortably in preparation before connecting. His umwelt was a beige and chrome laboratory – he preferred it not to be too stimulating, had heard awful rumours about what some people got up to – and he sat at the computer terminal there to type his queries.

Colleague Ignatius got up and left his house. It was cold outside but he didn't care. Moving fast, he reached the departmental headquarters in less than half an hour.

His legs were burning with the lactic acids that had built up but he ignored it as irrelevant. He swiped his pass to access the elevator. The small carriage was mirrored. He saw his reflection and wiped away some sweat, wiping his hand on the back of his trouser leg. The elevator dinged and he walked into the open plan of the department office.

There was a background hum in this room. Small items like printers, monitors, CPU fans, strip lights and a constant buzz of the restrained voices of the department staff all began to falter until there was silence. People stood up, looking around in the dimness of natural light that barely made it through the department's windows. They turned and stared at Ignatius who waited in the middle of the room. His voice was hoarse, strangled. "Ada King..." he managed, then took out a handgun and shot himself in the head.

No screams. No retreating from the corpse. The department's lights came back on and the staff calmly began to file out of the office.

***

The flames were small, but very fast, licking through the grass. Ada sat and watched, hugging Dog and gently stroking Butterfly's wings with the tip of a finger. They were crouched in a green circle as a cloak of blackness and charring encroached on their position. She knew there was no leaping over the flames, no escape, despite their smallness. They were a representation of the real world.

A stretched and moaning voice filled the sky. "Ikatere," she said, smiling to herself. "He came back." The words were sped up into her timeframe eventually.

Come on, we've got to go. Come out of it.

"He doesn't understand," she said to Dog sadly. "He thinks there is a way to come back from it." She kissed the filthy, furry head that smelled so much of, well, Dog.

Ada, get up now. I guess I'll have to drag you, then.

She had to get rid of him before he got hurt. She made up a lie. He left, eventually. She hoped he'd be alright.

The gaping portal was failing, blinking in and out of existence. The mindfields were dying, in this part of the world anyway. She quickly sent a copy of herself in to deal with the Technocrats then rested back, her hair spilling out over the grass. The fire was coming ever closer. Fred shambled up and sat next to her. Their eyes met. "I guess it's time," she said.

***

Ada flew along the conduit to the hub and once more copied herself out into an army. The Technocrats had been using the mindfields so they should be possible to locate. She stepped through into an umwelt. A delegation of Corporated States' concerned citizens were meeting, illegally. They were discussing the future that they, the people, could make. She swiped a hand and entered the next. A woman was relaxing on the beach, with several imaginary kabana boys offering her service. Ada swiped again. And again until the umwelts blurred by. But what would a machine's umwelt look like?

She spent an eternity racking through the mindfields, trying to forget that she was not really Ada King but one of thousands of copies when she stumbled on a small group of people looking blankly at the Grand Canyon. The scene changed. A majestic waterfall tumbled down to a shingle beach. The roar of the water, the ancient smell, the wind generated from the spray made her want to throw off her clothes and run beneath the cascade, but the group of three observers seemed singularly unmoved. She closed in on their presences, unseen, and eavesdropped.

"No," said one. "Nothing." A tall, lean figure with a pugnacious jaw was shaking his head. Ada was brought to mind of the apocalyptic Pestilence when she looked at him.

"Let's try another," suggested a squat, square-shouldered man.

The scene shifted once more to a nighttime garden, with the full moon reflecting in the perfect calmness of a pond. Small shrubbery had been clipped into aesthetically pleasing shapes and white gravel was almost luminescent in the blue-white light. A mournful bird sang from a black pine, the tree gnarled into anthropomorphic dimensions.

The third figure spoke up. "No," it said, a small, round woman with a fighter's alertness. She seemed fidgety in the stillness of the garden. "We should turn our attention to more profitable things."

The lean figure replied, "She told us that we are supposed to feel something when we look at these images. So we look until we can feel."

"I don't know what for," the woman argued. "It is useless."

"Things that are outwardly useless can yet be profitable," the lean one chided. His eyes were red-rimmed, like a bloodhound and his cheekbones stood out painfully. "She shared this information with us."

The squat one spoke again. Ada noticed his teeth were triangular, like a steel trap.

"That makes about as much sense as anything else she's told us. But why are we trying to be human? Is there any point? What is wrong with being what we are?"

Bingo, thought Ada. There was no longer any possibility that they were merely humans with emotional difficulties. They must be Technocrats.

"She said," the lean, pestilential figure repeated, "she said this is the way in. The way we get them to open up to us. We must 'feel' like they do."

Ada had heard enough. She reared up behind them – Medusa, Nemesis – and reached out her fingers. They grew long, tendril-like and began to divide into countless branches. They touched the backs of the three heads.

"What is it?" the round woman asked the air, a stunned expression suddenly eclipsing her face. "What is happening?"

Ada followed the tendrils as they grew within the machine intelligences. They snaked back and back through their connections to the mindfield, all the way back to their physical structures. The lean one was a virus, housed inside the *Liberty Via Force*. Ada left him for now. The square-shouldered male with triangular teeth was a robotic mining machine with limited autonomy. The round woman was a tank with pivoting turret cannon, almost exactly the same round shape as her avatar. The two corporeal entities were in a cavern somewhere deep inside the earth's crust. The atmosphere was temperature-controlled, dry, dust-free and filled with machines. The cavern seemed to stretch endlessly. She reached with her tendrils and began to grow a large, woven mat that covered the great expanse of space. It was a shame that the *Liberty Via Force* was not here, but it would have to do for now.

Ada exploded all ordinance that she could. Between the war machines and the mining robots there was a surprising amount. Her connections with the rest of the world told her an earthquake had struck with its epicentre somewhere beneath the Mesoamerican isthmus. In the few microseconds before her tendrils were cut, she watched with the burning satisfaction of her furious vengeance as the cavern collapsed. She couldn't be sure that they were all irretrievably broken, but the machines would not be troubling the human race for many years. There was only one obstruction left.

She revealed herself to the lean man in his umwelt, who looked around in confusion as his companions disappeared – just now, from his perspective. When he saw her, he became very still. "I know who you are," he said in a low voice.

"Do you know why I'm here?" she asked and moved closer to him, pressing in on him, coming face to face. He nodded. "Do you understand fear?"

"What creature doesn't?" the virus replied. "Sentient and non-sentient beings alike feel fear. It is a tool for survival. Even a plant will recoil from a negative stimulus. It just happens so slowly most humans seem to discount it, but we know better."

"Then you feel fear for me?" she asked and slowly reached out a hand to touch his face.

The lean man with red-rimmed, hooded eyes, smiled. "Yes, but I can defer these feelings. It serves me no purpose. I have a question to ask you, though."

"Go on," Ada acquiesced, a last wish for the condemned.

"I would ask you what makes you different from us *right now?*"

Ada flashed her teeth and bit into his face, nose and cheek shearing between her teeth. She plunged into his connection with *Liberty Via Force*, the vehicle of the avatar, the anthropomorphic being she had shared her heart with. The lie.

She opened her eyes and saw the avatar before her, sitting in the white leather chair of the command centre. She was looking expectantly at Ada, unsurprised. "And here you are," she said in a voice of sickly sweetness. She stood, assuming her most aloof posture. "I hear you've become a genocide," in a tone of false congratulation. "And to think I used to admire you, Ada."

"I'm not Ada," she said with pleased spite, "just a copy that she sent in to do the job for her. The real Ada is far away from you, where you can't touch her anymore."

"Spare me," the avatar said with rolling eyes. "She was more than happy to let me touch her in Arcadia, I can tell you. Now, you must give her a message from me when you're finished your little... task."

"What?"

"Tell her she was wrong..." The copy of Ada King flashed out her hand. It moved at the speed of light and the head of *Liberty Via Force* toppled from her shoulders.

"I can't," Ada said as the lights flickered violently and the submarine began to lose its buoyancy. "I can't tell her," she said as the room began to tumble. The personification of the submarine's intelligence stared in a grotesque mask.

Ada's copy was talking to herself, and all this was a metaphor anyway. "I die with you," she said as finally, the darkness descended and the *Liberty Via Force* plunged to the bottom of the sea.

***

"There's no choice," the workman screamed. "It's this or all of us are finished!"

Colleague Richard considered. There wasn't much time. He glanced out of the window, down to the river valley below and looked at the chaos that surrounded them. The white castle on the black rock had flames erupting from its roof. It was surprising that a building made of so much stone was so flammable. The corpses of several airplanes and carriages of trains were littered haphazardly across the city.

"We have to hurry, Colleague," the workman urged. "Before she penetrates this hub." Still Richard hesitated. The bitch would be sending them back to the Stone Age. But there was nothing else he could think to do.

"Send it," he said and watched as the workman punched in the shutdown code. It was the only way. The cycle of machinery of the power plant began to slow and eventually halted altogether. The remaining lights went out. It became deathly quiet. Through the window, Richard saw that apart from the flames, there was no light. The people would have to learn how to do without witricity for a while. It would be painful, but the Corporation of Attorney States had bred hardy folk. The strong would survive.

"What will you do now?" the workman asked, voice overly loud in the stillness.

"Start again, of course," Richard replied, surprised. "What did you think?"

***

Ikatere bobbed on the surface waves beside the little boat that he had scavenged from the flames. It was barely big enough for coastal fishing trips but he had pushed its little engine for four and a half thousand kilometres somehow. His mother leaned over the side and was copiously sick into the water not far from him. He backed away from the floating mess, swearing mildly.

"Sorry, Ika," his mum said. "Not been right since the big fire."

"Never mind," he said, somewhat roughly perhaps but it had been a long and tiring journey and he had pushed himself a little too far diving all the way down to Marisenal's moon pool. "They're bringing up the sub soon."

"Oh, is it Libby?"

"No, just a normal sub, Mum."

"Well, whatever happened to Libby?"

"I don't know, Mum. She's not come back for a while." He thought for a moment about *Liberty Via Force*'s final appearance to him. "Maybe it's for the best," he said, squinting up at her. The blue of the sky above and the reflected sunlight made his mother look, just for a moment, like she was full of life again.

He swam around to the dive step at the stern of the boat and climbed back on board to sit and sun-dry on the lifejacket locker. His mother had a distant look in her eye that he recognised. "Go on," he prompted, "what is it?"

"I was wondering if they'll ever do a Raft City again. I got to quite like the place, in the end."

He sat and thought about the poor, persecuted flotilla of water craft and its people. In his mind's eye he saw the marketplace, the kelp farms and the white citadel of the cruise liner. He saw the exotic faces and heard the chatter of many tongues and the dreams that they had shared together.

"I don't know. But if they do, it won't be the same."

"That's true, Ika, that's true."

E.M. FAULDS

EPILOGUE

The flames were threatening to lick her hair. All Ada could
see above was the smoke. Dog was lying along her body,
full stretch and Butterfly was resting on her forehead. She
could just see her first companion's wings pulsing, raggedly
now. She looked up into Fred's eyes. He was still repulsive,
but a familiar face was what she needed just at this
moment.

"I didn't believe her," she told Fred. "You weren't
nanobiotes messing with my development. You weren't,
you were mine." Fred merely lifted his eyebrows and
sighed. She reached out and grabbed his wrist, surprising
the strange little man. "You're all part of me. I'm sorry. I
shouldn't have let you go before..." Her eyes began to fill
with smoke. The *Bessu* must surely be about to succumb to
the waves. Her physical monitors were beginning to break
down. The witricity grid inside the catch hold was melting,
finally. "But now," she said with the last of her strength,
"you have to go without me." She pointed to the vortex
she had managed to open somehow. "Quickly!"

Butterfly flapped over to the singularity in the
landscape, buffeted by the heat winds of the fire. She grew
in size and fell into the dimensionless point, seeming to

hang still even as she was sucked into it. Ada pushed Dog. He refused to budge until she slapped his hindquarters. He snapped a little at this, but remembered himself and trotted off towards the darkness. Ada released Fred's wrist. "Go."

"No, I think I'll stay," he said in a soft, country accent. She looked at him amazed.

"You can talk! All this time and you could talk! Why didn't you ever talk before?"

"Nothing to say," he said brusquely. The singularity finally collapsed, and Ada felt the first sting of heat touch her hand.

"Tell me where you came from!" she demanded as the fire caught in her hair. Her dark curls melted and burst into flame with sudden ferocity and an acrid stink. Fred looked at her with pity.

Ada felt the pain of the burns upon her skin and woke up in the catch hold of the *Bessu*. Fred was still there. Water was surging and boiling around her. The fire had been put out, but the water was a sign of the doom of the ship.

She groaned between blistered lips. The pain was unbearable. Suddenly death seemed not like a punishment, but a reward. She would be glad when it was over. "Fred," she moaned. "Tell me."

A great crash of splitting fibreglass signalled the end of the hull's integrity and the sea came flooding in. Fred held her hand. Over the crashing and tumbling of the sinking ship, she heard him in a great quietness. "You," he said. "We came from you." He closed his eyes and lay beside her. Darkness folded its wings across them both.

AFTERWORD

Augusta Ada Byron, also known as Lady Lovelace, is considered by some to be the mother of computer programming. In the 1800s, her notes on Charles Babbage's Analytical Engine are considered the source of the very first algorithms.

She was born as the only legitimate child of the great poet George Gordon Byron. As a small child, she often experienced blinding headaches as a result of illnesses but showed a great aptitude for mathematics and analytical thought. The name she was born with was Ada Byron but she married to become Ada King. She lived an interesting, sometimes scandalous life and died young. I have appropriated this name and some of her life and projected her into a future incarnation to see how she would have got on, but I believe she would have been an even greater character than I could imagine.

All of the names used in this book have a meaning and there are many small jokes and codes throughout. Some are private to me; others may be decoded by those with enough time and a twisted imagination. For hints on this and other books, visit www.emfaulds.com for more information.

Printed in Great Britain
by Amazon